RATTLESNAKE WIND

A NOVEL BY

Lilith Saintcrow

Fireside

Published by Fireside Fiction Company
Brooklyn, NYC

Fireside has two goals:
to find and publish great stories regardless of genre,
and to pay creators well.

firesidefiction.com
ISBN: 978-0-9987783-8-9

.

CONTENT NOTE

Fireside provides content notes for its books to guide readers who may wish to seek out or avoid particular story elements. These content notes may contain spoilers.

Rattlesnake Wind deals with issues and themes of abuse in some of its myriad forms: domestic, psychological, and sexual. It contains depictions of racial and sexual microagressions.

A current list of all the elements covered in our content notes can be found on our website: firesidefiction.com/about/#content-notes.

CONTENTS

RATTLESNAKE WIND

"But Granny," the little girl said, the counterpane snuggled to
  her chin, "is it real?"

"Pfft." The old woman showed her strong yellow teeth.
"Tell me, devotchka, can you see the wind?"

"No." Warm and sleepy, still the little girl did not close her eyes.

"And yet, the trees move." One knotted, gnarled, ancient finger
  touched the smooth childish forehead. "Hush now, go to sleep."

Hush now, go to sleep
Or Baba Yaga will come get you

PART ONE: SUMMER

Doing Okay

T HE FIRST NIGHT WE SPENT IN THAT ANCIENT MOBILE HOME, the
wind mouthed its corners with a low whispering almost like words
from another room. Mismatched cardboard boxes everywhere, a stub of a
candle guttering on the small table with its spatters of gold paint under
heavy plastic film—because the wind's invisible fingers work their way in
everywhere, up at six thousand feet with nothing but the Rockies on one
end to stop it. It trips over the Appalachians, gets mad, trips again over the
Ozark plateau, tacks north a bit. By the time it reaches Wyoming, going
uphill, it's furious as only a drunk with a stubbed toe can be.

Mama, black hair lank and curly with sweat on her forehead, fiddled
with the stove while Raymond hunched over, digging through a black
Hefty bag full of our towels. I unpacked the silverware, and kept bumping
against Mama's soft, jean-clad hip. She gave me a tired smile each time,
blue eyes shadowed with weariness and her thin flannel shirtsleeves rolled
up almost to her elbows. Nobody to help meant we carried everything
ourselves, and Mama would do twice as much as we could, just to keep us
from being worn out. I did my best, but between her and Ray grabbing
things out of my hands *and* competing to see who could do most, I was
almost always the one rubbing IcyHot into everyone else's muscles.

"Gonna have to weatherstrip this tin can," Mama said, finally, stirring
the three jumbo cans of Chef Boyardee in her old battered red saucepan.
The stovetop ran a little hot, and the oven worked fine too so we'd have
cheap garlic bread with our candlelit dinner.

It was an occasion, so Mama caved to our pleas for the Chef. Well, *my*
pleas, Ray had wanted Spaghetti-Os since nobody was complaining about
canned food anymore. *I ate that shit in the mess hall, I don't wanna eat it at
home,* Daddy used to say, his eyes glare-bright and that small ticking in his
left cheek going once if he was just irritated, more than once if he was
mad. Outside, plum-colored twilight full of dust had descended, and I
caught myself listening for the burr of an engine or a car door slamming
outside, even though I didn't have to.

"I'll do it," Ray grumbled, even though nobody had nominated him for
the weatherstripping job. He was set on permanent complaint these days;
ever since Ray hit puberty he'd been addicted to rolling his eyes. He used
up all his portion of eyeroll-grimaces and mine too, and now, at a lanky

eighteen, he showed no sign of stopping or even slowing down. Mama told him his eyes were gonna fall right out of his skull one day, but he just kept right on.

I thought he sometimes secretly liked Mama scolding him.

I pushed my sweatshirt sleeves up and broke down the silverware box, familiar movements from last summer's job bagging groceries and stocking shelves. Mama didn't want me working during school, but now that I was sixteen I could do it without her signature. The only trouble was transportation, because out on the plains if you don't have a car you're what Daddy called SOL. *That's shit outta luck for you civilians,* he used to say, shoveling in Mama's spicy-sweet baked beans with Wonder Bread and grinning.

Things were a lot quieter without him around. More settled, even though we'd up and moved.

I stacked the flattened boxes and got plates down; the fridge was an ancient tan Kenmore monster but it worked like a charm. It wasn't Army housing, but it was okay. We could have lived onbase, I guess, but since Daddy was buried there—or parts of him, anyway—I sort of didn't blame Mama for not wanting to stick around. We were still able to use the PX and there were the doctors. And the child-care allotment, a few years of it at least since I was under eighteen. I didn't know how the amount of blood money changed monthly, but Mama told me not to worry about it just yet.

Ray poured milk, taking a deep swig out of the gallon for good measure, winking one blue eye at me as Mama sighed without turning around.

"Ray, that's a nasty habit." Wearily, she stirred the Boyardee with that special flick of her wrist, so she didn't break the ravioli open. She said she couldn't teach me that little trick, it was just something that came from practice.

My brother tipped me another wink as he slung the carton back into the fridge. His Captain America T-shirt was fraying under the arms, and you could see his biceps flicker as he moved. "It don't hurt nobody."

"It doesn't hurt anyone," she corrected, again. "You can speak like that in public, but at home—"

Of course, Ray just had to go one step further. "If I don't talk proper to a recruiter, they'll stick me somewhere nasty. I'll be a private anyway to start off with."

My sigh sounded like Mama's. "Can we please not fight?" You could barely hear me over the wind, but still, it stopped them like it sometimes did. I could never figure out why it only worked about sixty percent of the time.

"We ain't fightin, Dez." Ray set the three mismatched milk glasses on the table, and Mama started dishing. "We're just *discussing.*"

You're fighting. Mama might decide to go all in, if you poke her enough. "I'd miss you if you went away." Old familiar words, and I managed to turn the volume up for once. "We need you."

He was only half mollified. "More than you'd need an allotment and your own bedroom?" There were black arcs of engine dirt under his chewed-short nails, but Mama didn't tell him to wash his hands. Maybe she was beginning to pick her battles, or maybe she didn't notice.

"I got my own bedroom now, Ray-ray." I stuck my tongue out. "Besides, I don't want *you* ending up killed."

As soon as it was out, I regretted it. Mama just paused in her steady motion, then continued on. When the officer showed up at the door with the news, Mama had started crying. I wasn't sure if it was from grief or relief. I even made a song inside my head about it, *grief or relief, grief or relief,* just trying to pin down which one she might be feeling. Or what Ray thought about it.

It saved me from having to decide, too.

Ray shut up about the recruiter, thank God. I crowded Mama enough to get the garlic bread out and sliced it on an ancient wooden cutting board, the knife making fresh white scars, scattering salty crumbs. When we sat down and Mama said grace, Ray didn't even belch halfway through.

We were doing okay.

That night, I heard the whistling man.

· · ·

THE WHISTLING MAN

I had plans for my bedroom, but for the moment it was just boxes and milk crates, plus a sagging, narrow mattress on the tired blue nylon carpet. The two heaviest boxes were under the window, so I rested my knees on them and looked out at what, at first glance, seemed to be a whole lot of nothing.

Mama was doing the dishes tonight, and Ray was drying. I should have helped, or loitered to keep them from rubbing at each other, but there wasn't room for me in there too. Maybe she and Ray would get along better if I left them alone. Funny, she used to be his favorite person, but puberty made him an alien. Maybe it would make me one too, but it didn't seem to just yet. It just made me ache in my joints and other places, and made me worry about growing too much.

Clothes cost money.

Dusk was falling softly into night outside, the wind still singing along. The first thing we got used to when we arrived at this particular corner of the Army's far-flung tentacles was the constant air-hum. Wyoming wind just pours along, never stopping, just dropping down below what people can hear. Even in a row of Army houses you could sense the wide space outside, rolling hills covered with waist-high dry yellow grass beginning to green at the roots because the snow was sloppy-melting and pouring away.

It was fine when it was just Mama and me and Ray in the narrow, tall base houses, with layers of paint covering chips on every wall and banister. Then Daddy got the active orders, and a month after transfer he was heading off to whatever oil country we were taking over. That gave us some time to breathe. At least before he left he'd been in the post-move good behavior stage. It was when he came back on leave that the trouble always started.

We got the notification of his requested leave eight weeks after he'd flown out. Bracing and we braced ourselves for Daddy's upcoming TDY, but he didn't show up. Instead there was the tall ginger-haired officer at the door with the condolences and his hat held at a precise little angle in his hard white hands.

Mama started moving so steadily to get us offbase we didn't ask any questions. Maybe she was worried it was a mistake and he'd show up after all.

The wind sounded different out here. We weren't sandwiched in, with people on either side and the whole humming, neat little anthill of a base all around us with its regimented sidewalks and air of purpose. No matter where you land in the military, there's the blanket of regs and procedure to snuggle up in. It's nice and warm, until it starts suffocating you.

I tugged the flimsy window open. No screen, but it wasn't hot enough to matter yet. That was when I heard, long and low and liquid, a ribbon of silver melody. At first I thought it was someone's radio, but it sounded too, I dunno, *alive*. Then I thought it was a flute, but the quick rill of notes went too far on either side, up and down.

The front door slammed, I tensed and all my spit dried up before I reminded myself he was gone. Footsteps in the hall were Ray's, so it was probably just Mama taking the garbage out and lighting the one cigarette she said she was allowed to have after dinner. Smoking again, but with the way things were, well.

It was enough to make me wish I was old enough for a vice or two of my own.

Ray didn't bother knocking. He just poked his tousled head in the door and made that irritating *tsk tsk* sound. "You better close that. Dust'll get everywhere." All officious, big man of the house. Daddy would have been furious at him for growing his hair out. His eyes gleamed in the dimness, and the star on the front of his T-shirt was just a pale blur.

I made a face, using up one of my own quota of eyerolls for once, but he couldn't see it from the door. "Can you hear it?"

"Hear what?" A few moments later he was right next to me, bracing his knees on the boxes too. He'd complained endlessly about carrying my whole three loads of books, rubbing at his back as if it pained him like Mama's did. As if he hadn't bought a lot of them at garage sales or thrift shops for me, at least the ones he thought looked smart enough. *If it looks depressing or complicated or weird, I get it for you,* he'd say, and I would have to examine each one carefully while he watched.

He had a pretty good knack for it, too. He'd even brought me Kant once, in a leather binding. I couldn't get through the damn thing, but every once in a while I hauled it out and tried where he could see me. Only the first quarter of its pages had any wear at all. Some of the rest were still attached to each other, in that funny way they used to make books.

"Listen." I craned my neck, trying to hear better. Like birdsong, weaving in and out of the wind's low moan. The back end of the trailer looked out on a postage-stamp weed-filled backyard that faded into grassland on the other side of rusted barb wire. Scrub brush took advantage of every dip and hollow, trailing away as the windbreak's shadow narrowed. Everything rippled, grass turning its back like tired horses. There was even a roller, a real tumbleweed, skipping ahead of moving air. Once you focus, even a whole lot of nothing has its defining features.

I finally placed the sound. Someone whistling.

"What?" Ray had that look again, the one that told me I was stupid but he was willing to at least hear a little more. His lower lip pooched a little, and he craned his neck too, an echo of my posture. It made his face into a kid's again, for a brief moment.

"Whistling." *A bird? I don't think so.* It sounded wrong, like it couldn't possibly come from a beak.

"The wind, Dez." Perilously close to another eyeroll.

I imagined said eyes falling out and sounding like marbles when they hit the floor, and shook my head. "No." I pointed, chipped pink nail polish glinting briefly. Maybe now Daddy was gone I could wear something brighter.

A man-shape melded out of the dust and oncoming night, walking along with his head down. Tall and thin, just a man-sized shadow in the uncertain light. Indeterminate hair, a little longer than "normal" but not long enough to be what the locals still called "hippie."

Ray tensed a little. "What the hell's that?" Softly, so Mama wouldn't hear him swear. Even though he was practically adult now, like he kept reminding me. Some habits you just don't get rid of even when you hit magic eighteen.

"Just someone out walking." I found I was whispering too, as if we were eavesdropping.

Whoever he was, he was pretty good at carrying along a mouthful of music, marking time with his long loping steps. He was on the other side of the barb wire and crooked bleached fenceposts, and his path took him out of sight almost as soon as we spotted him, a long shallow hill swallowing him as a puff of dust slid by. Like a movie trick, now you see, now you don't.

The clear sweet tones remained, though, ribboning behind him and brushing against my open window. Vaguely familiar tune, but I couldn't quite place it.

"Weirdo." Ray shook his head. "Where's he going? No houses out there."

I didn't tell him there were no *houses* here either, just trailers and mobiles. "Maybe he's just out for a walk."

He jostled me, a half-unfriendly little motion big brothers everywhere perfect with long practice. "Yeah, in the wind." Remnants of teenage acne on his cheeks were fading away, bit by bit. Seen in profile he was almost handsome, but Daddy's heavy jaw and long nose didn't match with his thin shoulders and tall leanness.

Daddy always called him a milkman's son except for his nose, because Ray couldn't bulk up no matter what he ate. *Got to man up, Raymond,* Daddy used to yell, and that usually meant a week of him trying whatever new plan he'd come up with to magically make Ray over. Weightlifting, football, all sorts of things. But if the plan meant spending time around a yelling Daddy, which it usually did, Ray didn't want any part of it. Which was good, I guess, but his solution was to shut himself up like an oyster. A locked titanium shell, or a bank vault closed around a tiny pearl of a kid.

He slid the window closed as the whistling faded and the wind picked up.

I decided to grab the opportunity. "Will you drive me to school next year?"

"If I can. If I'm working, though, I might not be able to."

Well, crap. There went one part of my plan. "Where are you gonna work?"

"Everyone wants a mechanic."

"I'll bet they want you. You're really good at it."

He was, too. He could listen to an engine and tell its secrets, and whatever he touched fixed itself, seemed like. He used to take things apart just to find out what made them work—there was the time he fixed the oven, and Mama so scared he was going to blow up the house or burn himself to death. Neither happened, and she was awful proud of him afterward. She told Daddy; luckily, he was in one of his moods and just grunted. If I could have found the words, I might have told her that Daddy wouldn't like anyone doing something better than *he* could, and that went double for Ray.

"Yeah, well." Ray frowned, and you could see him when he was eight, picking at a scabbed knee and hunching his shoulders. "Got to get some money in."

It was weird to hear him say something so adult. "There's the pension. And Social Security for me. Mama said she'd find a job, too."

"Mama's a housewife."

As if I didn't know.

"She won't let me go back to the store. Mr. Ridge would hire me back, I bet." I crossed my arms, hugging myself. My elbow ached—I'd hit my funnybone a good one helping to get Mama's mattress in, and the bruise was vivid and fresh there. At least it was from just knocking against a corner, and not from... anything else.

"You shouldn't have to." Ray said it like he had a better idea.

So he was on Mama's side. I was hoping he'd see things my way. "I'm *sixteen*, Ray."

"You're going to college. Someone should get something out of all this shit."

The swear made me glance at the door, another nervous habit. We were both full of them. "I might not get there. It's a long way."

"You're smart. You will."

He sounded so sure, I could almost believe it. "What about you? You're smart too."

"I'm grease, not book-learning. I'm gonna get a beer."

"Mama won't like that." And I didn't like him getting so down on himself, but I couldn't say that or he'd laugh at me. Not in a nice way, either.

"Don't care." A kiss on the cheek, his familiar smell—engine metal, oil, fried food, pepper, whatever hormone makes boys smell faintly dirty even when they aren't—closing around me. "You can use the bathroom first."

It was sweet of him, but it meant I was the first one to find out the shower was tepid. Still, I took my time, and when I came out Ray and Mama weren't fighting at all. They were in their separate rooms, Mama with her TV on and Ray with his radio playing just a little louder than Mama preferred.

For our first night offbase, it went pretty well.

CHAPTER TWO

Go Play

COFFEE GURGLED, eggs hit the frying pan, and Mama coughed. It turned into morning smoker's hack. Even though she was trying to quit, moving had rattled her nerves, I guess, because I could smell the ghost of fresh tobacco clinging to her. "He's already gone," she said, swiping her hair back with one pale hand. She never did tan, not like Daddy. "There's a garage out on the highway he wanted to apply at."

"Before noon? Damn."

"Language, honey." She didn't crack down on me the way she was getting to on Ray. When it was just us, things were softer. She didn't have that perplexed, tired look so often. "I'm headed into Larston. There's that diner there, Marcie told me to come by."

Daddy never liked Marcie. *That loudmouth bitch*, he called her, mostly because she didn't give Daddy any admiring looks, and actually *argued* with him the first time she met him. About politics, she didn't know any better. She was divorced from one of Mama's cousins, and was sort of suspect—he called her a *freelove lesbian*, whatever that meant. I couldn't see how she was a lesbian if she'd been married before.

But it was Marcie who had stood by Mama at the funeral, holding her arm with a white-knuckled hand, and nodded at Ray when he put an arm around me. She had blue eyeshadow and a perpetual wad of pink bubblegum, but she was nice to Mama. That counted.

"I'll go with you." If it was the diner Marcie worked at, it was near the Sav-Mor, and I could talk to Mr. Ridge. I refilled Mama's coffee cup—that was always my special job in the mornings.

She sighed. "No, honey. You're not working at the grocery."

"But Mama—" *I could at least take the electric bill! Or something. Anything.*

Her shoulders came up, the old signal that she wasn't going to listen to any more. "No. Today you need to get some sunshine. It's summer, you should play."

I'm not twelve anymore. "Okay." I must have sounded resigned instead of mutinous, because she smiled and her whole face lit up. You could see what Daddy always called her "good looks." Even her hair was coming back, as full and black as it ever was when he was gone.

Maybe her cough would go away too, and the rings around her eyes. She might even gain a little weight, and her neck wouldn't look so scrawny-thin. She wasn't skipping meals like she used to. She even sat down and ate breakfast with me.

A little while later a car door slammed, a roostertail of biscuit-golden dust rose, and she was gone in the ancient maroon Chevrolet that Ray kept running for her. The Camaro was gone too, and Ray was probably thrilled to be driving that shiny black piece of metal. Daddy insisted it had to just sit while he was gone, always checking the odometer when he came back even when we didn't have the Chevy. Like two years ago when we were in North Carolina and Mama had to walk to the PX and back to get groceries or any little thing, and that one time she almost collapsed of heatstroke.

I wondered if Ray liked sitting where Daddy had in the Camaro, and decided I wouldn't ask.

I washed the dishes, being extra gentle with Mom's red and gold coffee cup. It had already been shattered once. Its cracks were rough veins, but Ray had sworn it would hold coffee, and it did. Nothing leaked out; Mama's face when she opened that sloppily wrapped present from under the tree had been a study.

I could have done some unpacking, but the wind rasped softly at empty corners and I caught myself just wandering up and down the hall, dodging boxes in the small living room. We hadn't been able to bring a lot of the bigger stuff. Like Daddy's leather couch, not that it would've fit in there anyway. Plus, Mama didn't seem to want any of it. I could do without seeing the shiny, worn divot on the couch-arm where Daddy rested his head when he was drinking, so I didn't mind, but it was…strange, not seeing half our furniture every day.

So I tucked my key in my jeans pocket and let myself out into a breezy blue day with high white pillows of cloud sailing overhead. The wind hadn't lost the edge of winter chill, but it smelled different. Greener, less yellow, somehow. You could tell things had shifted, our half of the earth leaning a little closer to the sun again. The mobile-home park was a giant horseshoe with cul-de-sacs blooming off, a spiny back curled around the meat of the manager's resplendently white mobile and its painted concrete foundation. The thing even had columns in front, a permanent porch wrapping around it, and the trailer that served as an office crouched at the far end of its shiny black driveway as if afraid to disturb its betters.

I kind of wanted to look at the pond to the side of the manager's place, but it was so glimmering-pretty. If I went closer it would probably end up being full of weeds or algae, or the white mobile would show up dingy and cracked. Sometimes I just wanted to leave things like that alone. Like Christmas trees. Ever since I was eight I never wanted to help hang the ornaments on a dying piece of wood. It made my head hurt, especially since Daddy never liked any decorations we had anyway. *So chintzy,* he would tell Mama. *So cheap.* One time Ray had said that if they were liquor bottles Daddy might not have complained, and my guilty laugh, caught behind my teeth, had made him blush.

So I went around the back, poking at loose places in the trailer skirting. I could even help patch them if Raymond wasn't in one of his moods where he was very conscious of being man of the house while Daddy was gone.

A listing, creaky back porch tried to cover up the fact that the cracked French door had plywood nailed over it and a bar dropped into brackets to keep the plywood snugged tight. On the inside, you could see the imprint of a body on that glass; Mama hung a shower curtain over that right off. The place was cheap enough, who cared what had happened here before?

The back yard wasn't ever going to be pretty. Mama liked gardening, but you just got things growing when the orders to move somewhere else came and the boxes had to be found again. There was the water bill to think about, too. Which made me wonder some more about that pond.

I didn't realize where I was going until I stood at the barb wire, brushing long strands of my hair back. Dark like Mama's, but my eyes were green, not blue like hers. Daddy called them Grandma Grim eyes, after Mama's mama, and Mama's mouth thinned each time he did.

I guess Mama's mama hadn't thought Daddy was good enough to marry her darling. I only knew her from pictures. There was a funeral announcement, too, with shiny black cord threaded through thick paper. Mama had taken us to see the casket, a two-day train ride, before we joined Daddy stationed in Germany. *My own mother*, she said later when he found out. *My own mother, for God's sake.*

The wind quieted. There was a thin ribbon of worn-down grass—a path, sliding quick and supple down the hill. It took a sharp right before it dropped out of sight, and I frowned. The dust back here was bone-white, shocking in comparison to yellowing grass. You couldn't see until you were right on top of it, and it made odd skips over tiny humps of earth, as if it got caught playing hopscotch and would resume the game the instant you stopped watching.

A junk pile—technically in the neighbor's back yard—creaked a little under the sound of the breeze as I hopped up on a rusty, side-lying fridge probably older than Grandma Avi, God rest her soul. Scoured and pitted by the wind, it was the first abandoned one I'd seen that still had its door, probably because there was a huge hole busted in its side. Looked like someone had thrown a serious firework in there and boogied, a sharp flower of destruction. Probably an M-80, they were real big on those in rural America, especially on the Glorious Fourth.

Of course, with the base around, someone might have gotten hold of something else and thrown it in the fridge, just to see what it would do.

On any other day I would have stopped to peer inside the dead appliance and figure out what the layers in its walls were made of, but today I was on a mission. I almost overbalanced as the junk shifted underneath me, grabbing at a tangled pile of metal next to the fridge that bit my left thumb a good one. "Ow!"

The whole pile shifted again, almost like a living thing. But I had my balance now and hopped down on the other side of the fence with a jolt. I had to look for a few seconds to find the path again, the grass shush-rippling in every direction. The white dust seemed different now that I was standing on it, but I wasn't quite sure *how*. Maybe more solid.

Sucking on my wounded thumb, tasting bright copper, I ambled down the path. Sometimes I wonder if that's where it started. Mostly, though, I think everything started when I was born.

Ray once said that's when Daddy started to get mean.

• • •

MORNING RAMBLE

The whistling man's vanishing trick was simple, like everything else when you look close enough. A gully split itself open, a green scar in the earth—there had to be water in the bottom. I checked the innocent sky—didn't look like any rain around for miles. You never could tell about gullies, though. Mama said a flash flood could drown you in seconds. Out of nowhere, a wall of brown-tea water, and you'd be tumbled to the bottom and held there like a rock.

The path meandered down, skipping from floury dust-dirt to rock shelf and back, layers of different stone and earth on the gully wall exposed just like the layers in the junked fridge. Sunlight gilded the geologic stripes, crumbling different-colored dirt and stone like book spines stacked vertical instead of horizontal. The rocks on the path were smoothly water-worn, pale creamy eggs. Green closed around me, and when I reached the bottom I was sweating a little.

Who would come down here in the evening? Maybe the wind skipped over the top and the dust didn't get bad. I almost wanted to go back and fetch a bandanna to breathe through, like a bandit in the old cowboy movies Daddy liked so much. *Shoot 'em up!* he used to yell when I was little, and I'd pew-pew at the screen, when he was in a good mood and I was cuddled against him on the leather couch. He only had one rule about Western movies—they couldn't have John Wayne in them.

John Wayne was for war movies. He wasn't, Daddy said over and over again, a *real* cowboy.

The path smoothed out, a ruler instead of a ribbon. A low chuckle to my left was a small creek. It wasn't storm season, but Mama would look thinmouth-disappointed if she found out I was hopping around down here.

She told me to go play. I'm playing. Right?

I almost grabbed a branch from one of the spiny green bushes, something to tear the leaves off of while I walked. Then I figured it wasn't fair. It wasn't like the bush had done anything to me, why should I rip one of its arms away? I kept sucking my thumb, like a baby. I'd probably get tetanus. Probably already had it. Was going to die in a hospital bed, all white and bleached, and maybe Mama and Ray would cry and say *we miss her so much* and stop fighting. I would look down from heaven with a big smile, like in that Christmas movie with an angel.

Except I didn't know if Daddy had gone to heaven. It was surely a sin to think of your father going to hell. Maybe heaven had different divisions, so you could visit people and leave while they were still on their company behavior. Who knew?

No, I decided, I probably didn't have tetanus. Mama made sure I had my shots. The path took a sharp, almost hairpin turn, and all thought of going back evaporated.

The creek, impossibly blue, ran along its stony bed. Aspens shook their long sleeves, leaves jangling. I blinked, rubbing at my eyes with gritty fingers, tasted dirt as well as blood from my stupid thumb. Had I come down far enough that actual trees grew here, invisible from above?

The real surprise was a round-bellied silver pig of a trailer nestled in the aspens, a faint thread of smoke rising from a stovetop chimney and unraveling before it reached the top of the gully. It glittered almost as much as the water, and surely someone wouldn't be down here if it flooded, would they? The place even had a low fence of stacked sandy rock and pieces of bleached-out timber, and behind *that* was a riot of green and red and blue and so many other colors splashing around.

A garden.

I considered this. Whoever he was, the whistler probably didn't like company. It was one thing to explore a damn valley—I looked over my shoulder, guiltily—but it was a whole 'nother thing to go near a strange trailer where a man lived. No way, no how, Mama might give me hell but Daddy would just plain...

Well, he's not doing anything to anyone. Not anymore.

The sunlight trembled. When I looked back at the silver pig, a thatch of white bobbed among the green. Not guy-shaped. An old lady, red shawl clutched to her shoulders, moving among the plants. Not painfully, just... slow.

She puttered around for a while, here and there, bending stiffly every once in a while. Picking, maybe, or weeding. Deheading things to make them flower again. Maybe just enjoying the spring sunshine, because being down here in winter was probably not a lot of fun. A whole lot of snow and not much else, especially with spindly naked aspens shivering all up and down the valley once they'd lost their leaves.

I realized I'd been standing there staring for a while when the old woman halted, and her white head swiveled.

She looked right at me. Something cried out overhead—a hawk, maybe, a high-pitched predatory yell.

My heart leapt up my throat, my liver revolved, and for a second I was the twelve-year-old Mom apparently thought I still was.

Because, like any stupid kid, I ran away.

CHAPTER THREE

We're Temporary

GETTING BACK THROUGH THE BARB WIRE WAS THE TRICKY PART. I got a scratch along my forearm, too—more tetanus—and dirt ground into my jeans. Later I figured out just to go a little in the opposite direction from the busted fridge, to where the fence listed so heavily I could simply step over. If I'd been smaller, I probably wouldn't have gotten a scratch, but Mama would have told me to stay in the yard. Or in the house, with strict instructions not to open the door to *anyone, alive or dead, you hear me Desiree?* Once I'd set out to ask her if anyone dead would come knocking, but got scared and decided it was better to just hide under my blankets at night, without sticking any part of me out that a monster could get.

I came around the white-and-blue trailer's front to find the black Camaro hunching in the drive, and didn't have to dig in my pocket for the key.

Raymond was in the kitchen, and I realized I was thirsty. My heart was still pounding, too, and my hair was a mess. I could still taste blood and dirt and fresh air, but the pleasantness of coffee-smell covered it up. My brother was grinning as the coffeemaker gurgled, a wide sunny smile meaning something had gone right and it was no doubt all a result of his grown-upness. He greeted me with a nod and a loud, "What the hell were you doing out there?"

"Exploring." I let the water run a little, shoved one of the cobalt-blue glasses under it. "You were up early."

He frowned, one of his patented Big Brother Expressions, but that satisfied smile wore through almost immediately. He just couldn't wipe it off his face. His hair was slicked carefully back, probably because he thought it made him look older. "You oughta be careful. There's snakes out there."

"Didn't see any."

He looked, in fact, just about ready to burst, but I didn't ask what had him grinning so hard. Most of having an older brother is *not* doing what he wants often enough to remind him you're not his personal cheering section *all* the time.

The coffeemaker burbled as it finished. He poured himself a cup, fixed me with a glare, and when I didn't move to get the milk he—wouldn't you know it—rolled his eyes, and decided to spill his news. "I got a job."

Now I felt a little sorry for making him come out with it. "Really? So soon?" I didn't have to work to sound pleased, either, which was a blessing.

He puffed up like a balloon, shoulders spreading wide and his arms out a little, taking up as much space as he could. "I fixed what they couldn't. Simple. Anyway, it's hourly instead of commission."

"So you're... pumping gas?" Just to get a little rise out of him. Because I didn't feel *that* sorry.

"Ha." He got the milk himself and sloshed his coffee into blonde, for once not taking a swig out of the gallon and making me remind him Mama wouldn't like *that*. "Got me part-time, working the front and organizing parts. They don't even have an inventory. Anyway, it's okay, the place I really wanted isn't open on Sundays."

"Huh." Was it a Sunday? Summer vacation messed up the week from front to back now, without weekends full of tiptoeing around the house hoping not to wake Daddy up and risk a trumpet-blast of fury. "So where is it?"

"Out on Highway 12, where it widens and there's Kretzger. Suburbs, kind of."

Now that was interesting. "Kretzger's got a thrift shop. And a church."

"Planning on getting God?" He wiggled his eyebrows at the thought.

As if. Mama didn't make us go to church anymore, and was it ironic to think *thank God* about that? Just as much as thinking that "getting God" sounded like catching a nasty disease. "What else is out there? More stores?"

"Nothing." But he was grinning again. "At least, nothing Mama would let you apply for."

"Dammit." I very deliberately didn't look over my shoulder, though my back tensed like I was going to.

"God, Dez, just be grateful." His good humor dimmed a little, his eyes darkening. Mama's were like that too, bright light summer sky when she was happy, darker stormy sky when she... wasn't.

I was grateful, I guess. But still. It was easy to get discouraged when your plans kept getting smacked down. "Can I go with you tomorrow?"

"Nah, tomorrow I'm going to the place I really want."

"Please?" I wasn't wheedling yet. But it was close.

"*Fine.*" Like I was twisting his arm, and he wouldn't love to bring me so he could brag both ways to an appreciative audience. "Now ask me what I fixed."

I figured I'd got what I needed. I could stand to listen to him now. Sometimes he even told me things about how engines worked. "So what did you fix?" Ray wasn't a *complete* pain. He never acted like a girl shouldn't know what goes on under a hood.

"Sweet little Chevy Nova. Temperamental. Older than Mama."

That's not nice. "Mama's pretty young."

"I guess." For some reason that made his forehead furrow. He took a gulp of coffee and probably burned his mouth. I pretended to be interested in the kitchen window while his face squinched up and turned red.

I figure people appreciate it when you don't watch them during something embarrassing. You act like you don't notice, and they get to salvage a little pride.

He stood there with his coffee, I drank my water, and for a little bit we could both relax. Once in a while it was hard with Mama. She was just... jumpy, and it's hard to take a deep breath when a static cloud of nervous collects in all the corners. You can't ignore it and you can't clean it away, so it just sits there and rasps all over you.

My voice surprised me. "Why wouldn't Mama live onbase anymore, you think?" I had my own theory, of course, but I wanted to hear his.

"Wouldn't or couldn't?" He shrugged. His T-shirt was black, and it had no holes in it. He'd really gussied up for job-hunting. "I dunno. Maybe *she* doesn't even know."

I was pretty aware that yes, there were things Mama didn't know, but I wasn't so sure it could be something inside her own head like that. "Is that possible?"

"Do you know why you do everything?" He sounded honestly curious, not like he was teasing or scoring a point or two.

I thought about it. "Mostly. Do you?"

He shrugged again, with that strange look on his beaky face. Faraway, like he was hearing music a few doors down, something he couldn't quite catch the melody to but he knew the rhythm was familiar. "We won't be here long. Something else will happen." A smaller sip of coffee, sucking in air at the same time to cool it down. "We're temporary."

There was nothing to say to that, so I just nodded. After a little while he retreated to Mama's room to watch her television, and I started making sandwiches for our lunch.

We're temporary.

He didn't know how right he was.

• • •

JUST KNOW

"Pays minimum, but there's tips." Mama all but glowed as she rinsed the greens, shaking them with quick flicks. Greens were good for you. "I start on Monday. Lucky that other girl had to move, Marcie said it's the first opening they've had in years."

"That's good." I dried off the stockpot, set it on the balky stove. You had to jiggle the knobs just right or things would scorch, but it wasn't any worse than the one at that base in Germany where Mama got burned so bad there was still a shiny scar on her arm. The memory ran through me and away, loud noises and a sickish-sweet smell. "Won't that make your back hurt, though?" Waitresses on TV were always talking about their backs.

"Oh, my back's fine, honey. Between some good tips and the pension, we might be able to rent a nicer place."

I slid past her, opened the freezer door, and held my breath while I got out a frozen cube of chicken stock. Mama promised she'd tell me how to make it as rich as she did when I turned eighteen, and I was looking forward to that. When I could breathe again, I decided asking her why she didn't stay onbase wasn't a good idea. Instead, I nodded. "Can I go with you? Not the first day, but maybe after?"

She glanced at me, rolling up the greens and pulling the cutting board out. "You are *not* working at the Sav-Mor, Desiree Elaine."

Two names, and the quiet way she said it, meant it was final. Even if I snuck out and worked without her signature, she'd get that disappointed look. I ran the block of frozen stock under the water to loosen up the plastic bag. It went in the pot, and I gave the knob the particular jiggle that meant *low heat, please and thank you.* "I want to help, Mama." Was it hard for her to understand someone might want to help *her* out once in a while?

"You do, baby. You're gonna go to college and be a doctor or a lawyer, and take care of your old Mama when she's feeble." She grinned, and a stray gleam of afternoon sunlight filled her pretty, tired face just like orange juice in a cup. "But before then, you don't need to be working at a grocery store with that Elon Ridge."

Something in the way she said the name was funny, and made me think about Mr. Ridge's big moist paws and perpetually flushed cheeks. He had his favorite employees, but he wasn't a bad boss, not like some of the stories Daddy told about bosses always trying to squeeze everything out of you in return for a lousy dime or two. "All right, Mama."

"You're young." She sliced the greens in her special pattern, and the good crushed-grass scent filled the kitchen. The backbones of the leaves fell away, cut neatly out. The wind made a dry rustling, like crickets in a paper bag. "School's your job right now, Dez."

It's summer. But I didn't say it. I just nodded, and watched the steam curling off the frozen stock. When Mama was my age she'd been working at a drive-in movie theater; that's how she met Daddy. I could recite the story in my sleep. *I looked up and saw a black-haired girl in a bright red uniform, and wouldn't you know, right then I was sure I was gonna marry her.* She finished high school, went into college and Daddy went into the military, but next came Raymond. Then me.

What was it like, to look up and just *know*? It sounded like the movies, and I always imagined it with soft piano music rising in the background, Mama turning really slow and smiling, Daddy looking straight at her with his most paralyzing look, the one where he was Paying Attention and you'd best beware.

I suppressed a shiver.

"You okay, honey?" The knife paused, the greens falling away in neat slices. Their backbones, swept off the cutting board, rejected as too bitter or too crunchy, lay in a variegated vegetable heap.

I nodded, and Raymond banged through the front door. I almost flinched, but there was no reason to be quiet now.

"Not as bad as I thought," he cheerfully informed us. "Just a couple things that need patching, and I can scrounge around for materials. It looked a lot worse than it was."

"Do we need plywood?" Mama was all practical now, gathering the greens and letting them fall into the stockpot, ribbons of plant matter. I reached up for the rice, measured it out with the battered yellow cup.

"It'd be nice. I can find it, though. And some galvanized. Might be able to find some caulk somewhere too."

"Find?" Her eyebrow raised a little bit. You could just *hear* it in her tone.

"Oh, Mama." He sounded downright aggrieved, but it was a reasonable question. "I got a job, I'll *buy* the caulk."

"Good." She didn't turn around, but I figured she was probably thinking *because if you come home in the back of a police car again we're going to have trouble.* I let the rice drift into the pot, a rattling hiss mixing with the wind. "Can you bring the laundry in, Dez?"

I dumped the rest of the rice and brushed past Raymond on my way out the door, hooking up the battered plastic wash basket. He smelled of fresh air and dust, and waggled his eyebrows at me, dirt all over his hands. I stuck my tongue out in return. As soon as I got outside the heavy greenness of approaching rain made me wrinkle my nose and squint at the sky. Big stacks of dark-blue clouds lurked in the distance, almost perpendicular to the faraway smudges of the mountains. The wash on the rickety line Ray had strung up across the backyard fluttered and snapped. Mama was probably giving Ray the talk about being a good influence on me, how he had a responsibility, and I might go back inside to a cold thick silence and Ray's sullen scowl.

Unclipping and folding was so familiar I barely had to pay attention. Instead, I was turning over how someone couldn't know something going on inside her own head, and it took a little while before a spiderwalk sensation went up my back.

Like I was being watched.

The back yard was just as small and dispirited as it had been earlier, and the wind ruffled the grass on the other side of the fence in long shoals. A blot of red caught my eye, and I stiffened, shading my eyes with my hand as a towel on the line snapped free and a rumble of thunder slid around in the distance. A greasy deep sound, like a bowling ball slathered with Crisco and turned loose on a slope.

The blot had a white patch on top, and I hunched my shoulders guiltily. It was the old woman from the gully, and she was looking right at me.

As soon as I spotted her, she turned, and even at this distance I could see how stiffly she moved. She sank down and vanished with slow shuffling steps. The wind freshened, and I had to hurry to get the rest of the wash off the line. Even when you can see it a long way away, weather sometimes sneaks up on you.

Under the wind was a buzzing, blurring sound I couldn't identify. I got everything into the basket, more or less, and retreated inside as the storm raced for us.

CHAPTER FOUR

Granny Bayaga

R AY FORGOT, and Monday morning I woke up to sunshine and an
empty house. Mama's note on the counter told me to put the beans on
to slow-cook for dinner. I did it just the way she always had, with the
chunk of cheap hamhock dug out of the freezer and the powdered garlic,
brown sugar, and a careful scant tablespoon of molasses. We had ketchup,
and maybe she'd bring home Wonder Bread, too. There's just nothing like
it for beans, all pasty and soaked with juice. You can make your own bread,
sure, and it's pretty good with beans. The best, though, is always Wonder.

With that done, I locked up again, and headed for the back yard.
Leaving the stove on probably wasn't a good idea, but I wouldn't be gone
long, right? Just a quick trip.

Just to see.

I found the hole in the barb wire this time, but I had to hunt around
for the path. Last night's rain might have shifted things around some, and I
wondered if the gully had flooded. Was that why she'd been up here?
Looking at the storm, maybe smelling the rain and afraid of it? It looked
like that silvery trailer had been down there a while, though. She wouldn't
be there if it was that dangerous, right?

But people did funny things. Built houses in all sorts of
places—swamps, earthquake zones, forests that could burn down. It was a
wonder anything stayed standing, really. The whole world was an accident
waiting to happen.

A flash between wiry grass gave me the path, and once I saw it I
wondered how I'd missed it. I went along, not really hurrying but not
ambling either. No reason to break my neck getting down there, but also
no reason to lollygag when I needed to keep an eye on the beans.

This time the slope down into the gully seemed steeper, more
treacherous. The rain had made everything uncertain. I had to jump in a
couple places, and the sound of the creek was way louder than it had been
yesterday. It was lucky the roof of the mobile didn't have a leak or two; that
would have meant Raymond up there monkeying around trying to patch a
hole and probably complaining about it endlessly afterward.

One thing about all the rain—there was much more green at the
bottom of the grasses, a whole hidden country of growth under the old
yellow fur of winter. I reached the floor of the gully and wound through

the aspens, imagining them shaking their new leaves last night. Had the storm reached down here, or had the gully walls kept it out? It was kind of like a castle down here, I decided, and was so busy building it inside my head and thinking about flooding that I was near the silver beetle of a trailer before I knew it.

Actually, I rounded a corner I didn't remember and found myself at the edge of its small clearing, jerked up short and staring at the fence. It was cobbled together out of all sorts of stuff—that bread-colored stone, scrap wood, pieces of sheet metal, long thin brown branches, barb wire, and juicy green hairy vines as thick as my wrist. On the other side the garden tangled, bright green and red and yellow and other colors too, and there was a puff of sweet tobacco smoke, not harsh like Mama's cigarettes but somehow mellow.

The little old lady was at her gate, puffing on a pipe of dark, fantastically carved wood and examining me with piercing, slanted dark eyes, her lashes thick and black. Her face was as round and brown and weathered as a walnut shell, and while some of the lines and creases on her looked like they were from smiling, there were others I wasn't so sure about. The red shawl looked hand-knit, and even though she looked stiff and a little hunched, her hands were deeply tanned and capable enough. She didn't look fragile, like Mrs. Silverstein at school or the shuffling women you saw in the PX when the government checks arrived and the liquor section took a hit. She looked vaguely Asian, and I wondered if she was somehow connected to someone at the base. Most of that part of the country is pretty Wonder-Bread-white, but in the military, you get all types. Daddy had hated some parts of that, but he said Asians were okay. *Hard workers*, he said.

We stared at each other. My cheeks were on fire for some reason, and my throat had dried up. I was suddenly, painfully aware of the silence all around us, and the fact that I'd probably been trespassing or something.

She just stood there, puffing on her weird, oil-grimed pipe. The sweetish smoke wreathed her head, and her scanty white hair was braided into a coronet. There were crescents of dirt under her yellowing fingernails, and the open gate she stood in was pieced together from the same scraps and bits as her fence. Except the vines. They almost cringed away from the gate itself. There was even an arch, built of thin discolored sticks lashed together with what looked like wire. They made a lattice, and something about them told me not to look too closely.

I remembered my manners. "Good afternoon, ma'am," I managed, but I sounded breathless. "I saw you yesterday. We just moved in, and I found the gully path."

Still she watched me, but her expression turned a little softer. I was beginning to think she was deaf or *really* foreign—the shape of her face was a little odd, her jaw too strong and those dark eyes with no difference between pupil and iris—when she took the pipe out of her mouth.

"Little girl. Do you know who I am?" Her voice was startlingly rich, what a choir teacher would call "contralto," and her teeth weren't stained. They were amazingly white, in fact. She might have been stiff, but her shoulders were broad and hard, and I got the idea she might have put together the fence by herself. She also had an accent, the shadows of an older tongue wearing through the syllables.

"No ma'am." I stood up a little straighter. "I thought you might have seen me yesterday and maybe—"

"Thought you were spying on a poor old biddy alone in the wilderness?" A smile creased up the nut-brown face, but her eyes were still stony-hard. "I might have. Don't get many visitors down here."

It pinched me, mostly because I felt guilty enough already. "I wasn't spying, I was exploring. Ma'am."

"Pert little thing, aren't you." She nodded, and jabbed the pipe stem at me for emphasis. "Stop with the ma'am. I'm Gran. Granny Iyaga, if you're feeling formal, and yes that's a *foreign* name. We're all strangers here, did you know that?"

"No ma—no, I didn't." I filed it away to think about later. Maybe she meant everyone was a stranger in America, or just on the plains? Or was she sort of, you know, metaphysical, saying everyone was a stranger to everyone else no matter—

"Hrm." She examined me again, from top to toes, and I was pretty sure I was a sight. I hadn't intended... well, I *had* been curious. Curious killed the cat, Daddy said, but satisfaction brought him back. Once I'd set out to ask him how exactly that happened, since it seemed like something worth knowing, but I'd lost my nerve before I even went downstairs because I could hear him breathing in that way that meant he wasn't angry yet but could be if you gave him any foolishness. "All strangers, little girl, except those who trooped across the landbridge first. Well, would you like to learn something?"

"Learn something?" *I go to school. And I'm not a little girl.* Still, to her, I guess everyone might look like a kid. The fine lines around her mouth when her lips were pursed were tiny gullies of their own.

She squinted at me. Maybe she was Japanese? "You deaf? That's what I said."

I decided that since I was here, I might as well ask. "The whistling man. Is he your son?"

She raised the pipe again and puffed at it, her expression turning from vaguely pleasant to remote in a fingersnap. Little wiry hairs, pure white, had worked loose of her coronet and glinted in the sunshine, curling vigorously. "A whistling man, eh?"

"I saw him the other night, coming down the path." If he wasn't related to her, maybe she needed to know someone was walking down towards her house at night.

"You saw him?" Not afraid, just curious. Of course, if she'd lived out here for a long time, maybe she had a shotgun or something.

"He had long hair. And he whistled."

"You heard him?"

"Yes ma—yes, I did."

"Huh." She nodded, as if it confirmed some private guess. "Well, then. Go home and tend to your beans, missy, and come back tomorrow. Early."

"Come back?" I probably sounded like an idiot. I didn't even think to wonder how she knew I'd left beans on the stove.

This time her mouth widened into a genuine smile, those teeth peeping out at me. Were they dentures? If they were, they had to be expensive ones. They looked real, and the canines looked...

Well, they looked sharp. *Very* sharp.

"Yes, come back. You can help me in the garden, and I'll teach you a few things. You want a job, don't you?"

"My mama says..." But I shut myself up and studied her in return. *Iyaga*. Maybe that name *was* Japanese, but it didn't matter. Money spends the same all the way around, as Mama said. What Daddy said was full of swears. "What kind of job?"

"Your mama says what kind of job? You got her in your pocket, a little doll, eh? Weeding, watering, helping an old woman. Thirty of your dollars a week, and you earn them."

It wasn't good money, but still, it was something. And close to home. "I can't come on Sundays."

For some reason, she found that funny. She wheezed, laughing in the gate, and turned from a leather-skinned statue into a merry old woman with tilted eyes, a red shawl, and an infectious chuckle. Wiping her cheeks, she finally chortled herself to a stop, and the aspens shivered around us. "Nor should you, little girl. I turn into a monster on Sundays. Come back tomorrow."

With that, she turned around, and shuffled inside the gate. I stood there, jaw hanging suspiciously loose, and gathered myself enough to catch at the gate's surprisingly solid weight. I swung it closed and latched it with a click, and she laughed again. She vanished into the green of the garden, muttering something to herself in a language full of consonants, even though I called "I'll be here tomorrow morning, ma'am," after her.

And that's how I started working for Granny Iyaga.

• • •

SO GRACIOUS

I heard an unfamiliar car—louder than the Ford, not as purring as the Camaro—grind to a stop in the driveway. I had every window open, bugs be damned, because otherwise everything I unpacked smelled like old bad memories and who wanted to come home to that? Maybe Mama and Ray wouldn't notice the smell, but I thought I'd be on the safe side. Plus, every new place smells uninhabited until the first time you open it up and give it a good airing. It's like washing the open space inside, cleaning it off so you can start putting your own marks down.

Two doors slammed, and I heard Ray say something and someone else reply. That made me curious, so I ran to the front window and peered between ancient brownish curtains. It was a dusty-blue Ford truck, the same as every other truck out here in the wild west. I was too late to see who was in it because they were already on the porch stairs, and Ray pushed the door open a little too briskly.

"—on in," he finished. "Dez?"

"In here," I called, and came around the half-wall to see a lanky blond guy behind Ray's patented wide, almost-fake smile that looked so much like Daddy's when he wanted to be charming. So he wanted to impress this guy, whoever he was.

"This is Alex," Ray said, tipping his head at the guy behind him. "Alex, this is my baby sister Dez."

"I'm not a baby." I folded my arms, and Ray had to push past me. I stepped aside from the other guy. He looked about Ray's age, with a beaky nose and prominent Adam's apple, already stubbling a bit on his cheeks. He wore what Ray called "the uniform"—white cotton T-shirt, jeans, cowboy boots. *And* a cowboy hat, a battered pale thing that he'd taken off, holding it in his left hand. I took in the engine grease on his fingers, added it to the sweat-band the hat had pressed into his forehead, the way his hair lay flat and the faintly perplexed look he was wearing, and came up with *what the hell?* "How do you do, sir."

"Ma'am." He blinked. His eyes were very blue, and there was a high blush of windburn along his cheekbones. He wasn't handsome, not yet. In a while, when his features settled, he might be. He was already shaving, that was for sure. "I mean, uh, miss."

"When's Mama coming back?" Ray was in the kitchen, and I heard the clink of cans.

Uh-oh. "Soon. She just went to the diner to apply." And some other places, too, but I wasn't going to tell him that. This looked like trouble, and maybe if he thought Mama was due back soon he wouldn't be able to get up a headstart into it. "Ray—"

He showed up again, with the five leftover cans of beer. Mama used them for cooking sometimes, and for sipping other times, and he wasn't supposed to get into it even though he did. He dangled them, one finger through the empty plastic ring, and his smile made sense now. "I promised Alex some beer. He got me hired at the place I wanted, remember I told you about it?"

I do. "Ray, you can't take those." I tried to sound firm and no-nonsense. I don't think I managed it, though.

"What, you want me to leave you one? Not gonna happen." He obviously intended to go so fast he escaped before I could say anything, so I planted myself squarely in his path and kept my arms folded.

"You know it isn't allowed."

"Relax, Dez. I'll be back after dark, don't wait up." He reached up as if he was going to ruffle my already-falling-down ponytail, and I flinched away, almost running into the new guy, who smelled like motor oil and fresh air. No tang of cigarette smoke, so at least Ray wasn't smoking again, but it wasn't going to be a happy time once Mama got home and found out about *this.* Even though I wasn't doing anything wrong, her disappointment would still collect in the corners, even worse than worry-static.

I glanced at the other guy, who was staring at me with a line between his sandy eyebrows, like he'd seen me somewhere before. No help there, and Ray would be furious if I embarrassed him in front of his new friend. "Ray, come on. Mama wanted you here for dinner. Your friend can stay, too." Desperate times calling for desperate measures, even though all we had to offer for dinner was beans and some cut-up franks.

"That's right kind of you—" Alex started, and Ray's gusty sigh was full of peppermint from his gum.

"I don't think Alex wants to hang around *here.* We're going driving."

And drinking. Wonderful. More desperate measures were called for. "Come back for dinner, then. You know how much Mama—"

That got me an eyeroll and the beginnings of a threatening glare. "You're turning *into* Mama. Come on, Alex."

The blond guy was still looking at me. He cleared his throat, and something in the way he did it made Ray stop.

"I'll bring him back for dinner, miss." He still held the hat, awkwardly, and it occurred to me that he'd taken it off to come inside, just like a soldier. "I don't want anyone's mama to worry." He didn't quite talk as syrup-slow as they do down South, but there was a definite twang there. You could just see him roping heifers or whatever it was they herded out here.

44

So there, Ray. But I winced inwardly. If Ray got snotty there would be a fight with him and Mama, and me not able to say anything because the rock would fill my throat and my head would go all dark inside. "Thanks, mister."

"It's Alex, miss." He even offered his hand, and I was so relieved that Ray didn't immediately jump in I gave him mine. Warm hard fingers, and I remembered my manners for the second time that day.

"I'm Dez. Can we offer you a drink of water?"

"Mighty kind, but no." He nodded, though, and didn't let go. "I'll have him home for dinner, Miss Dez," he said, and the way he was looking at me shifted a couple degrees. Into what I couldn't quite say, but Ray sighed and jangled the beer cans.

"Then we'd better get going." Ray gave me a glare that promised trouble later, but I was more occupied with tugging my hand out of his new friend's. I was blushing again, too, and that was weird. It was like someone had turned up my thermostat, or like the wind had just warmed and pushed a bunch of hot air into the trailer.

Still, the guy hesitated. "Did you want to come along?"

I almost lost my jaw, my mouth *actually* fell open. Going driving with a stranger with beer in the car? Even if Ray was there, Mama would have a purple *fit.* "No thanks, mister. Ray hates me tagging along."

He was still studying me, with that look like he was trying to read something in fine print. "You two aren't from around here? Reason I ask is, you talk real nice."

I finally figured out what his expression was. Maybe I had dust on my face or something, and he was trying to tell me. So I got my hand back and rubbed at my cheek, hoping I got it. "We're military." Same thing I'd said a million times before. "We were onbase, but our daddy...well." I almost said *he's gone to Jesus,* because that's what Marcie called it when anyone passed on. Funny, though, she'd just said *your daddy's past,* as in history. I couldn't figure out if she thought maybe Jesus wouldn't take him, or she meant he wasn't coming back.

"Aw. I'm sorry." He said it like he really was, too, and Ray made a restless movement. "Tell you what, Ray, why don't we go pick your car up and come back here? I'd like to meet your mama, if you don't me saying so."

Maybe he could read the desperation on me. At the moment, I didn't mind so much. Relief filled my chest, and I may have actually smiled. "That would be *great.* Mama is always saying Ray needs more friends." Which was a lie—what she said was *you need better friends than jailbirds, Raymond Sarpe, and I wish you'd find some.*

"You sure I won't be intruding?" Very nice, very hesitant. In his big blond corncob way, he seemed like a good egg.

"Of course not." *I'm just being polite, is all. And stopping Ray.*

"Might as well leave the beers here then," Ray piped up, and pushed them into my hands. His own smile was a marvel of forced politeness—he couldn't very well un-invite his new friend, now could he? I was so relieved I didn't even care about him being pissy later. He might even try to give me an Indian rope-burn. "We'll be back. Thanks, Dez. You're so *gracious*."

"Mama trained me well, I guess." I didn't roll my eyes, but oh, how I wanted to. They trooped out, Ray giving me a dark glance and Alex—I found out later he was Alex Carr, and that his daddy owned a chain of garages, which made him not quite local royalty but certainly *well-to-do*, as Marcie put it—looked at me again in that weird way, like I had something stuck on my face. As soon as they cleared the driveway I ran into the bathroom to look, but there was nothing but tangled hair and no makeup, white as a sheet except for the fading flush in my cheeks. Maybe I'd gotten something embarrassing rubbed away, for once. It was pretty charitable of the guy, all told.

I hurried to put the beer up and stir the beans, and wished I could call Mama to warn her. As it was, all I could do was put the dry part of biscuit dough together and hope.

CHAPTER FIVE

Partly Mollified

SOMETIMES MAMA JUST *KNEW* THINGS. At any rate, she arrived home with a couple packages of not franks but kielbasa, more milk, ketchup, and a whole clutch of sugar snap peas from Marcie's garden. Of course, when she walked in the door she'd already seen the Camaro and Alex's truck, and the boys were on the back stoop drinking and talking in that circuitous way males do, quiet laughter every now and again and strange primitive sounds. I was glad it was just two of them—more than that and boys get rowdy, like some law of physics fills them up with too much burnable testosterone.

Mama set the grocery bag on the counter, and I began hurried explanations.

"It's Ray's new friend from the garage, Mama. I invited him for dinner because..." I wavered on the edge of tattling, but Mama's sparkling eyes and broad smile deterred me.

"Oh, honey, you're so good. And making biscuits already, I see. Glad I thought we should celebrate a little." She hugged me, smelling of salt, fresh wind, but no sharp reek of cigarette.

It looked pretty good, and I decided I could guess. "Did you get the job?"

"I did!" The smile became a full-on grin, lighting up her face and easing almost every bit of anxiety lingering in me. "Mrs. Jalla—that's the owner—said that if Marcie liked me, that was good enough for her. It's been a dog's age since I waited tables, but—" She might have said more, but there were footsteps, and in through the front door came Ray and Alex, both holding bottles of grape soda—Alex had brought it, in lieu of beer.

Raymond was just going to *kill* me.

Anyway, now that Mama was home I didn't have to be the hostess, and I could just concentrate on rolling out the biscuits and tending the beans, dressing the sugar snap peas, and generally being too busy to talk while the conversation flowed around me. It was a relief, but every time I glanced at the table someone seemed to be looking at me. Mostly Alex, with that line between his eyebrows, but once or twice Mama with a puzzled expression, and often Ray, with that familiar almost-scowl that meant he was only partly mollified by how well things were going, since his guest seemed so impressed.

The oven ran hot, but I knew its tricks by now, and besides for biscuits you want it just this side of scorch. Setting the table, stirring the beans, Mama rising to help and being shooed back down, the vinegar shaken over sugar snaps sliced into ribbons, margarine and the salt and pepper, kielbasas slices browning, drained and stirred into the beans with the final dollop of ketchup. Alex leapt up to help me with the stockpot and almost got burned trying to take it; it thumped on the table and made it shudder. There wasn't room for everything, but at least I could put hot biscuits on every plate, and nothing burned or burst into flame. Mama said grace, and Ray might have rolled his eyes if Alex hadn't folded his hands and looked down properly, which meant Ray couldn't act like a doofus.

Maybe he'd turn out to be good for Ray. Anyway, I kept leaping up to refill plates and glasses, until Mama snapped at me to stop being a grasshopper and sit down properly. Which I did, but that just meant *she* started getting up to fetch for our guest. Still, I watched to make sure she didn't scrape her plate into the trash.

She didn't. She also didn't protest when Ray and Alex left to go driving afterward, Alex's truck growling a little before he cut the wheel and got past the Camaro and the Ford safely. I watched, a dishtowel limp in my hands; when they had gone I checked, and let out a soft breath of relief.

The beers were still in the fridge.

• • •

THE PROMPT ONES

Mama left early the next morning, so I just had to wait for the sound of the Ford to wither under the wind so I could tiptoe out while Ray's door was tightly closed. I locked up and ran for the backyard. The path was there, bright and shining under dawn light. That's one thing about the plains—if you manage to get out the door at the right time, you can see the light come up like thunder. A heavenly furnace on the far end of the horizon, layers of thick-smeared gold and red with indigo bands between, and even if there's no birds calling there's still the, I don't know, the moment just before an orchestra begins to play. Mama sometimes listened to classical on the car radio, and there was always that hush before the first wall of sound rose. If we still went to church, maybe I could call it holy. It gives the same kind of lift in your chest and behind your eyes.

Slipping and sliding down the gullyside, I left the mobile home park behind and by the time I got to the bottom I was hop-skipping like I used to on the playground. I don't know quite why I went so fast, but the aspens

48

were dark and the path went from side to side, and it seemed like I had to jump to keep up. It ended with me out of breath at Ms. Iyaga's garden gate, and I knocked cautiously once, twice, before opening it. I stepped through, vines rustling on either side of me, and the light intensified. The morning must have started sliding down into the gully after me, right on the heels of my battered sneakers.

There was a path of smooth river stones, just right for stepping. Between them, green moss like veins under skin. I made it a game, imagining the moss as lava. Ray and I used to play that a long time ago, in the base housing in Missouri and the summer of sticky heat that melted the roads and made Mama thinner than ever—and Daddy more angry.

A flash of red and white was the old woman opening her door and shuffling out, and for a moment I thought I was too early or something, because she scowled. Her strong knotty hands held a blue earthenware mug breathing steam; it didn't smell like coffee but there was so much else going on in my nose I couldn't tell. Damp earth, the dust-spiced wind, a medley of flowers and fresh green like grass had just been cut, a faint smoky odor I couldn't place.

I stopped at the porch steps. They were just as gray and weathered as her fence and gate, and looked like the same kind of piecework. The mobile was extra-shiny, though, a fat silver pig snoozing contentedly. There was even a crooked stovepipe chimney with a thin thread of whitish smoke rising from it, just like a painting. The skirting had a weird pattern of overlapping rings, but I didn't look too closely. My mouth had gone dry, because she was *still* scowling.

"Good morning, ma'am," I managed. "You said to come in the morning."

"That I did." She pulled a sour face. "I hate the prompt ones."

What? Did she want me to leave? "Should I come back later?"

"Well, you're already here. I suppose you know how to clean, little girl?" She sniffed, as if she expected me to say no.

I was born knowing that. "Yes ma'am."

"For the love of Hell, don't call me *ma'am*. It's Gran, or Granny, Granny Iyaga if you're formal. Say it."

"Yes, Granny Iyaga." It felt weird—I'd never called anyone *Granny* before.

She paused, one curling eyebrow—they were really fierce, a pair of wire-brush caterpillars on her face—rising just like Mama's *little lady, you're missing something* expression, and I realized what came next.

"And I'm Dez," I added. "Desiree Sarpe. How do you do."

"Ah." She nodded, cupping her hands more firmly around the mug instead of offering to shake. "Well, then. I like manners, little one. I don't abide rudeness, or slipshod work."

"Neither does my mama, Granny Iyaga."

"Your mama." The old woman squinted. "Black of hair and blue of eye, no doubt, and your brother just the same. You, though, you've got the jade. I wonder if that's why..." She halted, took a sip from the steaming mug. "Well, no matter. Come up, come in, you may have tea before you begin."

"Yes, Granny Iyaga." I'd decided discrumption was the better part of valor, like Mama sometimes said. The stairs looked rickety, but they felt plenty solid, and I followed her inside.

It didn't occur to me to wonder how she knew so much about our eyes.

· · ·

IN THE WILDERNESS

It wasn't coffee, it was tea so sweet and strong it could have been. It was the tea that added the spice-smell to her kitchen, a powerful warm scent. She put lumps of a brownish-black sugar in the bottom of the cups, muttering that in her day they had chewed it, but since the 'mancipation this was better.

I didn't know quite what to think of that, even though we studied the Civil War in fifth grade and again in eighth, and last year too.

Everything inside was round—the potbelly stove, the curved walls, the tiny dinette table where she ate her solitary meals. Her fridge was an ancient one, sort of like ours, with a curved front face and the habit of ticking loudly to itself, whatever brand name had been glued to the front long gone. The floor was a glossy sealed black that sometimes felt like metal, and other times like linoleum. I could never figure out which, even when I scrubbed or mopped it.

It wasn't very dirty, but there were some cobwebs, and a pile of laundry almost as tall as me to put into the ancient washer with its chipped white-enamel coat. Potted plants hung everywhere—philodendrons, airplane plants, others I couldn't name, African violets and cactuses and others crowding all the horizontal surfaces. A rocking chair of dark, age-polished wood sat next to the stove, and her washbasin had a pump handle instead of a faucet.

There was a funny dial on top of the pump, you pushed it to red for hot and white for cold. Most of the space in the kitchen was a gigantic butcher-block table piled with green things—bits of flowers, stalks and stems, branches and other pieces. More bleached, brown slivers of what I thought was wood but found out later... wasn't. Round, fat-bellied iron pots in different sizes—the only place I'd ever seen those was in camping goods stores. Of course, it was like she was camping out here, really, in the wilderness. I meant to ask her why she lived at the bottom of the gully, but it somehow never came up. I told her about Mama, about school, about Ray and his new job at the garage, and she told me... not very much. Just that she was old, and she lived out of the way so as not to have to deal with fools. "World is full," she muttered, knocking her pipe clean into a blue ceramic dish shaped like a fish. "Right to the brim, with fools."

I had to agree. "My mama says *her* mama said God loves fools and poor people, and that's why there's so many."

"She left out insects and dirt." But Granny's mouth twitched. Her accent was still hard to place, hard on the consonants, but funny sometimes as if she had cotton wadding packed into her cheek. "You listen to your mama, then?"

"Of course." It didn't seem possible *not* to, but then, Ray managed it. I almost asked if Granny had kids, but it didn't seem a polite question just at that moment.

In any case, she insisted I drink all the tea, even the sweet sludge at the bottom. "Keeps you safe," she muttered, then rose with a creak and a groan. "Start in the kitchen, child. Under the sink and in that closet, you'll find everything you need. When noon strikes, you go home."

I twisted in my seat to look for a clock, and she cackled a bit. It was the first sign of outright amusement she'd shown, and she shuffled for the door, surprisingly quickly. "Don't worry, I have the time here." She tapped at her tightly-braided white hair, and was still chortling when the front door opened wide and a wall of sunlight swallowed her.

At least she was a little less sharp-cranky. And thirty dollars a week wasn't much, but I could at least *help* with one of the bills.

I looked under the sink—ammonia, vinegar, rags, bleach, harsh powdered soap, two buckets. The narrow little closet she'd pointed at held two brooms, a surprisingly sturdy mop, and an assortment of other cleaning supplies. I whipped out the kerchief I'd stuffed in my back pocket, tied it around my head just like Mama during spring cleaning, and got to work.

CHAPTER SIX

Souls to Threadbare

R AY CUT THE WHEEL HARD, but he had the Camaro at just the right speed so the bump up into the lot didn't rattle teeth or axles. "Don't even know why I gotta take you," he said for the fiftieth time.

"We need groceries," I replied, for *my* fiftieth time, keeping a grip on my temper with teeth and toenails. "Mama said."

"*Mama said*," he sneered back. "If I'm late I'm gonna give you a rug burn."

"You're not late at all." My head hurt a little. He didn't work until two, so I had plenty of time to clean for Granny Iyaga and get back up the gully's side. Nobody asked where I went in the mornings—Mama left for the breakfast shift at the diner, and Ray was pretty much always sleeping in until noon. Which meant I came back just as he was yawning and bad-tempered before his coffee.

Mama had put her foot down about him working two jobs, and he made a fuss, but in the end he dropped the first place and went to work at Carr's Garage. I tried not to laugh at the name, but it was too much for me, and it just made Ray madder. He was getting more and more prickly about things like that.

The Camaro slowed to a decorous pace, and he parked it with prissy care in a dusty lot behind the garage. After seeing all the sky and grass crowding up on the trailer park, it was kind of a shock to be around buildings again. Across the highway—it narrowed to four lanes and had stoplights here, going through the suburb—was the Gibson Library, two stories of brick and pure wonder, and I had plans for getting me a card since it was part of the county system. There was a big shiny superstore there too—pharmacy, McDonald's, photo processing, flowers, you name it. The parking lot was huge and freshly painted, and I could almost *feel* the big store crouching there, ready to suck in everyone to empty their pockets down to lint and their souls to threadbare.

For all that, they had low prices, and I had Mama's grocery list safe in my pocket as well as the budgeted amount and Mama's grocery calculator. At the end of Ray's shift I could load the Camaro with bags, and then all I would have to worry about was dinner.

But before then, I could go over to the library, and read *all day* while he was working.

I waited for him while he locked the Camaro up and stood there looking at it for a second, like it was a puzzle he was trying to figure out. The blue coverall made him look older; there was a shadow of Daddy in his face even at rest now, and especially in the way he stood—back straight, thumbs near pockets, all military. That profile, heavy on the chin and nose, familiar and strange all at once.

We used to look alike until he got his Adam's apple. Later, well, not so much.

He finally nodded a little and gave me a sharp glance. I just stood there, bright sun beating down and making heatshimmers over the cars clustered up near the blue box of the superstore. There were homes around here too, developments full of cubes like tofu. All the same, and laid out on ruler-straight streets for the most part. When you had this much space, right angles made sense, maybe. If you could get on the roof of the superstore, you could maybe see skyscrapers glittering in the distance under a pall of smog. The city's tentacles hadn't achieved any height, they just...oozed, in perfect squares. Sweat prickled along my lower back, and I would have liked to be down in the gully. Granny said the water there was good for aches, and sometimes sent me to fetch a pailful. Summer storms kept it trickling along, and there was a place between two rocks that was just-right to fill the bucket, and if you were careful you didn't even get any sparkling sediment in it. I usually pretended I was panning for gold, back in the old-timey.

"Well, come on, and see the place." As if he wasn't dying to show me the brand-spanking-new building. Even though they only had him on part time, stepping and fetching, Alex had told his daddy about Ray's way with cars, and if Ray worked hard he could get a bay of his own. As ambitions went, it was a good one for him.

I bounced along behind him. There was powdered cleanser on my jeans, but I didn't care. A whole day to spend in the library, in air-conditioned comfort, reading until my eyes fell out. Maybe they'd have something... well, like a romance. I almost blushed at the thought, but I figured it was about time to expand my horizons and Mama read pink-jacketed books all the time, so they couldn't be *all* bad. Even if she did stuff them in her purse where Daddy couldn't see. *Them nasty books*, he called them. *How many times do I gotta tell you...*

I shivered and hurried along.

It was a nice place, as garages went, and I made all the appropriate noises to soothe Ray's ego. I had just about escaped when we rounded the corner into the waiting room—pretty ritzy, with a hardwood floor and dangly light fixtures that looked like Sno-cones—and there was Alex behind the desk, looking over the receptionist's shoulder as she tapped something in. "It just won't let me use that field," she said, and I half-recognized her from the Sav-Mor. Mrs. Gundiesson, with her permed cap of bright-red hair and her slash of crimson lipstick that feathered into the small wrinkles around her lips when she went shopping. "I am about to heave this goldurn thing through the window."

Alex, in coveralls that matched Ray's, wiped his hands on a dirty rag. There was a fresh scrape across his knuckles, it looked a little painful. But he leaned over Mrs. Gundie's shoulder and tapped at the keyboard. That line was back between his eyebrows, and if he didn't watch it, it was going to be permanently graven.

He looked older, too, but most of it could have been the black smudges on his cheek and the way his hair was messy, as if he'd forgotten himself and run grimy hands back through it. "There, see? You need to clear that one before it'll let you move on."

"You're a lifesaver. Why ain't you in here, instead of monkeying around with those engines?" Her big red plastic earrings swung, and I got a hint of AquaNet even this far across the room.

"Engines like me. These, not so much." He straightened, and caught sight of us, and the bottom of my stomach dropped out for some reason. "'Sides, dressing up makes me nervous. Hey, Sarpe."

"Hey, Carr." Ray nodded at Mrs. Gundiesson. "Ma'am."

"Hello there, Raymond." The lady squinted at me. "Is this your sister? My, isn't she a pretty thing?"

"Thank you, ma'am." I had to squish down all my impatience and be social now. "Mrs. Gundiesson? I remember you from the Sav-Mor."

That made her take a closer look at me. "That's right, last summer. Never a broken egg when you bagged my things." When she smiled, her whole face lit up, and it was cheerful to see even if I just wanted to get *away*. "Not like that other girl—Samantha? The blonde girl, with the long nails."

She was one of Mr. Ridge's favorites. Sam's nails were Lee Press-Ons, and she'd been so proud of them. I sort of wished we could afford them, but getting them knocked askew when you brought the cart in sounded painful. I shifted uncomfortably, searching for an answer that wouldn't show how much I hadn't really liked Sam either.

I didn't get far, because Alex came around the end of the desk, and he was looking right at me. "You gonna keep your brother on track today?"

Ray rolled his eyes, and a laugh caught me sideways. "He doesn't need me for that. I came to do grocery shopping across the lot."

"I can drive you home, after." He was still working his fingers around in that rag. "I'm off in an hour."

I glanced at Raymond, who was no help, plainly eager to get started. He coughed a little self-consciously and bumped me with his shoulder. "I'm heading in. Remember to get the right bacon."

"Yessir, I'll get your pepperbacon." I almost said *yessir I will get your damn bacon*, but with Mrs. Gundiesson there I couldn't. I was hoping that would put an end to the whole conversation, but Alex stopped about three feet from me, still working at that rag. He was going to need soap to get all that off, the dry cloth had done about all it could do.

"I'll drive you." Like he was daring me to turn him down.

So I tried. "It's okay, I'm going to the library."

"Well, then, afterward. No reason for you to stay here all day." Alex grinned, a wide open expression. "Unless you want to. I can teach you how to change the oil filter on a '89 Comeau."

"I already know how to change oil." There might not be a graceful way out of all this, and if I let him drive me home I could get everything put away and get a real dinner started. I could also lay on my mattress and read, if I brought books home. No air conditioning, but there was ice in the fridge. "I don't want to put you to any trouble," I hedged.

"No trouble at all." There was a younger Alex peeking out from that smile of his, and behind him, Mrs. Gundiesson was smiling too, a fond, half-rueful expression. She didn't look shocked or disapproving, so that was good. I was apparently acting proper enough. "I gotta go out that way anyway, won't do any harm to drop you off. I'm off in an hour."

"It might take me longer." I restrained the urge to dig my toe into the hardwood. Chill air played across my bare shoulders, they had air conditioning in here, too. "I don't want to make you late."

"Shoot, I can stand to be a little late. Go on to the library, come back in an hour, and I'll help you carry everything. It's a hot day."

I glanced at Mrs. Gundiesson again, but she was no help. Ray was already gone, probably to hover and watch the mechanics working, running to fetch something when they needed it, organizing, cleaning up. He came home with his head stuffed full of cars, and it was a nice change from his usual sullenness. Even if the self-important bug made him sharp. I imagined it was like a wasp, an angry little insect with a stinger, and when it came around to make you miserable you couldn't help but get all snitty.

"It's very nice of you," I said, politely.

"Good. Go on now, come back in an hour when I'm done." Alex nodded, and I backed up a step, two, doing math inside my head.

"I'll pay you for the gas," I said, even though it meant skinning the budget a little tighter. "I'll be back in an hour."

I got out of there, and didn't realize I was wearing a big stupid grin until I was halfway across the highway.

• • •

FOR THE BEST

He was full of questions—where we'd lived, how long, what I'd seen in different places. Daddy had been stationed all over, and reciting the litany got boring—Philippines, Missouri, New York, Virginia, Germany, Missouri again, North Carolina, and then here. He didn't ask about Daddy's passing but I told him anyway, and he offered his sincere condolences. Which just made it a little more difficult for me to decide between grief or relief, and he was likely to be shocked if I asked him which he thought I was feeling. He watched me work the calculator with an odd expression, and at the end of it, when I tried to give him gas money, he shook his head and looked serious. "I'm going that way anyway, Miss Dez. Don't pay it no mind."

I would have put my foot down, but he was already lifting the groceries and my bag of library books into his truck, and there was no way I could protest at that point. He even offered me his hand when I stepped up into the passenger seat, but I was fine even though it was jacked up high enough to cradle eggs during a roller coaster.

The windshield was a little milky, but when he turned the key the engine settled into grumbling smoothly. Maybe Ray had tuned it up for him, because it had sounded louder before. Or maybe it just sounded different on the inside, like a lot of things. I got myself buckled in and rolled the window down. With the wind coming in, it was too loud to talk. It didn't stop him from trying, but I acted like I didn't hear and watched the pavement slip away underneath us. Sometimes I smiled and nodded, though, just to keep everything polite and smooth.

At first everything around there looked flat as a table. When you got closer, or you drove along with the wind filling your head, you began to notice it undulated. A lot could hide in those shallow hills and dips, especially with the heat haze shimmering and the buzz of the radio indistinct under the roar of air protesting at being cut by such a blunt object. I was almost sorry when Alex slowed down—he didn't drive like Ray, I didn't feel like he was going to take it into his head to gun it and leap a ditch or two just because he could. We bounced into the mobile home park, and the owner's white castle in the middle was even prettier with the sun dripping thick as honey everywhere. The entire park looked dingier and more rundown by comparison, but comfortable. Somehow that light softens even discarded toys in weedy front yards and rickety slapdash porches going up to torn screen doors.

The radio turned out to be country-western, and someone was singing about a woman and a dog. All those songs blur together after a while. I probably heard this one in the box store, too.

Our mobile was a sorry sight, but at least the holes in the skirting were patched and I'd got some of the weeds out of the gravel driveway. Granny Iyaga said some things would grow out of the gully—succulents, tough plants that didn't need much water and could keep their own against the grass. She was going to teach me how to keep them, too, so we could have a sort of garden. Maybe.

The truck shut off, and I kept looking at the mobile. It wasn't so bad. The worst thing would be fixing that patio door, it was the kind of expensive that couldn't be patched. I didn't know anything about glass, and neither did Ray, but maybe we could trade with someone who did.

What *could* we trade, though? I'd have to ask Ray. He'd know.

I came back to myself with an internal jolt. Alex was just sitting there, quietly, his hands on the steering wheel. The grocery bags behind the bench seat had stopped their rustling, and I'd have to get the milk in before it warmed up too much more.

I searched—again—for something to say. Nothing quite fit, and I was abruptly aware of how quiet it was during the day here. Everyone at work, or inside watching their televisions during the long slow hot afternoon. At least it was dry heat, like an oven door opening, not the close wet fug of Missouri, and the sky didn't get that yellowgreen sickly color that meant tornadoes were on the way. Living there had been all sweat and fear, Daddy perpetually angry and Mama's hair coming out and the time I peed in my closet because I was so scared Daddy was going to come upstairs—

Quit thinking about Missouri. I cleared my throat. "Thanks."

"Welcome." Alex finally moved, but it was only to unlock his door. "I'll help you get everything inside."

"I can—"

"I know you can, but it's hot. I'll help."

I wasn't so sure Mama would like me letting anyone in while she was gone, but he was already out of the truck and I scrambled to get free of my seatbelt. It was just like unloading the car with Raymond, except Alex didn't roll his eyes or sigh when he hefted the heavy stuff, he just *did* it, and waited patiently on the porch while I fought with the door and got it unlocked. I would have carried more in, but he was already doing it, and in the end I didn't have to lift a blessed thing except my books, and I could start getting everything in the fridge right away.

First, though, I had to offer him a glass of water. He drank it on the front porch, as if he was afraid to come inside.

There wasn't much shade. He stood a little spraddle-legged, the way guys do, taking up space for themselves *and* their invisible friends. Hot bright sunny day, his blue eyes shaded under the brim of that battered pale cowboy hat, and his coveralls were full of dust and motor oil, but he looked happy. His eyes were bright, and he took long swallows of the water out of the cobalt cup. The wind was a whisper, but there was another buzz.

"Listen to that." He shook his head. "You don't go out into those fields, do you? You know what that is?"

"What? The buzzing?" It was just *there*, like the wind. What was there to know?

"Whole damn county's full of snakes. Rattlers. Big year for them, I guess. They'll try to get away before they fight, but you know to stay away from rock piles and stuff, right?"

"Of course." It was news to me, but I didn't want him knowing that. Mama hadn't said anything about snakes, just about flash floods and strangers knocking at the door. "I'm not scared of snakes."

"Out here you should be, probably." He took another mouthful of water, and he looked so dusty and sort of, I don't know, hangdog I guess, that I folded my arms.

"Come inside and sit down while you drink that." I had to put the margarine away too, and everything else that needed refrigeration.

"I'd like that." He drained the rest of the glass. "But I won't."

"Why not?"

"Your mama might not like it."

Now I felt like an idiot. Was *that* what he was thinking? "Oh. Well, I mean, you're one of Ray's friends."

"I know." He grinned, touched his hat brim, just like in a movie. "But I figure I'd better come back when your mama's home, Miss Dez. I kind of want to see what you got from the library."

That perked me up a little. "Do you read?"

"I'm *ignorant*, city girl. Not *illiterate*."

I stood there trying to figure out how I'd offended him, but he handed me the glass, touched his hatbrim again, and stepped down the rickety stairs. Just like a cowboy. He even had the boots.

Halfway to the truck, he stopped and turned around, peering at me from under his hatbrim. "Hey."

"Hey what?" *Is he mad? What the hell did I do?*

He hooked his thumbs in his pockets, and his hands seemed a little unsteady. Maybe he was tired from work. "Can I call you?"

"We have a phone," I managed, the rock in my throat sticking-dry. I couldn't see under his hat enough to gauge his expression. My heart had decided it was going to thump around like I'd just been caught sneaking one of Daddy's Hostess pies from the pantry when he was In A Mood. A bad mood, not just a silent one.

"I know you do." Slowly, as if I was a moron. "I'm asking if I can call *you* on it."

"I guess."

It wasn't until the roostertail of dust had died down after his truck and I'd gotten everything perishable into the fridge that I realized what he might have been asking and had to lean against the front of its cool enamel, my cheeks on fire for some reason.

It didn't matter, though. When he did call, he just talked to Ray and didn't even ask after me. I couldn't decide how to feel about that, but it was probably for the best.

CHAPTER SEVEN

Secrets

G RANNY IYAGA THUMPED A MEDIUM-SIZED CAST-IRON POT ONTO the butcher block, pushing aside a pile of fennel I'd gathered for her just that morning. Dew-wet and smelling of licorice, it lay there silently wilting, and she picked through it with her strong, rough fingers. I was beginning to get the idea that she didn't have to arthritis-shuffle around to get places, she just *liked* to. I was arranging the last of the laundry, some fine-spun cotton dresses that'd needed air drying. They didn't *look* like hers, but maybe they were old memories she didn't want to part with.

Everything inside the trailer was still round, and still full of plants, but it seemed larger in here now. Probably because I'd gotten the cobwebs down, and scrubbed pretty much every surface—including, very gently, a lot of plant leaves. I went around mumbling their names under my breath, because Gran didn't like to repeat herself and I wanted to remember; I kept checking out plant identification books at the library. Between making Gran's mobile shipshape and cleaning ours, I was beginning to think I was going to be scrubbing in my dreams as well.

But it was nice. Mama ate more often than not, and her inky black hair had all come back. It looked pretty, cut shorter than I could ever remember it being and framing her face, especially when she pulled it back with barrettes. Ray was getting more hours, too, and Alex sometimes came over for dinner. He didn't try to talk to me, which was...well, I didn't mind.

Did I?

I finished the last dress, fastening the straps to satin loops attached to the padded hanger to keep it hanging straight, and carried an armful of the pretty, gauzy things into her small, curvy bedroom with its big snow-white bed. The headboard, age-darkened wood fantastically carved with curlicues that almost seemed to move, probably weighed as much as the rest of the trailer. I'd given up wondering how she fit everything in here.

Her clothespress was ancient too, and smelled faintly nasty under the goodness of the cedar it was built of. I was going to have to figure out how to sweeten it in there, eventually, but next on my list was another lick at her old-fashioned, pebble-tiled bathroom. She didn't have a shower, let alone a bathtub, and it was a wonder she kept herself so clean with just a sink, a washbasin, and a commode.

I touched the green leaves trailing down by her bedroom door. "Philodendron," I murmured. Heart-shaped leaves, rhizomes—soon I'd ask her for cuttings, once there was a good moment. You always have to pick your time for asking anything, with anyone. When in doubt, just don't.

It's safest that way.

"What's she mumbling, over there? Ill-wishing old Granny?" The old lady laughed, one of her peculiar chuffing not-really-amused sounds. She had a lot of them. Her sense of humor was strange, but I supposed she'd lived long enough to get what Mama would call Peculiar. There are all sorts of peculiars, from the weird to the nutty to the actively batshit. Funny how old ladies get Peculiar, in all its different shades, but old men just get Mean.

"Philodendron," I repeated, but louder. "So I remember."

"Mh. Come here, child." Her black caftan swooshed a little; she wore funny triangular slipper-shoes embroidered with curlicues and strange symbols. I never saw her ankles. She wore leggings, always and ever, and they buttoned onto her slipper-shoes.

I made my way across the trailer, pushing my sweatshirt sleeves up. Down here in the shade of the house it didn't get oven-hot, it didn't even get more than warm. I didn't sweat while scrubbing like I did at home. Besides, this was a baggy, paper-thin sweatshirt, with USAF stamped on the front, the logo rapidly graying out to match the material. Ray had almost worn it to shreds, but it was too small for him now and I took over.

She'd finished selecting some of the fennel and bundled the rest, tying a knot in the rough cotton twine and handing it to me. I knew what to do by now, and hung it carefully on the drying rack by the ancient hutch that might have held china, but its windows were too dusty to see through. *Leave that alone*, she'd told me. *Even an old woman needs secrets.*

The *one* thing she didn't want me to clean, and it was smack dab in the middle of her living space. Go figure.

She beckoned me back to the big butcher block. Some of the fennel went into the cauldron, and a whole lot of other stuff—dried twigs I couldn't identify, mint, crumbly black stuff that stank, but of what I couldn't say. She glanced at me, her nut-wrinkled face pursed up tight. "You keep secrets, don't you, girl."

I suppressed a guilty flinch. I hadn't told Mama about my job. Instead, I slipped the worn notes Granny Iyaga gave me into Mama's purse, tucking them carefully in her billfold the way she usually did. They folded up nice and easy with whatever tips she brought home, and the worried look when she sat down with the bills two days ago hadn't been very bad at all. More thoughtful.

"Well?" Gran demanded.

"Yes, Gran." No reason to deny it. Everyone kept secrets. Like Mama, with the scar on her arm. *I burned myself on that silly stove.* Or Ray, with his black eye. *It was an accident.*

Or Daddy. *I ain't gonna hurt you.* Except that was less a secret and more of a flat-out lie. Grief or relief, I still couldn't figure it out. I was thinking maybe Mama hadn't either, with the way she sometimes cried in her bedroom late at night.

She tried to keep it quiet, but I knew. Maybe I was the only one that could hear her, because Ray didn't talk about it.

Granny's face wrinkled up even further, like she was thinking of something with a bad taste. "Well, I got a few of my own."

Well, duh. Anyone living all the way out here in the bottom of a gully had to have reasons.

My face must have done the talking for me, because she laughed again, and this time it *was* amused. The pot rattled against the table, and the plants stirred uneasily, their leaves touched by a breeze that shouldn't have been there.

"You remind me of another little girl. Vasilasa."

The name sounded foreign, so I just nodded. My hands were a little raw from the powdered cleanser, but her big double sink was as clean as the day it rolled off the assembly line now.

Gran's dark piercing gaze had gone faraway, softening just a bit. "Just like you she was. Big eyes and little doll in her pocket, that doll—" She trailed off in a foreign language full of rolling *a*'s and sharp consonants. It sure as hell didn't sound like the Japanese in the war movies.

When she stopped, a thin thread of vapor rose from the cauldron. It wasn't smoke, but I still inhaled as if to shout, to warn her, but the look she gave me could have cut right through the gullyside and kept going for miles through solid rock. "Hush, little Dasya. Come here."

I didn't want to, but I did at the same time. Like Daddy saying *don't make me come over there and get you.* My sneakers squeaked a little on that black, black floor. I knew almost every inch of it now, since I'd mopped and done a lot of the underneath-things spaces by hand, scrubbing like each speck of dirt or dust had personally offended me.

"You want to help your mama, yes? And your brother."

I nodded. My legs moved independently of me, bringing me closer and closer. The stuff lifting from the cauldron didn't have a color, but it had a weight. Like heat-haze, or very clear water, running so smooth you couldn't see the riptide underneath.

"And you work without complaint or shirking, even for Granny Fearsome in her—"

I couldn't hear the last two words in that sentence. It sounded like *chickenshit foozball,* but that almost certainly isn't right. Chickenfoot something.

Granny sighed, a deep heaving sound that stirred the plants in every corner. They rustled like they wanted to stand up and start talking, but *she* did, so they hushed. "Well, I don't know what would have happened if you came on a Sunday, child, but you came when you did. Besides, you saw that damn *chernyv'g*, and it's time, again." Gran blew across the top of the cast iron pot, and faint flickers danced upward, like sparks from a campfire.

My eyes had blurred as if I was crying. The smell was *that* powerful—pine sap, cold water full of minerals, juicy green fresh-cut grass. It filled my nose and my head, and I didn't have time to wonder before Gran grabbed my wrist and pulled my left hand forward. I knew what she was going to do, but it didn't seem important. She grabbed my right wrist too, and pushed both my hands into the thick gelatin smoke.

It certainly did have weight, that invisible shimmer. Gran let go of my hands and my fingers moved on their own, gathering it up as if I was wiping a table, folding it like laundry. Veins of warmth slid up both my arms under my sweatshirt sleeves, wicked little pleasurable shivers growing thorny-vine all the way up my arms, past my shoulders, tingling as they ran up the back of my head and under my hair, swallowing the rest of me in a rush of sparkles. My eyes brimmed over, trickles sliding down my cheeks, and Gran nodded, clicking her tongue like she did when she was deadheading the big sun-bright dahlias along one side of her mobile.

I don't know quite what happened after that. There was Gran talking to me, slow and low in that foreign language. Distant and dreamlike, except I understood every word. Inside my head we were both ghosts, and her ghost-hands held my ghost-hands, showing me how to make an invisible knot. It was sloppy and loose, so she tried again, and again. She kept going until I began to understand the knot, and when I could tie it myself her hands vanished but her voice continued, dripping knowledge like bright pennies down an old moss-choked well.

The trailer whirled, balanced on two stilts that were scale-ringed legs, and the things she told me made my heart beat slow and thick with syrupy terror and wild excitement all at once, like sneaking down to the corner store to buy forbidden candy with change culled from the couch cushions.

When I surfaced, there was nothing in the cauldron but fine white silverglitter ash. Gran pushed a mug of hot sweet tea into my hands, and looked down into my blinking, confused face.

"Secrets," she said, just once, and I understood.

• • •

STRANGER DANGER

The front porch didn't seem to sag quite so much. I sat with my arms around my knees, looking at the afternoon. Mama was due home any minute, and I'd decided beef stew was good for tonight. Cheap chuck and veggies I cut the bad bits off, but it smelled good, and out here I could watch the wind swoop through and hear all sorts of little things. The slow crackle of grass growing, the low soft brush of a bird's wings, little scurryings as the tiny animals and insects worked their way around giant human-made structures, looking for food and protection. The soft cool sound of the clouds sailing on a sky that was all compressed air molecules, a grainy sea we lived at the bottom of.

Got to empty the questions out before the answers come in, Gran said.

Ray would laugh at me for believing kid stuff. Mama would worry and maybe drag me to church if I told her what I knew now. She wouldn't want me to go see Gran again. That would make it sneaking. Or, really, it was already sneaking, but going after Mama had actually forbidden it would be double-bad sneaks.

I shut my eyes tight, but the afternoon was still there outside. The buzzing behind the house, grass full of slithering life, rose and fell in soothing waves. There was a flat tang of water, but not with the healthy smell of the creek. Instead, it was rank and foul, weeds clotted under the surface, and I knew the pool in the middle of the mobile park was probably a mess. I didn't even have to get close to it to feel the thump of disappointment.

Was that what growing up was? Finding out the shimmering pretty things were always rotten inside?

Be careful, Gran's foreign language whispered inside my skull. I still didn't know what it was, but the meaning inside the words spread through me like blood through a cotton ball. *You want to look, be warned. You might not like what you see.*

Well, you never did, did you. The world was just full of things you couldn't help but witness. Like Mama's face, paper-white, and Daddy's cherry red, and the sick sweet smell of roasting-pork-that-wasn't on a sticky-hot Missouri afternoon with the tornado sirens blaring...

I shuddered, opened my eyes again. The mobile park sweltered under late-summer sun. Dark clouds stacked on the horizon—the storms were moving in more frequently now. Autumn riding across the plains, and school approaching. Gran might let me come after school. If she did I was going to have to work triple-time to get everything cleaned for her properly, and our own house too.

Funny how I was thinking of the mobile as a *house*. Almost even that magic word, *home*. Moving around so much, always with the same breathless anxious static filling up every corner wherever we touched down, wasn't really optimal. I mean, it was fine, Mama was always there, and mostly Daddy was gone.

With him gone for good this time, there was a weird sense of...unsettled, almost. Like the ground might shift at any moment. It shifted enough while he was around, you'd think getting rid of him would make things stop whirling. Instead, it just made the invisible floor under everything we said full of strange pits and wrinkles.

The phone rang, a tinny echoing inside the mobile's depths. I barely heard it, bounced up, and for a second the world was a spinning plate around me, streaks of dun and tired paint and gleams from the metal on the mobiles clustered here on the almost-flat. I skipped sideways, ran into the doorframe, and made it into the kitchen on the third ring, breathless and with my shoulder a hot throb of pain. Scooped up the discolored ivory plastic, the chipped base of the phone familiar and heavy, the cord a tangled spiral I straightened with nervous fingers as I squeaked a hello into its black mouth.

"Well hello there." A smooth, oiled, male voice. I thought *telemarketer*, and was about to hang up. Then he said Mama's name. "May I speak to Edie, please?"

My entire body tensed up. "Who may I say is calling?"

A sharp-edged chuckle. "So polite! Tell her Richard's on the phone."

I covered the mouthpiece, made a sound like I was yelling for someone. Then I uncovered it, and found I was sweating all over. It was too hot, and the good smell of beef stew on the stove suddenly made my stomach clench. I was going to retch, I could just *feel* it. "She's busy right now. May I take a message, please?"

"*Very* good. I know your mama's at work, young lady. Please just tell her Richard called. Would you do that for me?" Oily again, a deep dark voice.

"Yessir," I mumbled, as my stomach cramped again. *I know your mama's at work.* Why would he say that? Was it a bill collector? We didn't *have* any bills past due, I knew it because I'd brought Mama iced tea and watched her pay them all, with a thoughtful instead of worried look, and she'd even given me a five for chores I'd slipped back into her billfold while she was in the shower. "I'll tell her."

"Good, good. You have yourself a nice day now, young lady."

"Thank you," I managed, but the connection cut, and the nausea broke in a fresh gush of sweat all over me. I put the phone down, very carefully, and now, despite the stifling heat in the mobile, I was cold.

It took a little while to warm up, standing there with my teeth chattering, with the stew beginning to smell good again. Rich and familiar, not spoiled and rotten. When I could move again, I bolted for the front door and locked it. The AC unit in Mama's bedroom wheezed, and I didn't dare turn on the one in the living room window until it was in the shade again or it might decide to melt or explode.

I realized I was hugging myself, like I used to when Daddy got to yelling. Forced my arms down and stood near the front door, listening hard as if the man might be sneaking around outside. *Stranger danger, stranger danger, don't ever let anyone know you're home alone.* I remembered singing that in third grade. That whole year Daddy had been in the Philippines with us in base housing in Virginia, and we had to sit near the phone every Sunday in case he could find some way to call. He sent Mama letters, too, with lists of instructions, little cartoons about the people there.

For a few moments I could almost smell that housing, the sour drains no amount of vinegar or baking soda would ever sweeten, the bread that had to be put in tupperware and sealed or the june bugs would get in. The banister I'd fallen and hit my head on, and Mama holding me in the Emergency Room, her arms shaking a little because she'd carried me, and Ray's persistent questions and whining because he was hungry.

It seemed like after Daddy came home from the Philippines things got worse. So I tried not to think about it, and even Ray wouldn't talk a lot about Virginia. He said when I was born Daddy got mean, but Mama could generally talk him around until he came back to Virginia missing a stripe and got orders for Germany.

That wasn't a good thing to think about. It was almost time for Mama to come home, Ray wouldn't be back until late. It never occurred to me *not* to tell Mama about the man calling.

Sometimes I wonder, if it had, would things have turned out different?

CHAPTER EIGHT

Questions

T HE NEXT SUNDAY WAS BREATHLESS-HOT, and I got up early enough
that Mama asked if I wanted to go to the diner with her. She had a few
hours during the after-church rush because one of the other waitresses
was sick, and since my only other option was tiptoeing around the house
so I didn't wake Ray up, I jumped at the chance. I couldn't even go down to
Gran's. *No Sundays,* she had glowered at me, when I tentatively broached
the subject.

Maybe she was religious. It didn't seem like it, though.

Mama didn't roll the window down and light a cigarette. Instead, she
turned the radio on low and hummed along with a screechy blues song
that might have been nice at a little higher volume. As it was I could only
catch half the tune, and that's worse than not hearing it at all, because
your brain keeps running around trying to make everything fit into a
pattern. It's enough to give anyone a headache, but I didn't ask her to turn
it up. I was busy with my thinking, looking out the window and watching
the grass rise and fall like waves.

When it switched to commercials, she glanced at me, then back at the
road. Already the pavement was shimmering, though it was barely past
dawn. Night still lingered in some of the cracks and hollows—down in the
gully it would still be ink-shadowed in places, and the creek just a trickle.
We hadn't had a storm for a while. Dog days, and there had been a to-do
with police cars and a firetruck on the other end of the mobile park Friday
night. Even dry heat can get to people after long enough, and the liquor
store less than five miles away probably didn't help. The end of the month
was coming up, too, when the money runs out and rent looms like a ghost
in the back of your brain, worrying at you with sharp dollar-sign teeth.

The reflectors ticked away on our side of the highway, little pops of
time marking our speed. Tick, tock. Tick, tock. The grass-waves were on a
longer tock... tock... tock, and I was busy trying to see if they would match
up after a while. The new seeing sat inside my head, and if I breathed
quietly and focused just right I could probably get the two rhythms to talk
to each other.

"Dez?" Did Mama sound uncertain, or just quiet?

"Hm?" My nail polish was chipping off. Pale pearly pink, hardly
discernible. The chips could be felt, though, and I could run my other

fingers over each one and imagine them, a map of scratch and ding. I hadn't been brave enough to buy another color of polish. Maybe next time we got groceries.

"Where do you go in the mornings, honey? Ray says you sneak out as soon as I'm gone."

Uh-oh. I'd been bracing myself for this. "I don't sneak, I just don't wake him up. There's an old lady. I do cleaning for her in the mornings. She's nice." Ray hadn't gotten me back yet for Alex's first visit, but I suspected he wanted to.

Older brothers play a long game.

"You're helping an old lady?" Again, thoughtful. Not concerned, and not angry.

"Mrs. Iyaga." *I don't think she's Japanese. You might know, though.*

"Where does she live?"

I hesitated, decided I could be honest in the least revealing way. "Outside the park a little bit."

"Ah." Mama took her foot off the accelerator as we breasted a long shallow hill. Dawn was over, but the east was still red, a sore stinging color. "Does she have a phone, this Mrs.Yaga?"

"No." I swallowed, hard, and didn't correct her about Granny's name. "But I can take you to meet her. She's foreign. I do her laundry and clean things, and she—"

"She pays you?"

"A little."

"I see." Mama's special silence wasn't worried, yet, but it was just the kind of quiet that could load up a guilty conscience with enough concrete to make it sink. "Dez, honey, why didn't you tell me?"

"I know you don't want me working." My throat threatened to close up. "But she's old, Mama, and it's not very much, honest." *And she teaches me other things.* Things I didn't want Mama knowing about.

Things that were *mine*, not hand-me-downs or Keeping Up Appearances, like Mama said Granny Avi was so good at. Granny Iyaga didn't care about appearances, it was the heart of things she was interested in, and once you got down to that heart, you could know something nobody else did.

Mama nodded, slowly, thinking this over. "I wondered where that was coming from."

I imagined Mama picking her way down the path, and what she'd think of Gran. If she forbade me, was I going to sneak anyway? I hesitated again, torn. "I can take you to meet her, but you might not like her. She's old and weird. She smells like old lady, and she's got a temper."

Mama's laughter caught us both by surprise, and it lasted a while. When she could talk again, I could tell she wasn't as worried. "Most old ladies generally do. How far outside the park does she live? Do you walk down the road?"

"No, Mama. I wouldn't do that. There's a path behind our fence. It takes ten minutes to walk down there. A lot less, really."

"I see." Thoughtful, again. "What's she paying you?"

"Thirty a week. I go in the mornings for a while, clean her house—"
—*and learn how to see things,* I added silently, *she's going to teach me more,*"—and come home for lunch. Then I do my chores and get dinner all put together. I help in her garden, weeding. She makes me wear a hat so I don't burn." *And tells me not to pull up anything useful. They're only weeds if you don't know what to use them for.*

"Well. And how did you find her?"

Was this why she'd wanted me to come along? So she could grill me? "I took a walk one day. I was bored."

"I know you get bored. So, was she expecting you today?"

"No ma'am. She says *no Sundays.*"

"Does she go to church?"

I almost rolled my eyes, caught myself just in time. "I don't know. Maybe. She doesn't talk about it."

"Well, good. She sounds harmless, I guess."

I wasn't so sure. But she wasn't anything Mama would have to worry about. "She's cranky, but I like her."

"You're a sweet girl. I wondered what you were up to. Do me a favor?"

Again I imagined Mama meeting Gran. It didn't seem like either of them would celebrate the occasion. Worse, Granny might think Mama was a fool. If she did, would she still want to teach me? "Yes ma'am?"

"Stop putting your money in my billfold."

"I want to help." My lower lip pooched out a little, just like a kid's. The reflectors kept ticking by steadily outside the Ford's window. I couldn't catch the hills, they needed more attention than I could spend with Mama talking to me.

Mama sighed. It wasn't a deep, hopeless sigh, though, it was just her *I am not going to argue with you* sound. "I know you do. And if there comes a time I need it, I'll let you know. Right now, I don't want you to worry about that. We're doing fine. Another few weeks of good tips and I might even get that patio door fixed. Wouldn't that be a sight."

"It would." Maybe I could change the subject now. "Ray likes his job."

"He certainly does. It seems like it's doing him some good. I wonder..."

I waited to hear what she wondered about, but she shook her head and turned the radio up a little. I guessed that was that, then, and went back to counting the reflectors as they marked off mile after mile. I had almost gotten the hills to match up before we arrived.

...

THE MISTER

The Souper Soup Diner had a wide dusty parking lot with plenty of space for the eighteen-wheelers rumbling right off the highway, two thick-necked cooks who spoke exclusively in grunts, and a yellowed, fading *No Hippies* sign taped to the door. Marcie declared me to be "getting taller all the time" and hugged me breathless, then set me in the kitchen with a tub of dishes to wash since the boy who usually did them was late and the trucker-rush—they got out early, even on Sundays—was filling up the diner. The owner, Mrs. Jalla, was dusky-skinned and wrapped in a bright red muumuu, and there were dots marching across her cheeks that looked like scars, as if someone had gathered up and sewed little bits of flesh into rosettes. Or as if someone had taken a teensy cigarette and burned her over and over. I found out later it was a medical condition, a type of lupus, which made me think of horror movies before I found it in a dictionary at the library.

Mrs. Jalla showed me the sanitizer, told me she'd pay me per dish, and I went to with a will. An hour later the real dishwasher—a weedy brown-haired kid with a prominent Adam's apple and a Metallica T-shirt, who smelled powerfully of spilled beer—showed up with a tale of woe and car trouble, and Mrs. Jalla read him the riot act through the steam and clatter while I kept washing. In the end, she gave him a hug he accepted with regular teenage awkwardness and she crooked her finger at me and handed me twenty dollars, despite my protests.

By then, things were hopping and humming outside, and I started helping the lean Mexican kid doing the bussing—Ramon. He clowned around and made faces at me when Mama wasn't looking, and Marcie thumped him with her hip once to get him out of the way, her big plastic earrings sparkling under the flood of sunlight coming through the big front windows. It smelled of grease and bacon, hotcakes and tired men, the burned note coffee takes on when it's sat in the pot for a while, and cigarette smoke. Mama moved like a swan through the noise and crowd; she was easily the prettiest woman in the whole place. Marcie, no slouch herself, cracked her gum and joked with the truckers, bursts of her laughter bright as a new penny in the hum. The other waitress, a short brownette with thick glasses and a habit of cocking her head while listening to an order as if she was a giant bird, didn't bother to give me the time of day, which was okay by me. I was busy enough.

She finally unbent enough to thank me for clearing five tables in a row for her, shook my hand once with a pale limp paw, and told me her name was Scatchard, and it was *Ms.*, thank you. I nodded and kept right on going.

The trucker rush trickled away, and two and a half hours had passed in an eye blink. Marcie sat me down at the counter with Ramon and put in an order for breakfast for both of us. "I declare, Dez, we're gonna hafta hire you too."

"Can't afford it," Mrs. Jalla sighed from the cash register, with a gloomy look. Ramon, next to me, muttered something under his breath. I caught the word *barata*, but I didn't know what it meant.

"Oh, hell." Marcie cracked her gum again. Her hair was just as impossibly big as ever, but not a single strand of it moved when she shook her head, making her earrings dance. "I can dream, can't I? Edie, look at how big that child is, I can't believe it."

Mama, sweeping her forehead with the back of her hand, was aglow with a faint sheen of sweat. She'd gained a little weight, and the exercise did her good. She had two barrettes in her hair today, both with bright fake diamonds on them, glittering against black strands. "Don't I know it. She's a good girl, too. Never an ounce of trouble."

"Not like Raymond." Marcie shook her head again. "He's settling down, though?"

"Seems to be." Mama retied her apron as well. Ms. Scatchard had two tables up front, and the rest were sparkling-clean. We had a little time to breathe before people came in to miss the church crowd, and then the church crowd itself would hit. "That Carr boy's a good influence. And so polite!"

"Which one? Alex, right? Nice and steady, even if he doesn't seem too bright. I get the idea he thinks more than he runs his mouth." Marcie grinned, glancing at me. "Always asks about Miss Dez every time I see him, though. Good taste."

"Oh, stop." Mama made a shooing motion and started filling napkin dispensers. Her back didn't seem to be paining her at all. "You see them everywhere. And Dez's too young for that."

"I'm sixteen," I piped up, but not loudly. Had Alex been asking about me? Why did I care? He was just Raymond's friend. And why would he ask Marcie, of all people?

Marcie's eyes were twinkling with her special brand of mischief. "Oh, honey, we were all too young. Which reminds me, what about that mister who's so sweet on you, Edie?"

"Marcie, for God's sake, I'm a widow." But Mama wore a peculiar, lopsided smile I'd never seen on her before. She moved away, and Marcie gave an eyeroll worthy of Ray himself while one of the cooks grunted her name behind the window.

"Widowed don't mean *retired*, Edie." She scooped our breakfast plates up—pancakes, bacon, eggs for both of us, but Ramon's eggs were over easy and mine were scrambled. "Here, kids. Eat up, and drink your milk. Good for you."

Ramon elbowed me. "Pass me the sugar, *chica*?"

I did, and settled into eating. The bell on the door chimed again, and I would have groaned, except Ramon repeated the elbowing. "Don't worry, it's a regular."

"Speak of the devil!" Marcie crowed. "There you are, Mister—"

A hiss from the kitchen swallowed the words, and I turned in on my spinning stool to see the new arrival.

Older gentleman in a gray suit, the maroon tie loosened a little so he didn't look starchy. Badger hair—white at the temples, black as shoe polish elsewhere. A neat little goatee, with a white patch just under his bottom lip, and he had very white teeth, sparkling as he smiled at Marcie. Eyes as cold and dark as leftover coffee, and my stomach cramped. Maybe it was just that I'd been going so hard all morning. I turned back to my now-tasteless food, picked up a bit of bacon, and nibbled at it.

That was when I heard him.

"Marcie, what a pleasure! And Edie, as lovely as ever." A rich, full, oily voice, like a politician on the radio. I'd last heard it coming through the telephone, crackling with static, and I turned cold all over again.

I know your mama's still working.

Marcie chattered at him, and that voice of his was like a river. He chatted back, and Mama ended up standing there and talking to him about how hot it was, didn't they all agree, the heat was dreadful, the dust too, polite things I'd heard a thousand times standing at the bottom of the counter as the groceries came down and the checker had to keep the conversation going.

I hunched my shoulders. What was he doing with our phone number? He wore wingtips, mirror-polished like Daddy's dress uniform shoes had to be. I knew because I kept sneaking glances. The bell on the front door kept jangling as people came in, and I kept trying to eat.

It was useless. My stomach had closed up tighter than a fist, and the air conditioner had finally gotten rid of the heat of so many truckers packed densely into the Souper Soup. Gooseflesh on my arms, prickling-painful, and when Ramon slid off his stool to carry his dishes back I decided to do the same.

"Dez?"

My stomach cramped again, and I turned around, slowly, dreading having to talk to the badger man.

But it wasn't him. It was Alex, in what had to be his Sunday best, which included a pressed summerweight suit in cream and a string tie, with his hair slicked back and a tentative smile lighting up his blue eyes.

I was so relieved I almost threw up, swallowed a hot wad of something acidic, and managed a squeaky hello.

CHAPTER NINE

In The Way

"**Y**OU TWO GO ON." Mama redid her sparkling barrette with swift fingers, and her gaze wasn't even on me. It lingered on a head of black-and-white hair, sitting by himself near the window and studying the menu as if he was in a five-star or something. As if he needed to take his time over the greasy spoon offerings. "Bring her home by four, Alex."

"Yes ma'am." He actually reached up as if to touch his hat brim.

I tried one last time. "Mama, I can help, you know."

"I *know* you can." Slightly irritated now. "But I didn't bring you along so you could be slave labor for the day, Desiree Elaine. The library's open, and this saves me a trip." She grabbed a coffeepot and strode off, and I was left with a slightly chagrined-looking Alex.

"I can just take you home, if you want," he offered. "I didn't mean to be trouble."

Well, you're not, but I don't want to leave her alone. "It's not that." Mama was filling coffee cups with a bright, set expression, and even though the badger-man was in Marcie's section I could tell she'd end up chatting with him again. When he looked up from the menu, it was to glance at my mama, way too casually. Almost like Daddy checking to see if he could find a mistake, but this man was smiling with those white teeth in the middle of that nest of goatee. "Do you know who that is? *Don't* turn and look—"

"You mean Mr. Vogg? Yeah, he's a lawyer. Business stuff." Alex frowned slightly, trying to look casual even though it was too late, he'd all but pointed at the man. "Why?"

I hesitated. "Nothing. He just seemed to know Mama."

"He's like that with everyone. Dad calls him a glad-handler." That line between Alex's eyebrows deepened a little. "Really, Dez, I just saw your mama's car and thought I'd see if she thought you wanted to go to the library. Are you working here now, too?"

Why do you care? You saw Mama's car and just came in? "Nope. Just came with Mama, because Ray was sleeping in." *And he's still mad at me over the beers, or something else. Hard to tell these days.* "He probably wouldn't mind seeing you, though."

"Well, I dunno. We talk at work, and when I call, well." He studied my face, searching for a reaction. There was none I could give but puzzlement, and Ramon bumped past me.

77

"You're in the *way*," he snapped, and that shook me out of my daze.

"Sorry," I called after him, and gathered myself to be polite but noncommittal to Alex.

Who was glaring after Ramon, those blue eyes suddenly uncomfortably piercing. "Does he always talk to you like that?"

"I just met him today. And I *am* in the way." I searched for a way to distract him, because that look on his face was perilously close to how Daddy's would get when he thought someone was *getting up on* him, as he said. "Let me just get rid of these. I'll meet you in the parking lot, all right?"

The troubling expression fled before it could really get settled on his face. "Yes ma'am." It turned into a grin, and one that seemed so genuine I couldn't help smiling back, relieved and nervous all at once.

• • •

LIBRARY TALK

It could have been awkward, but with the windows down and the oven-baked wind coming through at a roar, we didn't have to talk to each other until he cut the engine in the library parking lot. Behind the building, cottonwoods waved, and the box store's sprinklers across the highway were going despite the heat, making small rainbows all through the parking lot. It made me long for the shade in the gully, the gentle song of the breeze and the ever-present rattling buzz.

Alex almost leapt out of the truck, and was halfway around the front by the time I'd gotten my door open and hopped down, reaching back in for my book bag. "Damn, girl. You make it hard to be a gentleman."

"What?" *What the hell does that mean?* Owlish, I stared at him, yanking the bag free with a twist that threatened to tear the plastic.

"You're supposed to wait for me to open your door, right?" That string tie was of braided leather, and the catch was a chunk of impossibly blue turquoise that clashed with his eyes. Had he gone to church this morning? The battered, pale hat was back on his head, and under it his suit looked hot and uncomfortable, though the material was light enough.

I thought they only did that in movies. Like the schoolmarm riding into town on the stagecoach and having to hold someone's hand to hop down. "I'll cook to death in there on a hot day, though." I deadpanned it, and Ray would have gotten the joke, but Alex just frowned for a second, that questioning look back on his face. A too-long, awkward silence ensued, during which I found out the bag *had* torn, and ended up clutching the entire thing to my chest and staring back at him. "That was a joke, Alex."

"Oh." Relief dawned all over him just like sunrise out the living-room window. I watched, my own cheeks bunching up as I smiled back. "Good. I wasn't sure."

We just stood there, grinning at each other like damn fools, and when I stepped forward he moved away. I set off across the parking lot while he was slamming the door closed, hoping he wouldn't see the romance novel I'd stacked between two books on the Middle Ages. The cover was purple, not pink, but it was still a *romance*, and a pretty steamy one, too, about Florida and a police officer with a scarred face.

He caught up with me easily, those long legs of his capable of much bigger strides. "So... Ray says you don't want to talk to me."

"What?" It caught me flatfooted, the way he was always doing. "He never asked me if I did."

"Oh." Now Alex had caught my pace, I had to trot to keep up. "Jeez, you must really like books."

"Don't you?" If I could get inside and dump the current load into the return slot, maybe he wouldn't notice the romance. Maybe he didn't know what one looked like, but if Ray found out there would be no end to the teasing, and maybe tattling to Mama.

He made that short snorting noise teenage boys make when they want to dismiss something but not with any hard feelings. "Happiest day of my life'll be when I don't gotta go to school anymore."

"So what are you doing here?"

"I figure maybe you can explain books to me."

They're made out of paper, and you read them. "You want me to read to you?"

"No, I just want to talk to you, missy."

"Because of Ray?" My stomach was beginning to tense up. Had Ray gotten into trouble again?

"No. He really didn't tell you I called for you?"

"I thought you called to talk to *him*. He's your friend and all."

"I asked, but he wouldn't go get you. Said you didn't want to talk to me."

Why would he do that? Unless he thought this was getting back at me for the beers thing. "He hates me tagging along, I guess. Doesn't want me with his friends. He's older, you know." Then I felt like an idiot, because so was Alex.

The swinging doors opened, and blessed air conditioning ran all down my bare arms and through the holes in my jeans. My ponytail had loosened in the wind, but I fixed it as soon as I got my books in through the return slot without Alex even looking at them. Instead, he was looking at the shelves, the children's section with its brightly colored posters, the exhortations to read, the Books are Magic things everywhere, the card catalog under a bar of sunlight robbed of its heat and vigor by glass and the cool air pumped through vents. The building was old, and there were plaques to a rancher and an oil baron on its brick face outside. Since then, though, budgets had probably gone downhill.

"You seem a little more mature." The hat was off again, and he swung it a little uneasily. "You know?"

Did he mean I was more mature than Ray? *I* knew I was, but nobody would be able to inform my brother about it. "Mama says girls grow up faster." But it made me look at him a little closer. "How old are you?"

"Seventeen." He hunched his shoulders a little. "Graduate this upcoming year. Dad keeps talking about college."

Well, with their big business and all, it was probably a given that he'd go to college. "Mama does, too."

"Well, you're smart." He said it like someone else might say *the sun comes up daily*.

A tiny little warm worm wriggled in my chest. "How do you know?"

"I can tell by the way you talk. When you *do* talk."

I talk all the time. Just then, though, the rock was threatening to fill my throat again. Why was I so nervous? I stepped away from him, almost running into a round, gray-haired lady with a tartan bag shuffling through the front doors. "Beg pardon, ma'am." It came out in a breathy squeak, and I kept going until I was out of her way.

Alex watched, his forehead-line deepening yet again. He probably thought I was a complete idiot.

"I talk," I said, maybe a little too loudly. "See?"

"Yeah." His grin bloomed again, slow and steady. The turquoise on his string tie gleamed. It was probably real, not just a dyed stone. "So how about you show me some books, chatterbox?"

"What kind?" I meant to ask what he *liked* to read, but the words got tangled up between my brain and the back of my throat, mixed with the idea that he didn't seem too familiar with how libraries worked, and what came out was, "There's different kinds."

He looked about ready to unleash a Raymond-worthy eyeroll, but stopped just in time. "Your favorites."

That made me stop, again, examining him from tip to toe for any sign of irritation or pranking. He had his cowboy boots on, freshly polished, and it occurred to me that maybe he looked a little nervous. Especially the way his hat was sort of quivering, a little, in his capable hands with the shadows of engine grease under his bitten-short nails.

I'm ignorant, city girl, not illiterate. He was pretty smart too, but he probably didn't want anyone to know. And it didn't seem like he was playing a joke on me for Ray, or for anyone else, even himself.

"I won't show you my favorites," I said, finally, "but I *will* show you some good ones. Come on."

CHAPTER TEN

Open Gate, Go Home

T HE HEAT BROKE AT NIGHT RIGHT BEFORE THE FIRST DAY of school, but the hills were still burning under a white-coin sun. Even down in the gully it was warmer than comfortable, and I hauled bucket after bucket of water from the creek for Gran, trudging back and forth in the big, floppy, unbleached hat she made me wear so I didn't burn. *Summer water's best for old bones in winter, girl. Bring me more.*

I did, but I had no idea where she was putting it all.

She was on the porch when I brought the buckets back for the last time that afternoon, careful not to slop them on the path. Her usual sweetened tea was iced now, her ancient fridge clicking and humming as it labored. I brought them up the stairs, my shoulders aching, and she took them without a word, setting her tea down on the small table. I waited on the porch, waving a tired hand at flies who might have wanted to crawl into her glass. When Granny reappeared with a tray it seemed like the day was over. Now came the part I think I liked most: sitting with her on the shaded side of the porch, and at least one glass of tea while she told me things about how the secret world worked. Her voice, whispering and reedy sometimes, powerful as thunder others, but if other people were there listening I'm not sure they would have heard it. Some voices go right into your head without stopping at your ears, and Granny had a whole collection of *those*.

I waited until she was settled with a damp washcloth, patting at her forehead until she shooed me away just like a fly. "Sit, girl, and tell me what you so worried about."

I did, settling into the ancient deck chair next to her rocker. Between us, a spindly pale-painted wooden table was just big enough for the lidded pitcher of sweet tea, both our glasses uncomfortably wedged next to its sweating silver belly.

She waited while I got the words together inside my head. "School starts next week. I'll have to come after to clean."

"Cleaning's almost done." She sniffed, digging in her capacious pockets and producing her pipe and tobacco pouch. "Season turning, you go to school."

"Oh." I tried not to let the disappointment show, and she cackled, stuffing the pipe bowl with shreds of strong brown stuff she called *Mack*

Orca. I didn't know if it was a brand name, or what, but it had a fine deep smell and its smoke was good for all sorts of things. Granny even said it could cure rheumatiz, but the way she said it, with that one eyebrow of hers up and her mouth twitching, led me to believe maybe she was playing a bit.

"Oh, Dasya. Always so forlorn. You come in afternoons, for an hour. One hour only. Then you go home. I pay you, same as before."

"That's not right, Gran. I can't take the same amount for less than half the work."

She frowned at me, but I was used to her by now, and it didn't make me quake in my sneakers the way it could have weeks before. I just took a sip of my tea and felt my lower lip pooching, that sullen look Daddy disliked so much and Mama told me made me look older than my time.

"You take what I give you," Gran said, finally, in her queenly *that is that* tone. "You *learn*. In and out, around about."

"Secrets," I answered, and a chill went through me.

They were everywhere these days. Little bits of certainty popping into my head at the weirdest times, like knowing exactly when Mama would be home and what she wanted for dinner. Or knowing when Ray got off early but lied about it, and where he'd gone—dry gulch racing, or drinking with one of the guys from the garage. Alex didn't talk about it, but he hinted at being worried, and as much as I wished he'd tell Mama what Ray was up to, I also liked that he could keep a secret.

Alex. The biggest secret of all, how thinking about him sent a wire of warmth through me. The way I felt when he drove me to the library, like there was a balloon inside me filling up with happy. The zing that went through me when the phone rang and I knew it was him.

For every nice piece of surprise, though, there was a bad one. Like Mr. Vogg, calling Mama. The phone would ring and ring, and sometimes I just unplugged it. I didn't answer when I knew it was him, and Mama didn't cotton on. Still, sometimes he'd call after dinner, and Mama would take the phone in her room, and a sick weight filled my stomach listening to her murmured conversation. Wasn't *I* supposed to be spending hours on the phone, like every other teenage girl? Then I felt ashamed of my greediness, and tried even harder not to hear her soft voice, the quiet giggles, the whispers as if she was telling him secrets of her own.

Grown-up secrets.

There were other bad bits to the knowing, too. The parking lot at the box store across from the library was full of them. A dog locked in a hot car, a kid trotting behind an angry parent, hopelessness beating inside every step. Weeds and trash for each piece of glitter, and nothing I could do about any of it.

First you look, Gran said.

What would happen if you *could* do something, though?

"Secrets," Gran agreed, and her chin dropped toward her sagging bosom. Her pipe lit when she pressed her long left thumbnail into it and whispered a word; and two fragrant streams of smoke jetted through her nostrils. "*Ogon,*" she said, repeating the word a little louder, and I could almost see a spark trembling inside the word. Couldn't quite tell how to bring it out, yet.

Silence wrapped both of us in a nice warm blanket. When it got still like this you could hear the wind outside the gully, and a faint thread of buzzing. Alex swore it was snakes, but I'd never seen a single one. The wind and the buzz mixed with the aspen-rattles, the slither of the crick inside its bed, an occasional cry from a buzzard or hawk riding the thermals and looking for food.

Granny began to rock, back and forth, the slight squeak-thump adding a beat to the song. I stared at the garden and tried to figure out the best way to ask her how to change things. How to *help*.

A silver thread pierced the afternoon-song, drawing it tight, and I jumped a little guiltily, almost spilling my tea. Gran didn't cease her steady rocking, puffing on her pipe. The smoke ribboned away in long fluid streams, growing thinner and thinner as they skipped down the steps and curled into the garden.

That's him.

I opened my mouth to tell Gran, but something stopped me. The whistling wavered, turned shrill for a moment, then firmed. It shifted, coming from first one quarter, then another. First from down by the gate, then from behind the trailer, now almost vanishing up near the gully wall, now accompanied by a thump on the roof as if a raccoon was up there dancing, with skritching claws and a fat glossy tail.

I glanced at Gran. She just rocked, puffing away, and a gleam under her mostly-shut eyelids told me she was perfectly aware of what was going on.

Which meant there probably wasn't anything to worry about.

So I just listened, sipping at my toothrot tea. *Sweet to take bitter out of life*, Gran said. She brewed it in a big, age-blackened thing with spouts at the bottom and a teapot perched in a nest atop it, a piping singing appliance I could clean but not otherwise mess with. The more I tried to polish, though, the blacker it got, which worried me until I figured out that was its original color. Glossy ebony metal, polished to a mirror shine. Or it might have been, but for some reason, even though it was smooth and slick, I never saw a reflection in it.

The spillsilver sound went on. I imagined the Whistling Man dancing as he skipped all over the gully, winking out and appearing as it pleased him in the cottonwood and aspen shadows, balancing on water-smoothed rocks in the crick, working closer to Gran's house like a skittish animal.

Finally, the sound settled near the garden gate, and stayed there for a while. Gran's expression turned thunderous, but she just kept puffing.

The gate rattled, streams of silver sound sliding through the fractured pattern of struts holding its frame together. It slid into the garden, perking up the flowers and shivering the string beans on their trellis, the one I'd cobbled together from fallen sticks and twine against the patchwork fence. The sunflowers rustled uneasily, their big seed-heavy heads bobbing together, whispering about the new arrival.

Finally, Gran's steady rocking stopped, and the whistling did too. There was another rattle, the fence groaning, and she knocked her pipe against the railing on her other side, ashes and sparks flying. "Well, Dasya, go open the gate and go home."

Questions trembled on my tongue, each one of them stinging a little with warning. I set my glass down and managed a single inquiring look.

"Leave it there," she said, getting her tobacco pouch out again, her nails sharpened into yellowing points. "Open gate, go home. We have things to discuss, the *chernv'g* and Iyaga, things my Dasya has no need to hear."

"Yes ma'am," I whispered, and trudged for the gate.

There was nobody at the gate. I opened it wide and stood aside anyway, just like a kid playing house and inviting the invisible friend in for tea. A rushing breeze filled the aspens, rattling their leaves, and the buzz outside the gully grew deafening for a moment. I nipped through and the gate banged shut almost on my heels, and I ran all the way home without looking back.

• • •

APPLE BITES

The yellow bus heaved and snorted away from in front of the mobile park, leaving us stranded. It was kind of a shock to see how many kids from John Wayne High—of all the things about the school, the name was the only one likely to make you laugh—lived here. I hadn't seen hide or hair of them before, but I suppose being down in the gully all the time had cut into any socializing. As it was, I didn't talk to anyone, and I ate my lunch where I had last year, in a badly-lit corner of the lunchroom far enough away from everything else that nobody but the unpopulars sat there willingly. Some of the kids at my stop I already knew—Amy Hearness, who ran with boys and already smoked, Trace Fabrell, who wore a leather jacket and spoke in monosyllables when the teacher could get him to say anything at all, Cluny de la Rocha and Susan Small from my AP English and History classes. One or two populars too, like Mara O'Connor with her teased-to-heaven red-blonde mane, which was thought-provoking.

I hurried home through simmering heat, but the back of summer had broken and the nights were getting cooler. The hills were umber now instead of taupe, and I figured I had just enough time to bolt a snack and throw my jean jacket back on before heading down into the gully.

For the first day, it hadn't gone too badly.

I let myself in, and the phone was ringing. For once, there wasn't a tingle telling me who it was. I dropped my backpack and scooped it up. "Hello?"

"Dez! You're home." It was Alex, and I grabbed onto the counter to steady myself. "You were already gone this morning, and I couldn't find you after school."

That was a surprise. "You go to John Wayne?" I'd never seen him there, but he *was* older.

"Yeah." A pause. "Look, I thought I'd... you never gave me an answer. I can drive you. I'm not working now that school's in."

"I don't know. It's a lot of gas money." I opened the fridge, the tangled plastic cord of the phone stretched all the way across the kitchen. *Ray's still working. But he's graduated.* "You know?"

There it was, plain as day. We weren't rich. Even though Alex drove a beat-up truck, he always had spending money, and his daddy, well.

"Shut up about the gas money, all right? It's fine." There were muffled voices behind him, I couldn't quite make them out. "I'll pick you up at seven-thirty."

I hesitated. That would give me almost an extra hour of sleep in the morning, and the prospect of not having to sit on the bus was tantalizing. On the other hand, it was a debt, and I didn't know what Mama would say about it. "I'll have to ask Mama."

"Okay. Listen, are you doing anything tonight?"

"Studying." There wasn't anything to study, but I liked to look through the textbooks just in case. It kept me prepared. Raymond always teased me about it.

He wasn't teasing now. He was working, sure, but he wasn't home a lot when he was off. Mama sometimes remarked with a sigh that it felt like just us girls now. It might have been nice if I hadn't been so worried about what trouble Ray was getting into, for God's sake.

"It's only the first *day*." Alex probably didn't know how much like Ray he sounded. "Want to hang out?"

"I have to make dinner." And I had to get down to see Gran. "But you can come over. We can compare classes. Give me about an hour, okay? If I'm not here, just wait, I'll be back. I have a... a job I have to do."

"You guys work a lot."

"Only way to pay the bills." I didn't mean to sound sharp, but I couldn't tell if he said it admiringly, or if he was a little sniffy at the notion.

He paused for a moment, and I could have kicked myself. But when he spoke again, he didn't sound angry. "Okay. It'll be about an hour and a half. I got chores to do too."

"Okay." I tried to think of something else to say. *It'll be nice to see you* was too tepid, and *I've missed you* might give him ideas. "You want to maybe go to the library sometime?" *Way to go, Dez. He probably has popular friends, why would he want to sit in the library with you?*

"Just tell me when you want to go." I couldn't see him, but it sounded like he was nodding. "See you in a bit."

"Okay." I hung up, looked at the apple in my hand. I didn't even remember getting it out of the fridge.

It would have to hold me. Gran would be waiting, and the sooner I got out there, the sooner I could get out and be here when Alex arrived.

My heart thumped at the thought, I forgot a ponytail holder, and between big crunching bites I ran all the way to Granny Iyaga's door with my hair flying behind me and my feet barely touching the ground.

PART TWO: FALL

CHAPTER ELEVEN

Distracted

S HE MOTIONED ME INTO THE BIG RED HORSEHAIR CHAIR AND gave me a big metal bowl, creek water shimmering inside it. I sat, and she bent over, her strong ancient hands cupped over mine on the bowl's sides. "Little Dasya distracted," she sniffed. "I can smell it on you."

"What does it smell like?" *Probably like school, and sweat.* I examined the bowl—nothing but plain ordinary silvery metal, the same bowl she used for bread dough so she didn't get flour all over the counter. She never seemed to go for groceries, but always had what she needed in her cabinets, and sometimes I wondered about that.

Maybe the Whistling Man brought her milk and eggs.

Gran took a big, deep sniff, like a horse, and I would have laughed except her expression was serious. "Like young love. Dasya has a suitor."

Nope. But my heart made a funny twisting movement, and I started wondering if she meant someone in particular. "Boys are trouble." I knew *that* much, from Daddy's rambles and Mama's cautions. *Only after one thing,* Daddy would slur, when he took a mind to talk to me instead of yelling at Raymond. *You don't be no slutchild, Desiree. I'll tan your hide if you fool around.*

"Wise little girl." Her peculiar chuffing laugh. "Now, do you remember how to see?"

I can see just fine. But I knew what she meant—that funny knot behind my forehead when I concentrated, and the little bits of knowing came through. You could sometimes provoke them into showing up, if you tied the knot just right. Not too loose, not too tight. The summer had given me good practice. "Yes ma'am."

"Good. See in water. Look until you find." She nodded, briskly, and moved away.

Well, that was an open-ended assignment, wasn't it. But I settled in the chair and peered into the water, willing the knot to come.

It did, in fits and starts, but it was too tight. I breathed deeply, trying to loosen it. The day was still bumping around inside me, and I'd find myself thinking about what to make for dinner, when Alex would get there, if Ray was coming home tonight, if Mama would be tired, if that man Vogg would call. If Mrs. Garton the English teacher really meant she would grade harshly, if the aerobics class was going to be more trouble than it was worth, if I could maybe get a library aide spot. The populars didn't want to be library aides, they all wanted the easy assignments, like to the Principal's Dozen.

I kept breathing, trying to sweep all the day away, and Gran made a spitting noise from across the room.

I glanced up. She was shuffling to a high-peaked shape covered with canvas, and my heart was in my throat.

"Distracted," she muttered. "Here."

She twitched the canvas aside, and it was an old-fashioned spinning wheel I remembered polishing. She settled on the stool with a sigh, and after she got situated a hiss-thump-whirr began to fill the small round spaces. Every so often her hand would dip into a waist-high basket full of gray tangled stuff next to her, and thread slid through her gnarled fingers, collecting on the machine.

So that's how it works, I thought, dreamily, watching the wheel go round. A nice even rhythm, comforting. Like the rocker out on the porch, when she sat and smoked her oiled pipe, or the corncob one. Like Mama at her sewing machine.

She didn't sew anymore. Too busy.

The water trembled in the bowl. I looked down, and fell into it.

Front door slamming with a boom, and Ray-Ray's arms around me in the stuffy dark closet, its door not even open a crack. We could hear Mama crying softly downstairs, trying to keep it muffled. Ray-Ray's face was hot and salt-wet, and I had my whole fist stuffed in my mouth. Even that young I knew not to make a sound when that dark ringing silence filled up the corners, when Daddy's rage became bigger than the world.

Pulling back, I slid out of my small, small body and down the stairs, marveling at details—it was base housing, I could tell as much from the paint, thick and reapplied over and over until it becomes a hide instead of a skin. Everywhere in the world, base housing looks the same; you have to look harder for the tiny variations that tell you where you've landed. Heat shimmered everywhere, and the old heavy dark wood of the balustrade somehow said Germany, we're in Germany, we're in the same bedroom because Mama and Daddy have the other one.

Ray was only four, and he kept whispering to me, to my small, shuddering, helpless body. Important big-brother things. Don't make him angry. Be quiet. I'll protect you. Be quiet.

As if everything depended on that, just being as still and small as possible.

The stairs came to a jolting end. The kitchen was strange, seen from a high-up angle, and the worst part of the strangeness was Mama on the floor, curled into a ball, trying to get enough air in. Sobbing like a little kid, and a strange unsteady feeling went all through me. It wasn't right for Mama to sound that way.

Footsteps. The door opened again, and a black cloud came through it.

"Teach you a lesson," *he slurred.* "Straighten you up." *The cloud stalked to the stove, and I could only catch glimpses through it. A familiar heavy-duty green watch, his boots that Ray had to polish, the wedding ring on his left hand a thin malicious glimmer. There was a snap, and a ring of bright blue flame popped into being on the stove.*

Ray's hot whispering in my ear. The black cloud pulled Mama up by her hair.

"Now you know you got to be straightened out," *the black cloud said.* "Whore. Talking to men all the time. You think I don't know what you'd do if I let you? Say it."

"N-n-n-no—" *Mama, very softly, she couldn't breathe.*

I didn't want to see what happened next. I knew what it was. That scar on Mama's arm, and her wincing as she smoothed cream on it. Burned myself on that damn oven. I should be more careful, shouldn't I.

Mama looking down at my solemn, upturned face, Ray's silence, his expression shifting between disgust and fear, and the lie was big enough to choke us all. The rock in my throat, big as a boulder, big as the moon.

A sizzle, and Mama screamed, a high short sharp sound. The black cloud roared at her to be quiet, and I squeezed my eyes shut, burying my face in Ray's neck. I was two years old, and that was when the stone lodged itself inside my chest, and it would never come loose.

"Enough."

The bowl fell with a spinning clang, and creek water splashed all over the floor. I gasped, and Gran had my hands in hers, clamping down hard enough to hurt.

"Enough, Dasya," she repeated. "Good girl. No more today."

The entire trailer looked foreign for a moment, and Granny Iyaga was a stranger with a hooked nose and yellowing teeth, a green gleam in her dark, catlike eyes. It passed, but not before the apple tried to crawl up my throat in a hot, bilious rush. She bent, far more swiftly than an old woman should move, and had the bowl in front of me as I heaved.

I didn't *quite* throw up. But it was close.

I swallowed bile and half-digested apple, a tiny tremor going through everything inside me, as if I'd been feverish like I used to get, the world going at a slightly higher speed than I could handle. Gran touched my forehead with one finger, right above and between my eyes, and that helped. At least, it pushed the unsteadiness back, and when I could sit up she took the bowl away. "*Very* good little girl. Go home now."

I'm not sure I want to. "I'm sorry." The words tumbled out. "I'll clean it up—"

She turned, and those green sparks far back in her depthless eyes winked at me as she blinked. She snapped her left-hand fingers, jabbing her hand at the pool of creek water on the black floor, and a *fwoosh* of steam went up, thinning into the air.

My jaw dropped. The unsteadiness came back, breath leaving me in a high hard huff, as if I'd just been punched.

Those dark eyes narrowed, but it was still Gran. She examined me curiously, as if I was a stranger now.

Or as if she wasn't quite sure what I was going to do.

I swallowed, very hard. What were the right manners for a situation like this? Nothing Mama had ever said seemed to apply.

If this was where all the looking led, I wasn't sure I wanted to keep doing it. "I guess..." The rock was back in my throat, and I was hard put to produce anything but a sort of squeaking breathless whisper. "Is...is there anything you *do* need me to clean, Gran?"

The moment stretched out, long and elastic, and when it snapped she was the regular, brisk Granny Iyaga again. "Cleaning is done, Dasya." A faint ironclad smile, not showing her teeth, and I couldn't remember if they were white or yellow. "Go shut Granny's gate, and come back tomorrow after school."

"Yes ma'am." It took me two tries to get to my feet, but I managed it. "Can I... can I bring you anything? Tomorrow? Groceries, or... anything?"

Did I imagine her shoulders slumping, ever so slightly? She turned back towards the kitchen, shuffling along, the bowl held out in font of her as if it was a pot pulled from the oven. "No, child. Go on."

I hesitated, but she said nothing more, and I made it out the door, through the gate, and halfway up the gullyside before I heaved again, almost losing the apple. It took me a few minutes to get myself situated under the cloudless sky, its blue deepening into autumn instead of summershade, the buzzing rattles in the field above filling my head with a whispering roar.

. . .

NOT A GOOD IDEA

A white box, sitting on the porch. I stopped and stared, my mouth full of sourness, and glanced around. The mobile park was just the same. The Cranstons across the street had all their doors and windows open, country music blaring, and down the cul-de-sac the Marples' dogs were expressing their displeasure with something or another. There was a spume of dust as a yellow delivery van pulled away, and I climbed the steps as if I was as old as Gran, holding onto the shaking banister. Ray had promised to fix it, but he hadn't yet.

The white rectangle was a florist's box, and it made me queasy. I had half a mind to just dump it in the garbage, but Mama might see that and there would be trouble.

I unlocked the door, and crouched to examine the box. It was from Jim P. Vogg.

The badger-haired man with the rich voice, the one who kept calling. My mouth went dry, and that was when Alex's truck made the turn onto our half-dirt street and purred over the shallow rises masquerading as speed bumps. I grabbed the box, holding it as far away from me as I could, and got down the stairs all in a rush. Around the side of the house, I felt glass inside the plain white cardboard, and a scratching. The smell told me it was roses, but the scritches against the inside of the box made me think of tiny claws and sharp teeth, scrabbling inside a cage, just aching to get out and scuttle into a dark corner.

Like a rat.

I didn't realize I was running until I almost hit the back fence, the box flying in a high, wide arc into the field. It hit with a crunch much louder than it should have been, and the buzzing from the sere, undulating grass became a roar for a moment, a wall of sound.

Everything inside me turned over, from apple to bone, and it was like being struck blind—a white flash, nothing but darkness for a few seconds afterward even though I could hear the buzzing and the wind in the grass. Slipping and slithering, and a high piercing sound, as if the Whistling Man had decided to lay music aside for volume, a screeching of torn metal and broken glass tinkling onto pavement.

When it passed I found myself shivering under a flood of warm sunlight. For a moment my breath clouded up, like it does on cold mornings. A door slammed, and I backed away from the fence, slowly, carefully, as if the barb wire was going to come after me.

Well, you know, it could happen. All sorts of things could. It doesn't even take Gran to show you anymore. What had I just done?

I'd protected Mama, that's what. I let out a long shaky breath.

"Dez?" Alex, at the front porch. He was probably knocking at the door.

I turned my back on the whispering grass. "I'm back here. Hang on."

There was something happening in my head I didn't like. It wasn't the knot, or even suspecting strange things about Gran, or the just-knowing. It was just plain logic.

If I wasn't crazy and things with Gran were weird, it stood to reason that there were other weird things out there in the world. Which brought up the question, just what was that man Vogg?

And why was he so set on my Mama?

"You okay?" Alex peered out from under his hat, leaning against the corner of the mobile. The sunshine went diagonally down him, and for a moment, the shadow over his face reminded me of a black cloud and a burning smell. "What's wrong?"

"Just something nasty I had to get rid of." I tried for a smile, but it felt weak and watered down even to me. My hair was a mess, and I found out I'd put my jacket on inside out. *Way to go, Dez.* "It's... it's good to see you."

And it was. Those blue eyes of his just seemed to make everything more solid. More real. Of course I sounded like an idiot, because I'd seen him a couple days ago, but the way his face lit up I didn't so much mind.

"You too. You sure you're okay? You look..."

I probably had vomit all over my jeans, my jacket was all messed up, and my mouth was sour. Heat stained my cheeks, and I skipped past him, hoping he couldn't smell anything bad on me. "Just hungry, I think. It's hot."

"It is." He ambled along behind me, and the dim, relative coolness of the kitchen was a relief. "Hey, you painted in here."

"Oh yeah. Mama likes cheerful colors." I did the cut-in, and she did the rolling, neither of us talking much because of the heat and the smell. We had it down to an art form by now.

"You're really good at this sort of stuff, Dez. You know? You make everything pretty." He accepted a cobalt glass full of water, and his fingers were live wires, because they sent a zing all the way through me.

It's just paint on cheap paneling. And it doesn't cover up the fact that we live in a trailer. "Can I ask you something?"

"Sure. Anything." He took a huge gulp of water, and the windburn on his cheeks was pretty red. Or was he blushing? His T-shirt and jeans uniform was just the same, and his arms were tanned. I caught myself looking at his biceps—long lines of muscle definition under brown skin.

"I... I just..." I grabbed my grits with both hands, as Daddy would have said. "Do you know what's going on with Ray?"

Some of the water might have gone down the wrong way, because he coughed a little. A momentary flash of disappointment, like he'd been expecting me to ask something else. Or like it was just awkward, which made the worry a tight ball under my ribs.

"Uh." His eyes were watering big time, too. Blinking rapidly, he cleared his throat again. "Ray? He's... hanging out with Matt Stark. One of the mechanics. Older guy. I..." He looked around, not really seeing the kitchen, just hoping for somewhere to rest his gaze, I guess. "Look, Dez..."

"He's drinking, isn't he." I didn't want to believe it, but there it was. I stripped out of my jacket, but maybe I shouldn't have, because I only had a tank top on underneath it. It was a lot cooler, but my arms felt naked now. "He smokes to hide the liquor smell, but it's all over him." *And the knot in my head knows.*

"Stark's a drinker." He stared down into his glass like there was an answer to a question I hadn't even asked in there. "Listen, I wanted to ask *you* something."

"Sure." I leaned against the cabinets, mostly to hold myself up. My legs felt awful rubbery. The first day of school was turning out to be a real doozy.

He set his glass down on the counter, just far enough back from the edge to show he'd been raised right. "I know you'll need to ask your mama."

Is that a question? "Huh?" I folded my jacket over my arm, carefully. There was a hole under one of the arms. Had it been inside-out all day? No, because I'd put my key in my pocket when I left this morning.

"Homecoming's next month."

"Yeah?" I restrained myself from saying *so what*, because he wouldn't have understood I was honestly baffled. Ray would've, but he wasn't here.

If Ray was drinking, well, Mama wasn't going to like that. She didn't like him smoking, but he was over eighteen. *Don't do it in the house,* she told him. *Your sister doesn't need lung cancer.* And then Ray had said something to her too low for me to hear, and the silence afterward was like the moment after a slap. Cold, and ringing, and I had curled myself up tighter in my bed and wished they could just stop rubbing at each other.

One of these days, they were going to strike sparks, and who knew what would catch fire then?

Alex was still talking. "Are you going to go?"

I shrugged, wedging my hip into the cabinet corner. My knees were getting a lot stronger. I just had to breathe. If I could just get a couple minutes of quiet, I could get back to normal. "Big waste of time. All the populars standing around congratulating themselves. Bad music and cheap decorations." *And girls getting knocked up in the parking lot. Daddy always talked about that. Prom preggers, he called it.*

"Oh." The line between his eyebrows deepened. "I, uh. Well. If you're not going, I... would you go if I asked you?"

The world didn't quite stop spinning, but it may have slowed down a bit. *What?* "To Homecoming?"

"Yeah."

This was not helping me gather myself. "I'd need a date," I managed, blankly. *What's going on?*

"Well, I'm asking you, Dez. So you can, uh, draw a conclusion from that, right?"

"You're asking *me* to Homecoming?"

He didn't quite roll his eyes, but it was close. He seemed too big for the kitchen all of a sudden, holding that stupid hat of his and working the brim a little with his fingers. "You can say no. It's fine. I just thought—"

"*Yes.*" It burst out of me, a little too loud, and I almost clapped my hand over my mouth. "I, I mean, I'd love to. If you're asking." *Oh, Jesus. What did I just say?*

If I could have took it back I would have. But he smiled again, this grin leaving all the others in the dust, like he was a kid at Christmas having just unwrapped one of the shiniest toys ever. "Really?"

No. I took a firmer grip on the counter. Dances weren't for people like us, and I knew it. Didn't he have a popular girl to take? One of the cowgirls with teased-out hair and the tight jeans when they weren't wearing cheerleader uniforms? They all wore sweater sets on the same days, like there was a calendar in their heads that told them Tuesday was twinset day or something. Their daddies went to barbecues and other weird Americana events with his. They had their own language full of bird chirps and *no, really?*

And sarcasm. They walked down the school halls in packs, and by God you got out of their way if you knew what was good for you.

Alex Carr was planning on putting me right in the middle of them. "I'm asking." He kept grinning.

"Your friends." I had to look away from that bright open smile, at the sink where breakfast dishes listed to the side because I hadn't washed them yet. "Don't they wonder why you're hanging out with me?"

"They're nice people, Dez. You might like 'em. They know I've got a girl, but they don't know..."

Got a girl? My eyes probably couldn't have gotten any rounder. I wished I'd had a chance to brush my teeth, I wish I'd thought about it before I said yes, I wished I'd just said no. "Oh. Look, your friends don't know who I am, or that we're... friends. Right?" *Because you never take me to meet them, do you. You never even asked.*

He "had a girl." Well, he never talked about her. Maybe she went to a different school. Maybe this was a revenge date or something, because I was disposable.

"Friends, huh?" That dimmed his grin a bit.

I swallowed, hard, against the sourness in my mouth. "Yeah. Second thought, it's not such a good idea, Alex. Take someone else."

"I want to take you."

"So your friends can laugh at me, and you feel ashamed of hanging around with a girl from the mobiles? Or maybe so you can get back at this girl of yours?"

That baffled, wounded look, as if he'd never thought about it. "Why are you acting like this?"

"Because I have to." Didn't he *understand*? We weren't in the same pay grade, we weren't even on the same *planet*, really. "Don't tell me you don't know." The rock was back in my throat. Everything was blurring, going way too fast.

"I thought you were just shy." His hat dangled from his free hand. He moved, and his elbow bumped the water glass, but it didn't fall. It just rattled a little. "I didn't know you thought... that."

"You go to school. You have to know." *Don't be a dipshit.* But that was a cruel thing to say, and I wasn't going to say it, was I?

"I thought you just, you know. You were shy." He was staring at me like I'd just turned into an insect.

Everything on me trembled and the rock turned around, fitting itself in my windpipe with a click. Nothing could get out past it, so I just stared at him, and he stared back at me. His hands had dropped to his sides, and that stupid hat of his moved a little against his trouser seam, as if he was shaking too. Next he'd get angry. Maybe like Ray, with a black look, slamming out the door and spinning tires screeching, or pulling into himself until you were no more than a fly buzzing around in another room. Or maybe he'd get mad in a different way.

Like a big black cloud. *Got to straighten you out.*

He just stood there. My breath came in little hitching gasps, and I waited for it. For whatever he'd do.

"Hey. Oh, shit. Hey. Dez. *Dez.*" He was too close, and I flinched, the door to the cabinet where we kept Mama's pasta pot and saucepans slamming with a hollow bong as my knee ran into it, one of my elbows coming up to protect me in case he...

Alex stopped dead and inhaled sharply, like he'd just got a good idea. "Jesus. What's wrong? Come on, sit down." His hands were on me, but they weren't hard bruising clamps.

He all but dragged me across the kitchen and pushed me into my regular chair, and since he'd been over so much he knew where everything was. Water splashed, and he came back to me with the threadbare purple washcloth, clapping it against my forehead. The coolness was a shock, but the bigger shock was the knot tightening inside my head—there was no anger making him into a black storm cloud. Nothing but worry, a bright blue wash of it tinting everything in the kitchen before I blinked it away, water dribbling down my cheeks and splatting against my tank top.

"Jesus." He was suddenly smaller, because he was crouching in front of me, one hand holding the sopping washcloth to my forehead and the other bracing him against the chair leg. "You gonna faint when I ask you to prom, too?"

Something cracked in me. I was surprised he didn't seem to hear it. Laughter bubbled up through the shifting mass in my throat, and small, perplexed smile bloomed on his face.

I peeled the washcloth away from my face. I had to touch him to do it, but he didn't seem to mind. In fact, his hand curled over mine, and I ended up with him crouching in front of me and holding *both* my hands around a washcloth dripping onto my jeans.

My mouth worked for a second, but nothing came out. He nodded, as if I'd spoken. "You keep everything closed up in there. Just locked all up, all polite. Sometimes you peek out, and I get to hear what you're really thinking."

"Sorry." Husky, like I'd just finished crying.

"I don't wanna scare you, okay?" Soft and earnest, a stray gleam from the window sliding over the top of his flattened blond hair. His hat had ended up under the table somehow. "That's the only reason I haven't taken you to meet people. Because you get those big eyes and you get all polite, and that's how I know you're scared." A soft pause, while he peered up at my face. "It just about kills me."

That doesn't sound good. I swallowed again, trying to dislodge the rock. It didn't want to go.

"I like you. I don't give a rat's ass what any of my friends thinks about it. If they ain't nice to you, they ain't my friends, and that's that." He nodded once, sharply, as if he could just make it that way by saying so. "Okay?"

There was a whole list of things I wanted to say, but the rock wouldn't let me. Still, I managed to whisper. "Your girl?" Now, of course, he'd laugh and tell me he was just kidding, he already had a girlfriend, ha-ha on me.

"Ray said you weren't interested, he warned me about hurting his baby sister. Boy's got a temper. I been trying to figure out if you... How you..." He stopped. Looked like he'd run out of words too.

Oh. "I like you," I whispered. "I like you a lot."

He looked up, and I tipped forward. I smelled spearmint gum and fresh air and dust, and the oil and hormones of a guy who washes every day but still sweats in the sun. A healthy heat-haze enfolded me, and he did something so interesting with his tongue that a bolt of something clean, and warm, and fascinating went through me. I finally found out what his hair felt like, because my fingers tangled in it, and I ended up with his gum and wet jeans and his forehead against mine, both of us breathing heavy.

Only got one thing on their minds, Dez. You fool around I'll tan your hide.

But Daddy wasn't here. Neither was Ray, and Mama wasn't due home for a few hours. I could do whatever I wanted.

Or *he* could.

I closed my eyes. It was nice there, I decided. Nice to feel him shaking just like I was, nice to have the knot inside my head loosen up so I could think straight. Nice to hear him say my name, just whispering it. I could have stayed like that for a long while, but there were things to do.

"I h-have to make dinner." I swallowed the splinters of the rock. It went away a little more easily than usual. "And clean the kitchen. And..."

"Can I help? I know how to wash dishes."

"You're a *guest*." I sounded scandalized.

"A good guest helps out. Come on, Dez. Can I stay? When your mama gets home, I'll ask her if you can go to Homecoming with me. I'll even promise to bring you home early. Okay?"

All I could do was nod.

CHAPTER TWELVE

Dinner Guest

BY THE TIME THE FORD BOUNCED INTO THE DRIVEWAY, my teeth were brushed, the kitchen smelled of pot roast and a breeze was sweeping the day's heat away. We were on the front porch, Alex with two nails in his mouth as he concentrated, swinging the hammer just right each time. I let go of the railing when he nodded at me, and it was fixed. *Little scrap lumber will do that right up, and brace the step too,* he'd said. *I did a summer with a carpenter. Liked it a lot.*

I guess his daddy told him working would keep him out of trouble when he wasn't in school. I could have pointed out that it never worked for Raymond, but oh well.

Mama looked tired, but she was smiling. "Well, look at that! You're handy to have around, Alex."

He palmed the nails and gave her one of his polite smiles. "Thanks, ma'am. Dez said I'd better work for my supper."

"My girl drives a hard bargain." Mama's smile was a marvel to behold. "How was the first day?"

I must have looked blank, because with everything else, school seemed an afterthought. "Fine. Just the same."

She hitched her purse higher on her shoulder. "I brought some things home. We're having a guest for dinner."

Another one? "I did pot roast." So there should be plenty for everyone, we just wouldn't have much in the way of leftovers. Whatever we did have I could put over noodles or rice, and we'd be okay for another day or so.

"Bless you." She smelled of salt and fried food, a faint tinge of sweat and the high lemon-yellow tang of excitement. The wind, mouthing the corners of the mobile homes, made a low sliding sound like a growl. That should have warned me. "I need to clean up, can you—"

"I'm on it." I headed for the Ford. "Who's coming over? Marcie?"

"No." Mama's smile lit up her whole body, a wonder to see with her black hair glowing with blue under the westering sun. "It's Mr. Vogg."

My heart began to hammer as if I was in the kitchen again, or running up from the gully. I kept going, peering in the backseat of the Ford for the grocery bags. She'd gone to the high-end grocery in Salsville, not the box store.

The fresh stick of Alex's minty gum in my mouth had turned to a dry tasteless wad.

•••

DISCIPLINE

A shiny black car sat next to the dusty Ford and Alex's truck, gleaming sweetly. It had tinted windows, and tires so glossy they looked fake. Mr. Vogg didn't wear a suit, at least, but his chinos had a sharp crease, his hair stayed in place even under the breeze, and his wingtips had sharp points, polished carefully. He kissed Mama's cheek and presented her with a big handful of flowers—roses.

Red, red roses like blood clots. I didn't see him looking to check if his other ones had arrived, and a hard fist clenched in my stomach until I pulled out the breadboard and began slicing the fancy bread Mama brought. Alex, next to me, cut up tomatoes for the salad, and something about him just standing there, his elbow occasionally brushing my arm, made me feel a lot steadier.

There were only four chairs at the dinette, and I kept getting up and running to fetch things. Partly because the table was so small... and partly because Mr. Vogg sat right across from me and I could smell his cologne through the pot roast and mashed potatoes and bread and salad and the bottle of wine he'd brought, which Mama seemed pleased at and said *just one glass* but I knew she'd have two and turn soft and maybe laugh that sweet childish giggle of hers that made her sound younger than me.

But that didn't matter, because halfway through dinner I looked up, my knee pressed against Alex's, and I heard a familiar sound. An engine purring nice and sweet, a familiar burp as he did the usual trick of downshifting to slide into a parking spot. "*Ray!*" I bumped the table, leaping up, and Alex grabbed at my milk glass before there was a Spill Event.

I suppose I thought everything was going to be all right now that he'd come home for dinner, for once. The wind had changed a little, growing cooler as the sun slid down over the Rockies, and someone else in the park was barbecuing. The good smell of smoke and meat warred briefly with bad memories, and I pushed it aside.

He slammed the Camaro's door and pitched his cigarette aside, pushing up the lip of his cowboy hat. He'd taken to wearing one lately, and with his lanky tallness I guess it looked okay. His coveralls had been broken in but good, now, and his hiking boots were a new pair.

"Ray!" I threw my arms around him. "I haven't seen you all week! There's dinner. It's pot roast. I did the potatoes the way you like them."

He stiffened, but he didn't push me away. "Looks like you're having a party."

"First day of school. Didn't you know?"

"That's why I'm here."

My heart swelled up with happy air. He'd remembered. "Alex is over. Mama has a guest." I waited a beat. "It's a guy from her work. Customer."

"Huh." He squinted at me, blue eyes gleaming under the hat brim. "Been a long day."

"I know. You didn't come home last night."

"Lay off, Dez." He shook free of me, and the happy in my chest faded bit by bit as I watched him stamp up the porch stairs. The banister didn't sway when he grabbed it, but maybe he didn't notice. He banged the screen door, too, and if I couldn't tell trouble was brewing before, I sure knew now.

I ran after him, the wind lifting my hair and tangling it together, almost like clawed fingers. As soon as I got inside I braced myself for the awful.

It didn't look like much. "Pleasedtameetcha," Ray mumbled at Mr. Vogg, who had half-risen to offer a handshake. He didn't even look at Alex, said nothing to Mama, stamped down the hall, and his bedroom door closed so hard it rattled the whole mobile.

The silence that followed scraped all over me. Everyone was looking at me as if I'd yelled. "He's really tired," I managed. "He's been working a lot."

Mr. Vogg settled back in his chair. *Ray's* chair. It didn't even squeak like it usually did. "A difficult age for a young man," he said, smoothly, and Mama's face eased a little. "It's good that he works so hard. Teaches 'em discipline."

"He's a hard worker," Alex chimed in. "He's magic with engines. There's pretty much nothing he can't do with one."

Mama straightened up and tried to beam. She was always so proud of him. "He's always been like that. Taking things apart to see how they work, and he can put them back together too. Once he took apart my oven."

"Now *that's* interesting." Mr. Vogg had an odd smile. Very white, even teeth, but his mouth turned down first before the corners went up to make it a grin. Like he had to drag a frown all the way around to make it into something else. His shoulders moved under his polo shirt, a movement too subtle to be a shrug. "He'll go far in life, with those talents."

Mama's smile had relaxed still further, became natural. "I hope so. My Dez, too, she's smart. She'll go to college."

"Did you go to college, Edie?"

Mama's expression changed just a little. "I did. For a while."

I knew *that* story. She'd gotten pregnant with Ray, Daddy had married her, and she always thought she'd go back. Mr. Vogg's face perked up a little, as if he couldn't wait to ask another question. Maybe he was curious, but it didn't feel like he was. It felt like he was searching for something, the way a lady at the grocery will inquire when she's hungry for gossip.

I searched for something to steer the conversation away. "I might join the Peace Corps." Not like I ever would, but it would give them something else to talk about. Hopefully. It came out too loud, too desperate, and my throat had gone dry once again.

Another long silence, this one embarrassed instead of painful, and Alex's mouth twitched slightly. Looking at him was like catching a rope, and something liquid-hot spilled all through me.

It felt good.

"Really?" Alex sounded genuinely interested. "I'll bet they'd send you somewhere and have you teach kids. You'd be good at that."

And just like that, the conversation had something else to rest on. I wasn't the only one propping it up.

Mr. Vogg started talking about charities young people could volunteer at, and Mama, maybe happy nobody had started yelling, laughed at some of his jokes. At least he made her feel good, but I ended up not being able to eat much. The empty space where Ray should be wasn't even halfway filled by Alex, but he gave it a good try, and he even helped me clean up afterward while Mama and Mr. Vogg sat in the living room on the pink loveseat a neighbor had set out with a Free sign on one of the hottest days of August. Carrying it in had been a chore and a half, but worth it—even though the thing was studded with cigarette burns. It was still something to sit on, and I brought them coffee in the only two mugs that matched while Alex dried the plates. Mr. Vogg's fingers brushed mine as I handed him a mug, though I tried my best to avoid it. A small greasy shudder went down my back, but nothing else happened, and I mumbled a "you're welcome" and fled.

It wasn't until later, with the house empty of everything but Mama sleeping and Ray doing whatever it was he did in his room with the door closed, that I realized Alex hadn't asked Mama if he could take me to Homecoming.

Maybe he'd changed his mind.

CHAPTER THIRTEEN

Standard

S CHOOL WOUND THROUGH A COUPLE WEEKS, finding its rhythm. The cafeteria was a fishbowl, a hubbub of healthy young animals sloshing and bouncing around inside under a thick layer of the wet-gelatin reek of industrial food and the sharp tang of industrial cleaners. There was a sort of comfort to being tucked in a dark forgotten corner—the closest tables were all taken up by stoners in flannel and their harder-edged cousins, the tougher of the unpopular classes. Nobody wanted this chair because the back was broken, but you could sit against the half-wall and use another chair as a table, sort of, somewhere to rest a backpack while your lunch sat in your lap and the current book—a thick heavy one about sorcerers in a fairytale England—shielded you from casual commentary. Mama had bought me new blue-and-white sneakers because I'd worn the soles right off the other ones, and I felt bad about that even if I was glad to have new shoes.

I ate without tasting, absorbed in the part where a man with thistledown hair began wrapping his spiderweb conspiracy tighter and tighter, and I didn't notice the hush building in a bubble around me until the knot inside my head gave a twitch and I jerked, almost spilling my free milk carton onto the floor.

"I wondered where you ate lunch." Alex had another orange plastic chair, and my first thought was wondering if he'd yanked it out from under one of the stoners. Or maybe, being Alex, he'd just *asked*. "Hi."

I stared at him while he settled down into the chair about an arm's length away from me, as if it was the most natural thing in the world for him to penetrate the pariah belt. "Um. Alex."

"Did you forget I was picking you up?"

No, I thought you'd be mad at me, so I just caught the bus in the mornings like usual. I shook my head. With him suddenly sitting there, the rest of the caf had drawn away, as if a camera had pulled back and shown all the space around us. Or *made* a bunch of space, a solo country.

It was like he carried around his own planet, and I wondered what it would be like to be that *sure*, to be born expecting the world would accommodate you if you chose to step out a bit of line.

"I tried the library, and even behind the bleachers with the smokers, and pretty much everywhere," he continued, settling his backpack on the floor between his cowboy boots. "Everybody said they'd just seen you, or that you had a different lunch."

"They said that?" *They probably don't even know who I am.*

"Oh yeah. Brian Saldano swore you had second lunch, but the office said different. I was an office aide last year, did I tell you? Anyway." He took a deep breath, and I got the idea he was nervous, again.

So I closed the book and set it on my backpack, and picked up my sandwich crust. "*Freshman* have second lunch."

"I keep forgetting you're sophomore. Hey, listen. I wanted to talk to you."

My throat closed up. I started sliding everything back into my brown paper bag, which was good for a couple more lunches. The plastic bags could be washed and reused, too. There was nothing to be done about the half-full container of apple juice, though. "About?"

"I didn't get to ask your mama about Homecoming." As if he'd been sitting on the question for a week and a half.

Is this the part where he lets me down easy? It was easy to not pick up the phone, if I unplugged it and only put the jack back in when I knew Mama would be calling. I wasn't *quite* avoiding him. I just spent time in the gully, sitting and looking at the creek after my hour was up and Gran shooed me out. The water had slowed to a tiny trickle, a dry autumn even though clouds clustered around the mountains in the distance, white and gray smudges like a faroff headache. "That's okay."

"That's why I'm heading over to the cafe after school." He examined a safety poster stuck above the lockers across the wall, a kid on a skateboard with gel-spiked hair reminding everyone to *Look Both Ways Because Safe Is Cool.* "You want to go with me?"

"I can't. I have my job to go to."

Why did he look so damn *interested*? "What kind of job?"

Everyone was probably wondering what the hell he was doing talking to me. "It's... an old lady, near my mobile park. I clean for her, look after her." *And she teaches me things you wouldn't believe.* "I can't take you to her."

"Doesn't surprise me. I could take you home and wait for you, maybe? Then we could both go?" Questions tumbling out like the creek in its channel slipping over stones.

"I have to make dinner." I picked at the seam on my jeans. Someone laughed all the way across the cafeteria, a high bright shout, the sound punching through the rest of the noise. "Alex..."

"I thought I'd take you and your mama out for dinner."

"Oh." *Is that even legal?* I wasn't so sure about it. "I... but if you're just sitting around and waiting for an hour, you'll get bored."

"I'll bring something to keep me occupied. Come on, Dez, stop shooting me down."

Why wasn't I telling him to get lost? It would be the safest thing to do, right? He was in a whole 'nother world from me, and I knew it, even if he was playing like he didn't. Still, I had to be gentle. That's the thing with anything man-shaped. You have to smile and play nice, so they don't turn into black smoke. "I'm not. Really I'm not. I just—"

"You really think my friends are gonna be mean? Or that I am?"

He kept switching around. Normally I had no trouble keeping up, but I wasn't braced for this. And the knot in my head was so tight nothing could get through, the way it usually was at school. I didn't *want* to know what all those other kids were thinking of. "I just... we've moved around a lot, Alex. It's pretty standard everywhere."

"Huh." He nodded, thoughtfully, scratching at his chin. They made the boys take off their hats inside, and without it his hair was soft and springy, just enough curl. It was a good look on him. "Well. What if we're not standard?"

Everyone thinks they're not. I opted for questioning, since it would give me time to think. "Your friends?"

"No. You and me."

The warning bell blatted, a sea-change rippling through the caf. Clatters of trays hitting metal, catcalls, and a burst of laughter from a flock of cowboy popular girls, all in the school's green and blue cheerleading uniform, their fake tans all the same shade of orange and their bangs hairsprayed high enough to catch low-flying aircraft. I stuffed the book and my crumpled lunchbag into my backpack. Next was AP History, and I was fairly sure there'd be a quiz on the Opium Wars. "I don't know," I finally hedged. What was he aiming at?

"Because I don't think we're standard." He hadn't moved, still looking at me with that strange expression. That line between his eyebrows was a permanent fixture, and the irrational urge to reach up and smooth it away all but made my hands itch.

Instead, I found myself smiling. "You don't?"

"Nope." The line shallowed out, and he smiled back. Had he actually been worried? "What do you have next?"

It was pretty strange to think someone might be worried *I* would get mad. "History." Milk sloshed as I tossed the box in the garbage can—another reason nobody sat here. But you can get used to anything you try; I'd just stopped smelling it.

"I'll walk you." Alex's mouth had relaxed, and there were little bits of actual gold in his hair, glowing even under fluorescents.

Why? "What do you have?"

"Life Skills. You think you could teach me how to sew?"

I was sure he was joking, but he said it just like he said everything else, and I hitched my heavy backpack higher on my shoulder. "I'm not good at it. Mama is, though. She'll help you out." I didn't ask why he didn't roll his eyes and groan at what Mama would have called a Home Ec class. He actually sounded a little excited about sewing. "I can get out her machine, too."

"You teach me to sew, and I'll drive you to and from school."

They'll teach you in Life Skills anyway. But for once, I just swallowed hard and agreed. It wasn't a fair trade, and I don't like being charity.

But from him it felt different. Maybe he wasn't standard after all.

· · ·

FIRST MENDING

Gran shook her head, sucking on her teeth. Today she moved even more slowly, as if pained in her joints. I'd seen her be as spry as she wanted before, but my suspicion of her putting on a show faded as I finished drying the dishes she'd washed. She told me not to, but I dared to deploy an eyeroll of my very own and carefully swabbed at each mismatched piece, from the thin porcelain plate with its gold rim to the thick uneven mug with cracked glaze and funny backwards letters that looked hand-painted. I'd found those letters, or ones like them, in the foreign-language section at the library. A funny word.

Cyrillic.

"Go sit down. I'll make you tea."

"Dasya never makes it sweet enough." But she shuffled away from the butcher-block table, piled high with herbs both dried and fresh, flowers, and cooling jars of preserves. A fury of pickling and canning had descended on her, and instead of looking into the bowl I saw shapes in steam, or the bubbling surface of hot strawberry jam. More often, a soundless whirl would descend on me, and the next thing I knew Gran would be holding my hands in her gnarled paws and saying *that's enough, Dasya. Good girl.* There would be a whole rack of things I didn't remember putting through the water bath, or jarring, or chopping, or washing, or anything else.

"I'll bring you the honey jar, Gran." I dried the champagne flute, its thin bowl sparkling now instead of full of reddish crusted stuff.

"You don't know how to run the *samovar.*" Downright petulant.

"I can boil water just fine." Both hands on my patience now, and for the first time I wondered how much of the hour I had left. Wondered if Alex was waiting in the driveway. He'd probably left, tired of hanging around for a girl who kept shooting him down. And it would be a good thing, too. He wasn't in my range, my class, my pay grade.

Whenever he was out of sight, I got to thinking he was a mirage. Probably the safest way to consider the whole thing, but it made a hole open up in my ribcage, one I didn't like. Nothing like the hole of missing something you knew you were better off without.

Gran made a spitting sound and jostled past me for the sink.

The champagne flute fell, turning end over end, and hit the floor with a musical tinkling crash.

My horrified gasp almost drowned out Gran's harsh, cawing laugh. "Distracted, Dasya. Too distracted."

"I'm so sorry—" The rock lodged in my throat, and the old woman turned. Quick as a snake, she grabbed my wrist, and her fingers turned into a vise, grinding the small bones together unmercifully. I might have yelped, but I heard, clear as day, a horrible thundering voice.

You shut your mouth, boy, or I'll shut it for you! And Ray's trying to snuffle quietly after the storm was over.

Daddy hated crying. My mouth glued shut, pressure rising inside my chest, my eyes hot and grainy as they bugged out, refusing to fill with tears.

My first two fingers popped out, and Gran hissed furiously. The sound became a buzzing rattle, like the song from the fields of high grass, turned slower and sleepier now since the days were no longer oven-hot. But it was still there, seething at the tough, pale, tangled mat of grass roots you could rip up at the edges like lifting a carpet. Underneath, the crumbling earth was dry, crying out for rain as everything above turned sere.

"Stupid girl," Gran hissed. "*Use it!*" A fresh squeeze of my wrist, the bones shrieking as they were ground together even harder, and a wire of something hot slid through me from the top of my head down to my heels, branching out through every nerve. I *felt* them light up, just like the plastic overlays of "The Nervous System: Your Body's Messenger" in middle school, terrifying to think of the skin stripped away and everything underneath exposed to dust and grit.

She let go of me and I snatched my wrist to my chest, stumbling back. Stared at the floor, cradling my throbbing hand. Black spots danced over my vision, and I whooped in a long breath full of baby powder, old-woman sweat, heated fruit-sugar, and the rough brown scent of autumn on the open plains with its hint of smoke even if nothing's burning.

The earth just exhaled the smell, a perfume that came from too much sun, too much tough grass, too much space.

My lungs just couldn't get enough air. I fetched up hard against the butcher block, rattling the racks of preserves. Slowly, the gasping faded, but I couldn't stop staring.

Gran bent, stiffly, very slowly. She touched the champagne flute with a callused fingertip.

The whole, *unbroken* champagne flute, sitting on the floor. It gleamed as if it hadn't been shards just a few moments ago. My arm ached all the way to my shoulder, my temples shrieked with pain. I blinked, several times, and my dry eyes finally decided to leak a little. My cheeks, hot as if they'd just been slapped, throbbed too.

"Oh, Dasya," Gran whispered. "See what you have done."

My breathing evened out. Gran lifted the delicate glass, whole as if it had never hit the floor. She examined it, critically. "So many of them, they come to Granny Iyaga, and they wish for curses and vengeance. They come asking for blood and breaking." A small, sad shake of her head. "My Vasyas, my Dasyas, not so common. Not so common at all." A smile split her weathered face, teeth gleaming sharp-white, and I made a small sound, holding my wrist to my chest.

That brought her terrible, benevolent gaze to rest on me, and I wasn't sure I liked it. But it was, after all, only Gran. Now I knew she was Russian, and those pretty, sleepy eyes meant she was from the steppes. I didn't know much about Russia except Daddy said they were all Communists, but at least I'd found a few encyclopedia entries.

Granny Iyaga set the flute in the drying rack, gently, and shuffled for a cabinet. "Some arnica, Dasya may have bruise. First mending's most difficult, always. Then you shall go home, safe and sound."

"Is this what you do?" I whispered. "You... fix things?"

"Pfft. Granny *teaches*." She disappeared into the tiny round bathroom, reappeared with the jar of arnica and mugwort paste. "Dasya *does*."

Um, okay. I swallowed, hard, and when she got close I almost flinched. She just took my wrist, gently this time, and smeared the paste on it, and the immediate relief made my eyes well up even more.

"Is a hard thing. Is very hard. My Vasyas and my Dasyas are always hardest." She capped the jar again, and stood, looking at me. "Now go home, Dasya, and do not come back until it is time."

"Until... what? Did I do something wrong?"

She shooed me towards the door. "You will know. Go, do not come back until time. Someone waits for Dasya above, go, go. Go, before Granny loses her temper."

That broke any remaining courage I had, and I fled. All the way up the gully and into the backyard, all I could hear was her familiar, rasping, sometimes-terrifying cackle.

CHAPTER FOURTEEN

Hypotheticals

T HE ROAR OF THE WIND DIED DOWN, and Alex took the turn into the diner's parking lot slowly. The truck still bounced—not even the best shocks would make that beast ride smooth—and I took my sneakers down from the dash, uncurling slowly. Everything on me felt tender, my wrist was sore but not puffing up and my stomach wasn't as happy as it could have been. But Alex, as usual, made everything seem... safer. More solid. The knot in my head could relax a bit, too.

He cut the engine and I blinked. The sun was a glare against the diner windows, and inside it would probably be a little warmer than comfortable. I couldn't tell if Mama was having a good-tip day—they came in waves, she and Marcie always said, and you never could tell.

Of course I didn't say that *I* usually could, nowadays, when I wasn't feeling all shaky inside. There was just no point in it, any more than there was a point in telling Alex about Gran. I'd had enough time to wash my face and settle a little bit before he drove up—he'd gone down the road to get gas, and I was just grateful she'd let me go early, I guess.

But she told me not to come back. Why would she do that? I hadn't done anything *wrong*, really. Unless dropping the glass in the first place was—

"Dez?"

"Huh?" I shook off the woolgathers and found him looking at me from the other side of the bench seat, his seat belt still on and his hair still violently mussed. "Sorry. Been a long day."

He raked his fingers back over his hair, trying to get it to sit down so he could resettle his hat the right way. "I guess. Hey, before we go in, can I ask you something?"

"Sure." I took a look at the parking lot—not too full, not too empty. So far so good.

"You ever had a boyfriend?"

My jaw threatened to drop. A nervous laugh spilled out of me. "No, never. I mean, well, I read a lot. And we move around, so... yeah, no." *I'll tan your hide,* Daddy whispered in my head. *Don't you be no slutchild.*

I was coming down more on the *relief* side of my Daddy-gone-song every day. Which probably made me a bad person. I decided to worry about it later, because this conversation was heading into dangerous territory and I needed all my wits in proper order, as Mama would have said, to navigate.

Alex measured off space on the steering wheel between his fingers. No engine grease on his hands now, but they still looked rough. Dependable. He had chores at home, too. "I wondered. So if I asked you, would you say no?"

"Ask me what?" *To Homecoming? We already did that, and you sort of seem stuck on the notion.* He hadn't asked Mama yet. There was still time for him to change his mind.

"For God's sake, Dez." A little too loud, and my heart gave a terrified leap before I figured out it was just irritation, and he calmed right down.

Then I realized what he meant. It was a day for jaw-dropping, all right. "Oh. You mean, you?"

Was he *blushing*? You couldn't tell much with his tan. He wasn't fake-orange like the cheerleaders, or burn-prone like me. "Yeah, *me*. I know I'm not your brainy type."

"I don't have a type, really." I took a deep breath. "Are you asking?"

"What would you say if I did?"

Oh, no. You don't get to make it all my idea. "Are you asking?" At least, whatever this was, he didn't get to make it my fault, either.

"Sure." Offhand, as if it didn't matter, but a reddish tint had worked down to his neck. I studied this, fascinated by the way his Adam's apple bobbed as he swallowed. Did boys have a rock in their throats too? What made that stick out the way it did?

"I suppose I'd say yes." I could still back out if he started laughing. If it was a joke, well, good one on me, and I'd get out of the truck and sit in the diner until Mama could take me home.

"You *suppose*?" Alex sounded baffled, but there was no hint of anger.

"Well, you're only talking in hypotheticals, so—"

"So you're my girlfriend."

Oh, what the hell. It could be a stupid decision, but nobody else from school was around to see, right? "Hypothetically." I hit my seatbelt release, and scooted across the seat to elbow him before he could get any ideas. "Unless you really want to ask me."

One second I was there, the next I was tangled in his seatbelt and he was kissing me, his fingers in my hair and things were going pretty amazingly until I slipped and my elbow whapped the horn. The noise scared both of us—at least, I jumped and almost bit his lip hard enough to hurt. It didn't matter, though. He laughed, so did I, and he asked me straight out and proper.

Everything inside me blew up like a balloon again, and for the first time since I left Gran's that afternoon I started feeling okay.

So that was how we walked into the diner holding hands, and Mama looked up from ringing out a man with bandy legs and a fuming cigar to see us. Her hair was pulled back with pink barrettes this time, and both electric light and sunshine polished her skin, glinting off her grandmother's pearl earrings. For a second she just looked baffled, but then she smiled, wearily, and a muscle way down deep in my stomach relaxed with pure relief.

It tightened up right afterward though. Because sitting at the smoking section of the counter, holding a cup of coffee halfway to his mouth, was Ray. He set down the mug and slid off the stool, and for a second his face was just like Daddy's and everything inside me turned cold and loose. *Don't you let me see you with no boys, Desiree Elaine.*

I should have checked the parking lot for the Camaro. I should have seen it.

"Dez!" Mama slammed the register drawer and beamed at me. "This is a nice surprise. Hello, Alex."

"Ma'am." Alex's blush had faded. He hadn't seen Raymond yet, though, so that was good. "I've asked Dez to Homecoming, and I wanted to ask your permission."

"Homecoming?" Mama's smile turned into a sunbeam. "God, that takes me back. Of course, Alex! We'll have to talk about curfew, and—"

The bandy-legged cigar-smoker slid past, and the knot in my head quivered a little. I didn't want to see what was in his head, so I jerked it tight. Then Ray was almost right next to me, and his expression—set and strained—was new. "Hi, Ray." I said it a little louder than I probably should have. "Didn't know you were off work."

He stopped short, and that dangerous expression broke up like ice in warm water. Mama almost bumped him with her hip as she came around the counter for a hug, her familiar smell enfolding me in tenuous safety. It meant I had to drop Alex's hand, but maybe that was okay.

"Early," Ray said, and cleared his throat. "Carr."

"Sarpe." Alex offered a handshake, and maybe he winced a little when Ray squeezed. Or maybe it was a small expression of effort as he squeezed back. "How you?"

"Oh, you know." Ray shook his hand twice more, smiling faintly. He looked a little like Daddy when he did that, and it was enough to chill me even in Mama's embrace. "So you're taking her to Homecoming?"

"If it's all right. You bein' man of the house and all."

"You're going to need a dress," Mama said in my ear, her gold hoop earring pressing against my cheek. "Fabric store. We'll go this weekend. I'll measure you up, and make you something nice."

"Can't say no to my little sister." Ray finally turned loose of Alex's hand. "As long as she's happy, Carr."

"I'm sure if she ain't, you'll be the first to know." Alex's chin lifted a fraction.

"Count on it." Ray's smile was more of a tooth-baring grimace. It occurred to me that he wouldn't know a damn thing about how I felt one way or another because he was never home to ask, but I didn't think Alex meant it that way.

I mean, he was too sweet to mean that, mostly. Wasn't he?

In any case, Mama went right on through the awkward silence. "It's a day for good news, I guess. Ray got a promotion, and I—" She glanced over her shoulder, dropped her voice. "—well, I'll tell you later. This just puts the cherry on the cake."

It was one of Daddy's phrases, but it didn't sting coming from her. Flushed and sticky in the blue polyester uniform, her hair drying in fine thready curls against her sweating neck, Mama was just... beautiful.

No bruises anymore. Was she coming down on the *relief* side of the song too? It took a while after someone... left... to make things settle, I guess. *Did* Mama even know what she felt, or what was going on inside her own head? It was just like Ray to say something like *that*, something that turned everything over and made me wonder.

Alex wanted to take us all for dinner, but Ray said he had to go meet a guy about a carburetor and Mama had decided to pick up a few more hours. "You two go on. You deserve a break, Dez. How's your old Mrs.?"

See what you have done, Dasya. "She's okay. Canning a lot of stuff."

"It's the season for it. I wish..." But Mama simply shook her head as another customer—a trucker with a baseball cap instead of a cowboy hat—ambled up. "Go on, you two. Alex, thank you. She'll let you know about the corsage soon."

"Thank *you*, Mrs. Sarpe. I'll bring her back tonight by eight."

"See that you do." Mama's smile was sunlight.

Ray didn't stop to say goodbye, just banged out the door and was gone in a cloud of dust by the time we made it outside. I stared at his taillights until he took the right on Capasca, and looked up to find Alex doing the same thing. "He's been working a lot," I managed, a little lamely. "He's tired."

"Yeah." A flash of... was it trouble? I didn't want to find out. "Your mama said he got a promotion."

"I guess. Did you know?"

For a moment, the trouble intensified, then it vanished. "He doesn't talk to me now that school's on. Maybe he thought I was older."

Or maybe he was nice to you to get that job. "I dunno." That seemed to finish everything up. I surprised myself then, by reaching down and grabbing his hand. "I'm glad you're not. Older, I mean."

He nodded. For once, that line between his eyebrows smoothed out, and it was nice to see. "Me too. Let's go."

. . .

MENDING

Now that I was sixteen, the doctors added things to the regular checkups. Like cold metal stirrups, and those awkward questions about Are You Sexually Active, rushed through by a bored nurse who more likely than not would look at you like you were a bug underfoot if you said *yes*. I figured kissing didn't count as *active*, and this time I went in when Mama did for a checkup. Aside from me having grown a bit there was nothing to report. I sat in the waiting room, a book about homeless kids in Europe open on my knees, and watched people come down the hall. Freshly enlisted with their high-and-tights exposing pale scalps, the older wives with their set looks, pregnant women clutching copies of *What To Expect*, not a lot of kids my age. Instead, there were a bunch of younger ones. They mostly behaved themselves, except for one kid who kept poking at his little sister and making little *foo* noises until she, being only about a year and a half, started to howl. Their mother, a harried-looking brownette filling out paperwork, was probably new to all this.

The clock ticked on. It was Mama's night to make dinner.

Marcie wasn't precisely *angry* that Mama had given notice at the Souper Soup Diner. But she did think Mama was being a bit hasty. *Edie, you don't hardly know this man, and he offers you this job? Too good to be true generally is, you know.*

Oh, Mama knew. But being a secretary downtown, while it meant a longer commute, also meant more pay that wasn't tips, and sitting down. And Mr. Vogg hadn't quite gotten Mama the job, he'd just told her there was an opening—she went down and interviewed, wearing the blue silk-and-wool skirt and blazer that still fit her, even though it was from before my being born. *That shorthand and typing in high school turns out to pay more than anything college did,* she'd remarked at dinner, and smiled at me.

No more white boxes on the front porch, though.

There were pinpricks on my fingers, a tingling like when I had to hold the gray watered silk for Mama. The dress was beautiful, but I still felt a nervous flutter each time I looked at the sewing table. Something like before a rollercoaster takes that first plunge.

Which made me think about Gran. *You'll know,* she'd said. But I didn't. All I knew was that instead of running to the gully after school, I was lying on my mattress reading, or doing homework at the table. Or I was riding in Alex's truck, the windows only half-down now, and finding out what kids around here did for fun.

Like hanging at the mall. I thought kids only did that in movies, and I didn't like looking at all sorts of things I'd never need or be able to afford. It was only fun because Alex was there, really. I liked it better when we were just... driving, aimlessly or not, on the ribbon back of the highway.

I shifted uncomfortably in the hard plastic chair, tried to sink back into the book. It wasn't working.

Maybe it was that this waiting room had no window, and the linoleum had long black scuffs where someone had jabbed their bootheels down. The magazines were always armed-forces publications, sharing space with brochures on immunizing your kids and exercise being the fountain of youth. All faded, dog-eared, tattered. Probably better off as origami, really.

The knot in my head quivered a little. Nice and tight, as if I was in school. I still kept wondering...

Like the brownette mother, her teeth aching and her kids climbing on her, the younger one snuffling snot all over everything. It wouldn't take much—just a small push in the right direction. A light touch, like Mama shaking the greens in her particular way.

The first mending is the hardest, Dasya.

Nobody even noticed. The mother, swiping at her hair against her forehead, took a deep breath. She dug in her purse, and out came a tissue. With the snot wiped away, the little girl smiled up at her, and the older kid patted at his sister instead of poking. Now the mother's hair was threaded with gold, and her shoulders eased. The ratty T-shirt she'd been wearing had become a faded peach sweater, obviously old but neatly mended and well-kept, and her eyes sparkled as she smiled. "There you are. Just be patient a little longer."

I breathed out. My wrist cramped a little. It didn't matter, because the older brother was grinning now. "Sissa be *fine*," he stated proudly, and clumsy little-boy hugged the baby again. "Sissa gonna be fine."

The knot inside my head tightened up. Breathing afterward was the hard part, taking all the anger and pain and desperation and painting its edges with glue, fitting it together until it made something softer. Something *whole*. Ripples spread out, the magazines a little less dog-eared, the round, frowning nurse at the counter shrugging at the new recruit anxiously holding his sheaf of papers. "Let me check that for you," she said, wearily but kindly. "I've seen a million of these."

The new recruit, a jug-eared, nervous guy Ray's age, swallowed very hard. "Thank you ma'am. I... really, thanks."

It took so little to make the world so much better. It didn't matter that each small change sparked a headache. And the dreams—seeing how things could have gone without the nudges, watching the bad and the nasty gather in corners. Dreams stitched together by a river of breathy melody, a long-haired shadow capering through sleep's rolling country.

I bent forward, pretending to tie my shoes, but really just waiting for the shaking and dizziness to go down. *Everything costs, Dasya. One way or another.*

I was still staring at my toes when a shadow fell over me, and I looked up to find Mama standing there, paper-white and shaking. For a second I thought she'd somehow seen what I'd done, and my mouth fell open.

"Desiree." A tight little bullet of a word. "We're leaving."

I scrambled to gather up my book and my backpack. "What's wrong?"

Her jaw clenched tight, and some of the color was beginning to come back into her face. Still, the way she stood there—shoulders stiff, purse clutched to her belly as if it was a watermelon, "Nothing. Let's go."

"Mama—" The world was sliding sideways, with me on it. The knot in my head clenched itself, a spike through my temples.

"Nothing is wrong." She already had her car keys. "It took a while. We're going home."

"Okay." I hurried to keep up. She was moving at a nice determined clip, and the halls around us were a blur. "Mama, are you all right?"

"I'm *fine*." Her tone gentled, and she finally slung her battered leather purse onto her shoulder, its cheerful fringe swaying. "We're just late, that's all."

Late for what? I wasn't going back to school; I'd been signed out before lunch with a Medical Slip. Alex was coming by later to take me to his house for dinner for the first time, and I might have wanted to talk about it now that the poking and prodding and weighing was done.

But I knew better than to question when she was moving like this, arms stiff and her long legs marking off time. Just like she'd been moving after Daddy... died.

If I hadn't just done a touch to fix up things in the waiting room, I could have maybe seen what the knot would tell me about what Mama was feeling. But all I got was the headache mounting another notch when I tried to concentrate.

So I just hurried after her, breathless and head-tender. We plunged out into the first afternoon autumn was breathing a chill across the plains instead of long syrup-slow Indian summer. We didn't talk all the way offbase, and when we got home, she made a pot of coffee and sat down at the table with the bills, a haze of strain and static all around her filling up every corner of the kitchen.

I stood in the middle of my room, my hands turning into fists and my head full of nails and scratching, and tried to breathe.

• • •

COMMOTION

Alex popped the truck into park while I stared at the house. "You okay?"

The place was *huge.* Cream-colored, with a red-tiled roof, sort of Spanish-looking. Sprinklers were going—the lawn was a huge expanse of clipped green, and there were neat masses of purple and blue flowering bushes under every window. The driveway was black and glossy, sealed and new-looking, and there was a shiny red truck as well as a big crouching black beast of a hemi-dualie-something or another, with *Carr Mechanics* plastered all over it. An American flag glared from the back window, to leave no doubt that this was a red-blooded truck owned by a red-blooded, go-gettin' man. Next to it, Alex's old, battered blue pickup looked a little scruffy. There was also a brand-new red sedan, but that was pulled into one of the four garage spots—the only open one. It crouched in front of racks of organized, color-coded Rubbermaid bins I was suddenly sure were full of Christmas decorations, not to mention Thanksgiving, St. Patrick's, Labor Day, and any other holiday you could name. Probably craft supplies, too.

I shouldn't have worn jeans. My mouth had gone dry.

"Hey." Alex cut the engine. "Dez?"

"Fine," I managed. *Oh, Lord. Everything in that place is probably vacuumed twice a day. The dishes probably all match. I am going to do something wrong.* There was absolutely no way I was going to get out of this without embarrassing myself, and my head hurt. "Just, you know. Doctors."

"Yeah. Sports physicals are the worst. It only took one to convince me I didn't want to do any of that."

"Yeah?" I knew he wasn't on any of the teams.

"Yup." He blew out between his lips, almost a whistle but not quite. "Dad was a little disappointed, but I think Mom was relieved. Then Kevin started doing all that stuff, and it was reversed. You'll like them. Dad's loud, but he means well."

"Okay." Our mobile would fit in their four-car garage. His mother probably used potpourri, for God's sake. Then there were his brothers, I didn't want to forget their names. "And there's Kevin, and Charlie."

"They're assholes," he said, promptly, and I almost laughed. "But you know, brothers."

"Yeah, I know." My fingers were twisting each other together, tighter and tighter. I didn't belong in Alex's world, no matter how nonstandard he thought he was. "I just hope I don't do anything embarrassing."

"They know you're shy." He half-turned, watching me across the acres of bench seat between us.

Great. "Okay." I didn't bother protesting that I wasn't shy, I just liked to keep myself safe.

"So don't be worried."

"I'll try." I managed a smile. "They probably think we're making out in the car."

"You want to?" He actually looked hopeful, and this time I didn't just *almost* laugh. I flat-out giggled, and his smile was a reward all its own. The sprinklers chugged outside, and I wondered about their water bill.

If it'll put off going in there... But then, they probably would take one look at me and know *mobile home.* My head gave one last pound of pain, and through the half-open window another sound intruded. The sprinklers made a rhythm, and underneath it a silver thread ran, a whistle skipping along like the creek at the bottom of the gully. I saw the champagne flute again, fine thin glass glowing against Gran's black floor, and something eased inside me.

If they didn't like me, I knew where I could go. Even if I didn't go to Granny Iyaga's trailer, I could sit next to the creek in the gully and feel the clean immensity of trees and grass and stone all through me. No matter how rich they were, they probably couldn't mend things.

That, too, was all mine. The whistling faded into a murmur just at the very edge of hearing, and I reached for the door handle.

"Don't!" Alex waved both hands, to get my attention. I didn't flinch—well, not much—when he did. "Dad'll tear me a new one if I don't open a lady's door, okay? Hang on."

The slam of his door made the rest of my headache disappear, and watching him walk around the front of the truck seemed to take forever. He couldn't make an engine sing the way Ray did, but he kept his truck running. His hair was longer now and messy, and that line was back between his eyebrows, and he was in jeans too. So at least we'd match, even if I was wearing Mama's wine-red sweater with the V neck. I'd thought it looked sophisticated, at home. Now I was just glad that it smelled comfortingly like her perfume. Whatever happened, I could go home afterward.

Out beyond the sprinklers, the tall yellow grass took over. That would be where the Whistling Man was, sliding leggy and lean between the stalks, right on the border where weeds would grow from the runoff from the carefully nurtured grass. Maybe he was checking on me for Gran, or maybe he was... something else. Who knew?

Gran probably knows. Is it time?

But then Alex was at the door, and I had to get moving. I slid out, he grabbed my hand, and we both braced ourselves.

• • •

I'd expected...well, some hairspray. Maybe big earrings and cowboy boots. Instead, there was a round dumpling of a momlady with twinkling blue eyes and a messy blonde ponytail bent almost double, doing her best to restrain a wriggling cocker spaniel who really, *really* wanted to make my acquaintance judging by his dancing and whining, his nails scritching madly against shiny hardwood floor.

"Butch... oh, hi, you must be Dez, sorry, he's... watch out, he's really friendly, but—"

The dog leapt at me, barking excitedly, and I crouched too, so he wouldn't get scared. This put half of me out the front door, and the dog's ecstatic wriggling was matched by a furious baying from deeper inside the house.

"Is she scared of dogs? Alex, you *did* tell her about the dogs, right?" Flushed and deft, in a chambray workshirt and jeans herself, her bare toes painted bright crimson, she didn't look like a cowboy mama. "Oh, honey, he don't bite, I swear, he's just—Butch! *Mind* yourself, now!"

"It's okay," I managed over the baying, yipping, and general commotion. "I like dogs."

The noise resolved into a basset hound almost tripping over his own ears to get past her and at me, and I began to laugh at his floppy face and high-volume excitement. The knot inside my head relaxed a little, and the sheer clean joy from both dogs was enough to make the world straighten up just fine. I ended up sitting down against the long etched glass panel-window next to the door, both dogs cavorting over my legs and doing their best to clean my face, while Alex got the door shut.

Mrs. Carr sagged with relief. "You must be Dez. I'm Libba, so happy to—Butch, *quit* that! Jesse, *down!* Happy to meet you. Sol—that's Kevin's girlfriend, she's scared to death of dogs, even Butch. He's just excited, that's all. Oh, honey, aren't you sweet. They like you! Alex, you *did* warn her about the dogs, right?"

"RELEASE THE HOUNDS!" someone else yelled, and a skinny, straw-haired boy who looked about twelve bounded down a flight of stairs that could have starred in its own MGM musical. It had to be Charlie, the brother in middle school. His jeans were torn up around the knees, his shirt clearly a hand-me-down and splattered with dried paint, and he looked about as happy as a mischief-making middle-schooler ever could.

I didn't feel so underdressed anymore. The basset hound got his nose in my hair and got a mouthful of whatever he thought was so interesting there, and Mrs. Carr lunged forward. "*Damn* it, dog, last thing she needs is you eating her hair! I'm sorry, honey."

"It's okay," I repeated. "I like dogs."

"Is it her? It is! Alex is in *loooooove!*" Charlie hit the bottom of the stairs and took a running leap. He hit the floor going full-bore, and crashed into Alex. I winced, and trooping down the stairs came a mild-looking German shepherd and a beak-nosed, slightly younger version of Alex, with big raw hands and his sandy hair cut aggressively short.

"Cool it, pipsqueak," the new arrival called. He was in chinos and a polo shirt, and his face was vaguely familiar—freshman basketball, maybe?

The dog ambling behind him gave me an intelligent look, like she could tell I'd started the ruckus but was willing to let it slide. She paced towards me, and in a few seconds had both of the other dogs minding their manners while she calmly, tail wagging and ears perked, sniffed at my extended fingers. "Hello," I said, low and soft. "It's nice to meet you too."

"Looks like Daisy likes you." The guy on the stairs—Kevin, the middle brother—grinned from ear to ear, an expression of such pure dopey goodwill it was hard not to grin back even though Alex was occupied with wrestling Charlie, whose high-pitched, screamy laughter threatened to drown everything else out. "Hi, I'm Kevin."

"How do you do," I managed, properly, and glanced nervously Alex's direction. He was occupied, so it was his mother who gave me a hand up from the floor. "Thank you, ma'am."

"So polite! None of that ma'am, though. You can call me Libba. Alex has told us all about you, honey."

"Oh." Now I had to start worrying about what he'd said to them, brushing a little at my slobber-covered jeans. I might have felt even more self-conscious if Mrs. Carr hadn't been covered in dog hair too. "Good things, I hope."

"Oh yeah." Kevin's grin looked like a permanent fixture. "He can't shut up about you."

Charlie broke into even more hysterical laughter. "Finally has a girlfriend! We thought he was *gay!*"

"Charles Frederick Carr, get off your brother and mind your manners!" Mrs. Carr glared, and that restored order just as quickly as one of Mama's quick-snapped *I'm looking at you, Desiree!*s "Come on in, honey. Frank's out back with the grill, hope you like barbecue. You're not a vegetarian, right?"

"No, ma'am. I eat just about anything." Besides, Mama said it didn't matter, you were polite when someone was feeding you, period, the end, even if they gave you fancy French snails. Which had brought up the question of just who would offer anyone French snails, but I figured in France they were probably like popcorn.

"Hi!" Charlie barged up to me. "I'm Charlie. Do you kiss Alex?"

I couldn't help myself. "I'm Dez. Do you kiss your mother?"

He cracked up again, doubling over, and Mrs. Carr laughed too. It was a nice sound, even if it did echo under the high ceilings. I wondered how they dusted the big beams up there—oh, they probably had people to do the cleaning.

People like me. Or Mama.

"I thought you said she was *shy*." Kev mock-punched Alex's arm, and the German shepherd herded the other two dogs away in a yipping ball of commotion, since I was standing up and presumably much more boring now.

My stomach eased a little, and in here, I couldn't hear the whistling outside. Mrs. Carr drew me along, quizzing me about school and what I liked to read, and I began to feel cautiously hopeful.

Maybe this wouldn't turn out so bad.

CHAPTER FIFTEEN

Almost Contained

I sat in the middle seat on the way home, and Alex kept his arm around me the whole time. "I told you they'd like you."

Everything inside me was glowing, the way it did when I was around him for a while. "Is your dad always that serious about meat?" Frank Carr seemed to view the scorching of dead animal flesh the way other people saw church rituals. If it wasn't for the soft padding of fat on him and the belly laugh, he might have scared me stiff, he was so loud and *definite* in all his opinions. Even his red polo shirt was bossy, mostly because it was so *large*. And his belt buckle had a gigantic horseshoe on it.

Alex laughed. "Oh yeah. Especially when we have guests. You'll know he's relaxed when he drinks beer at the grill instead of cracking one when he sits down."

What else could I say? "I like your mama. She's nice."

"She taught English for a while. You're probably her favorite now because you knew who all those people were."

"*Those people*," meaning, pretty much every author I'd ever read for school. "Everyone knows who Jane Austen is."

"I don't."

We'd talked about her for a good half-hour, though. "Weren't you listening?"

He waved one index finger, lazily, lifting it from the steering wheel to brush the question away. "That stuff just never sticks in my head."

"But you read." I knew, because he'd checked out books at the library.

"I like mysteries. And westerns." He didn't blush this time, admitting it. The truck's hum was an old familiar friend now, and I was comfortably full of smoke-juicy meat and a potato salad Mrs. Carr promised to write down the recipe for. *Next time you come over. Got to make sure you come back so I can introduce you to Proust.*

"Well, that counts."

"If you say so, Dez."

"I do." I pressed my lips against his cheek and the truck shimmied a little, as if it had the happies too.

Alex's arm tightened. "Don't distract me while I'm driving."

"Thought you liked that."

"I can pull over." He sounded hopeful at the thought.

I had to laugh. "No you can't. Mama wants me home by nine. If I'm late she won't let me go out with you again."

"Then don't distract me."

A heady thing, to be able to affect someone else. "What if I like to?"

"Damn, girl." The haze of feeling from him, deep and clean, took all the chill off the night air and made the radio—playing softly, a country song with wailing guitars and a strange backbeat—a low sweet blur of sound. He didn't blast the music like Ray did, and his hands never turned hard and hurtful. He didn't flinch when his father yelled at the grill, trying to get it to behave, and Mrs. Carr didn't flinch either. She just rolled her eyes and told him to mind his language with a young lady present.

It made me wonder what it would be like to live like that. All that space and the color-coded Tupperware for the leftovers, stacked in a fridge that didn't wheeze. A sleek new dishwasher, and two sinks—scraping the plates over the garbage and rinsing them even though Mrs. Carr protested I didn't have to, their garbage had a lid you had to hold up with a foot pedal, in shiny stainless steel. Everything was so clean, even Alex's messy room with the posters tacked up anyhow. He had a desk for doing homework, too. An actual *desk*, with a tensor lamp and a cup for sharpened pencils.

Pulling into our driveway, he turned his head a little and kissed my temple. The truck's engine idled, a familiar song now. He set the parking brake carefully, and before he'd finished doing that I was kissing him.

A fascinating new country, his hands on me and our mouths sharing heat, greedily gulping at each other and somehow managing to give back as much as we took. The porch light was on, the sky was purple, and maybe Mama was peering out through the window, to make sure things didn't go Too Far.

Or maybe she wasn't. Maybe she was still in her bedroom, thinking about whatever the doctor had said.

That splashed cold water all over everything, and I pulled back. Rested my forehead against Alex's, and our breathing matched, deep and fast. One of his hands had worked under my sweater, the skin of his palm against my back.

"I should go inside," I whispered.

"Yeah." A hard swallow, his Adam's apple bobbing. His eyes closed, and a little sweat on him.

I did that. What else could I do to him? For him?

With him?

"Thank you for inviting me." Now I sounded like a priss. "I like your family."

He heaved a sigh like he was relieved, a warm draft touching my chin. "Good. I mean, you're... Mom'll be sad if we break up. She likes you a lot."

"She just met me."

"It didn't take me long to like you, either."

My laugh tangled with his, just like my breath. Another kiss, and then I had to tear myself away. He got out to open my door, and by then I knew enough to let him. He was just the same, and I hadn't embarrassed myself.

At least, not much. Not more than usual. I hadn't dropped anything. If I had, though, I wondered what those people would do if I mended it right in front of them.

Oh, I knew I never would. But it was still sort of fun to think about, a dark sweet candy with a trace of bitterness in the center.

Alex even walked me up to the door in the fragrant darkness. The wind was full of soft rustling. Stopped, his thumbs in his jean pockets and his shoulders a little slumped. He was built broader than Kevin, but leaner than his dad; you could see his mama in his face. Especially around his blue, blue eyes. "See you tomorrow morning."

"Okay." I went up on tiptoe to kiss his cheek. Swapping spit with him on the front porch probably was a little too far. "Goodnight."

"Goodnight. Go on in, Dez."

I'm not going to get attacked on the front porch. It might have irritated me, but instead, it made me feel... safe. Almost contained. Like his personal planet included me. "Yes, sir."

"Ha. Hey, Dez?"

Thought you wanted me to go inside. "Hm?"

"Still going to Homecoming with me?"

"Haven't changed my mind yet." I didn't even feel like I was lying. Did being so nervous you wanted to hide from the whole damn thing constitute changing your mind? I wasn't sure.

"Good." He leaned forward, pecked me on the cheek, and backed away as I got the door open. "Tomorrow."

"Tomorrow," I echoed, and shut myself safely inside. Listened for the truck's rousing, and listened to him drive away.

It smelled like heat and dust inside. I tiptoed down the hall. Mama's door was open, and though it was dark and quiet, I could tell she was awake. "Mama?"

"Huh?" The sound of her moving under the covers. She did a good impression of being just-woke, sleepy and slurred.

"I'm home. It's eight-forty-five."

"Didja have a good time, honey?" Hopeful, as if she hadn't been sure I would.

"I did. I like his parents. Did you have dinner?" The little breath of roasted margarine and Kraft in the kitchen told me it had been grilled cheese, which meant Ray hadn't been home at all. I could go back to the kitchen, to get a glass of water, and check the trash to see if she'd actually eaten.

"I did. Glad you're home, go to bed."

"Yes ma'am." But I hesitated. "Mama?"

"What?" Was that a tinge of fear? Bright like lemon against my tongue.

"I love you."

Her relief was blueberries, bubbling in a crisp, hot and tart. "I love you too, honey. Night."

It wasn't until I was done brushing my teeth and tucked in that it came back—that thread of silver melody. The wind rose, mouthing my window, and I suddenly knew what the doctor had said to Mama.

I shivered under my covers as the Whistling Man prowled and capered outside, his song turned sharp saw-edged. I saw him behind my eyelids—perched on the sagging barb wire like it was a tightrope, his hat gone and his lank hair whipped into an electric mass. I fell into a thin troubled sleep as thunder rolled in the mountains, and my last thought before the darkness was simple enough to make me cold again.

It's time.

. . .

A MAN'S QUESTION

I ended up taking the bus home the next day—well, later I would tell Alex I didn't see him after school, which wasn't precisely a lie, but close because I deliberately hadn't been looking. I hopped off first at our stop and ran.

Not for home, though. I cut behind the Amberson's, casting a quick glance through their yard to see if anyone was in our driveway. It was empty, but I still didn't even stop to throw my backpack into my room. I had to nerve myself up, or I might not do what I knew I had to.

The aspens had changed into autumn colors, but the path was still there, and still bone-white. It took me a few moments to find it, and I began to have the odd idea that maybe, just maybe, it was *hiding* before it burst into sight under the sere, shaking grass. It stuttered, but I was going fast enough that I could guess where it would jump next, and I only fell once, rolling down the gullypath and tasting blood when my teeth clicked together around a little bit of my tongue.

It was damn lucky I didn't crack my fool head on a rock.

Overhead was gray, a wide lens of cloud. The weather systems out on the plains are massive, American-sized like the cheeseburgers. Sometimes I thought about the clouds in Missouri, cotton-packed between slumping dispirited houses. Or in Germany, although I was too young to remember, or so Mama would say.

I wondered. Was it remembering when you saw it in a bowl of creekwater? What exactly was *remembering*? Did just knowing something had happened count?

It was one of those questions I would want to ask Ray, if he'd ever been home.

I finally spilled onto the bottom of the gully and ran along its floor. The creek was still a thread; the storms hadn't broken from the mountains yet. The water had a high-pitched cranky sound, not the chuckle of summer.

Gran's gate was open. I skidded to a stop. Slick with sweat, my ribs heaving, *feeling* the path behind me shift unhappily. Had it wanted to throw me off? Was this a warning? A freshening breeze wandered through her garden—peapods brown now, ready to be shelled to plant for next year's crop, the crisped remains of flowers neatly deheaded. The blueberry bushes had turned bright scarlet and yellow, painting themselves for winter before everyone else. The aspens were still green, but it was a tired drained color, not the juicy lushness of before.

I stepped under the rose arch. I'd trained the vines up over it myself, trying not to see that under the living green, the weathered brown arch was made of bones lashed together with weird gummy strips. Hips swelled fat and secretive on the vines and rosecanes, Gran told me they wouldn't bloom from old wood so you had to cut them back almost savagely if you expected to have petals for candying or an attar to bottle—*pure youth*, she said, *useless to Dasya now, but later, you may want, oh yes.*

The moss-rivered rocks were solid underfoot. I climbed the porch steps.
What if she says no?

If she did, I'd—

The door creaked open. Gran's face appeared, a wrinkled moon losing its summer tan and yellowing like old paper. Behind her, the familiar dimness of her little round house. She watched me for a long few seconds, black eyes taking in every detail, her mouth pulled tight.

Maybe it was seeing her after so long, but I didn't think so. She looked *younger*. Streaks of black in her thickening hair, combed back tightly into a bun. Her cheeks softer, plumper, the wrinkles around her eyes less deep. If I didn't know her, I might almost think she wasn't the same woman.

But there was the familiar odd shape of her mouth, the eyebrows—groomed now, not long curling tangles—raised just slightly, the tension in her bony hands. They could so easily be claws—did all old ladies have paws that looked dangerous?

Or just her?

"Dasya." A single word of greeting. Soft, the sibilant slipping between her lips.

"Gran." I had to swallow twice, my throat was so dry. "I've come." *She looks mad. Maybe she is.*

"You want something from old Granny, do you?" She ran her tongue along her teeth behind closed lips, the bulge moving in strange ways.

"It's Mama. Her ladyparts, the doctor says cancer." My own hands wrung themselves together, scrubbing. I barely realized I was doing it. "I... Gran..."

Her teeth were strong and white now, and they crept slowly from behind her bloodless lips. "Tell Granny what you want, little Dasya." Her eyes *sparkled*, but it wasn't with humor.

No, this was something else. The green sparks sputtered in her pupils, and I was suddenly very glad I'd stopped at the edge of the porch.

"I... Granny..." I sounded about five years old. I grabbed myself with both hands, as Ray would say, and it spilled out. "Granny, can you teach me to mend that?"

Silence. The breeze rattled dried plants, fingered my hair. Gran's expression changed, millimeter by millimeter, softening like the clay she told me to take to the creek in its metal bowl, working it with my hands over and over until it was a slurry instead of a brick.

Finally, her thin shoulders dropped, and the softening became a slump. "Serves old Granny right," she muttered. "Teach old Granny to assume. Come in, Dasya. Come in, come come, we shall talk."

I hesitated. "I don't want to be trouble, Gran."

She made a spitting noise, as she usually did when I said something she considered idiotic—or a man's question. *What's a man's question? One you already know the answer to, Dasya. Now do as I tell you.*

I never quite worked up the courage to ask her what a woman's question was.

My heart calmed down, and I wiped at my forehead. Inside it was cool, and dim, and when she shut the door and turned to face me, I was suddenly sure everything was going to be all right. I maybe even cried a little, but silently, just taking a big sniff every now and again to pull everything back up inside my nose.

Granny opened her cabinet, and I got a confused look of things quivering inside. She snapped a word that made them all settle down, but then the cabinet door slammed again and she shuffled into the kitchen, carrying a bowl.

It wasn't the usual big metal bowl. Instead, it was black, and she pumped water into it, muttering under her breath and making that spitting noise again when I opened my mouth to ask if I could help. "My Dasya is a good girl. Sit, now. Sit there." One crooked finger pointed at a spot on the floor, and I folded myself down. Sniffed again to try to clear my nose. My stomach ached. So did my shoulders—well, pretty much every part of me. The tang of blood and crying-snot mixed far back in my throat, coating my insides with a funny loose feeling.

The bowl was obsidian, and Gran only put a few cups of water in it. It was so big the water made a thin, small puddle at the bottom, and she settled it on my crossed legs, plucking at my hands and fingers to get them situated just-so, then squeezing so I knew to hold it.

Then she settled back onto her haunches, sighing a little, and fixed me with her bright, beady glare. The silence thickened once again, until she broke it. "I do not give this gift lightly, girl."

I nodded. The rock was back in my throat, but everything was so loose I managed to get the words out. "Thank you, Gran."

"She thanks me!" For some reason, she found this funny. At least, she wheezed out a cascade of laughter, leaned forward, and clamped her hands around my wrists again. "Look into the water, little Dasya. Hold tight."

I looked down. Nothing but my own face, white rings around my eyes, my hair messed up and smears of dirt on my too-pale cheeks.

Then it happened. Between one breath and the next, I was gone, and the next morning I woke up in my own bed, the alarm clock buzzing and everything in between just... blank. There were leftovers in the fridge, a note from Mama telling me she'd be home at five sharp...

...and on my nightstand, a creased note on a torn page of college-ruled school paper. I opened it up with my heart thudding along, as if I'd been running again.

Hold on. Be careful.

It was my own handwriting. I tucked it into my pillowcase and looked at my hands. There were red marks around my wrists, prints of ancient, spidery fingers. Knowledge bloomed inside me, soft and sure. Getting the conscious me out of the way so she could fill me like one of her jugs, pouring secrets in. Strong secrets, good ones, and others not-so-good but just as strong.

You had to have both before you could do *anything*, she said, and I knew it was true.

The note held three more sentences.

I give you all, Dasya. I teach you everything. The rest is up to you.

"Thank you," I whispered, and went to go get ready for school.

CHAPTER SIXTEEN

Awkward

A LEX WAS JUST THE SAME, cheerful and easy, and he drove me home after school with the windows up because it was finally too chilly to have them down. The sky was a bruise as storms raced hop-skipping across the plains, and it had begun to feel natural to scoot across the bench seat and buckle myself in the middle, sitting as close as I could while he drove. We bounced into the trailer park, and the wind, full of golden dust flashing under sunlight, sent tumblers rolling out of our way. "So Craig flicks another paperclip, and Marsellus just *loses* it. Ol' Edmonton had to peel them apart, and haul them down to the office. But at least we didn't get a quiz."

Safely buckled in, bouncing on the seat, I touched the radio's volume knob. "Why don't they like each other?"

He slowed, braking gently. "Craig's an asshole."

"Oh."

"He keeps calling Mars things. You know." Alex's mouth drew down. "Kind of like my dad. He doesn't like, you know, black people."

"Oh." What could you say, to something like that? "My daddy didn't either."

"You miss him, don't you." Alex took the sharp right up my street.

How can you say *no* when someone asks you that question? You're not *supposed* to feel... whatever it was I felt. Like the sneaking sense of gladness that Mama's hair had come back, that nights were quiet now, that the static didn't settle in the corners and there was no black cloud or shiny spot on the arm of a leather couch. No broken bottles, no broken skin, just a quiet I still couldn't learn to trust completely. Maybe if it lasted another few years I could begin to think that there wouldn't be any more yelling or sobbing or awful thundercracks of rage.

There also wouldn't be the steady paychecks. *He's a good provider*, Mama had always said, sometimes as if she wanted to convince herself. No sitting on Daddy's lap while he watched Westerns. *Pew-pew-pew! Shoot 'em on up!* None of those times when he took us for ice cream, so cheerful and soft and gentle we could all think the worst was past and the nice Daddy would stay with us for a while.

Grief or relief? Grief or relief? Best just to shut up.

Alex nodded as if I'd spoken. "Yeah, Ray is always talking about your guys' daddy. How good he was."

What? My jaw threatened to drop, and to cover the confusion I stared unseeing out the window.

That was why I didn't see the gleaming black car in our driveway at first, right next to Mama's Chevy as if it had a right to be there. Alex pulled up to park beside it, and while my stomach clenched, it wasn't the nausea and cramping I'd had before. "Wonder what *he's* doing here." Popping out of my mouth like bad candy, my teeth hurt for a moment. Like they wanted to sink into something.

"He seems sweet on your mama." Alex stamped on the parking brake, cut the engine, and his hand brushed my knee. "Can I come in?"

"Sure you can." The squirming sense that maybe it would be better to have someone else there while Mr. Vogg was inside with Mama turned rose-red with guilt. It wasn't fair to use him, was it?

He steadied me as I hopped down, though I didn't need it. I guess maybe he liked doing it, though, because his hands lingered a little, and he dropped a nuzzling kiss on my temple before I laughed and slid away, hitching my backpack higher on my shoulder. The porch steps didn't wobble, but when I swung the screen door out and jiggled the knob, it was locked.

Mama knows I'm coming home. I fished for my key, keeping the fist in my head clenched nice and tight.

It wasn't enough. Something was wrong. The door opened reluctantly, swung wide, and I took a deep breath.

Coffee. Dust, and a faint whiff of frying—Mama had done chicken last night, though Ray hadn't come home for his. She kept stubbornly cooking as if he'd show up, and we ended up with a lot of leftovers on days he didn't.

A trace of cologne hung in the air. Sweetish and sharpish, and my nose wrinkled before I could stop it. Under the chemicals mixed to make a man smell like something good, there was a whiff of something blind and white-fuzzed in a dark corner. Potatoes left too long, or an onion caving in on itself. A breath of rotting musk, too, as if a skunk had been run over on the highway.

With the windows all closed, you could also tell the carpet was cheap nylon full of old cigarette smoke and the fug of desperation. Green glass—a wine bottle on the counter near the dishrack, sticky-empty. Looked expensive, and on the dinette table a pickle jar held a bouquet—red roses, baby's breath, some leafy green things, and a crimson ribbon. Dishes still on the table—soft stinking cheese with cold blue veins, strawberries, bread crusts. A small shiny-foiled box, the kind that holds one or two chocolates nobody in their right mind would pay that much for.

A soft sound, from the hallway.

"Um." Alex caught on before I did. "Maybe we should wait outside?" The words pitched deliberately loud, warning.

"Dez!" Mama appeared, coalescing out of the dim living room. The curtains were drawn in there for some reason, and another, cleaner musktang filled it wall to wall, spilling out of the doorway and into the weird open space leading to the kitchen. I blinked, because there was something behind her, a looming wave with pale spots. "Home already?"

Her hair, longer now and mussed wildly, poured over her shoulders and her blouse was askew, the top two buttons undone. High color in her cheeks, and for a moment she looked my age, her eyes sparkling and a half-guilty grin curving her pale lips. Over Mama's shoulder, Mr. Vogg's face swam into focus.

His hair wasn't disarranged. His eyes gleamed flatly, like an animal's. His mouth was red and full, and as I stepped back into Alex, startled, the glow over his irises vanished. Trick of the light, maybe.

Maybe not, something in me whispered.

"Alex drove me." My lips were numb. "I thought you were at work."

"We had an early day." Slightly embarrassed, and I was suddenly very sure Mr. Vogg's hand was at the small of her back, almost like Alex sometimes put his on me while we were walking or standing waiting for a door to open. One of those touches that doesn't look like much, but can send a flush all through you.

Don't touch my mama like that. The knot inside my head tightened, this time coarse and splintery instead of smoothly braided. The splinters pricked behind my eyes, and the world swam for a moment, came back.

"It's Carr, isn't it? The eldest one." Mr. Vogg moved past Mama, oilysmooth, offering his hand. His socks were black, and probably more expensive than anything I was wearing. Why didn't he have his shoes on? "Pleasant to see you again, young man. How's your father?"

"Very well, sir." Alex shook, briefly, and I found myself staring at Mama's bare feet. Red nail polish—when had she done that? *I don't have time for that sort of thing,* she'd always say at the drugstore, while I looked at lip gloss and lacquer, all the candyjewel colors. "I'll tell him you said hello."

"Do just that. Hello, Miss Desiree. How was school?" He offered his hand to me, too, and my skin crawled.

So I pretended not to notice. "Boring. Alex, you want some coffee?" I slipped aside, leaving Mr. Vogg's badger-paw to hang wilted in the air. I might catch hell from Mama later for being impolite, but nothing, not even her disappointment, would make me touch *him*.

And thank God, Alex followed me back into the kitchen, and he didn't say anything while I fumbled with the coffeemaker. Mama walked Mr. Vogg out, and her soft murmurs were so familiar—the one she sometimes used when Daddy was in a good mood that might break into thunder at any moment.

Alex waited until the screen door banged shut. "Wow. Awkward."

"Yeah." I poured the water in, flipped it on, and grabbed at the counter. "Alex…" What could I ask him? How did you politely ask about something like this? What did he think?

He beat me to it. "You want to come over for dinner?"

I shook my head. "Mama might need me."

"I can ask her." A little insistent, a little too soft. Like he was trying to tell me something else.

What I really wanted was to run down into the gully, maybe knock on Gran's door, maybe only sit by the creek and shiver a little as the wind mouthed the changing aspens. Mama was going to ask me if I liked Mr. Vogg, and it was yet another question I couldn't answer honestly. Why did people bother even *asking*, when they knew you couldn't say anything true?

Maybe just to make themselves feel better.

"Okay." I tried not to feel like a coward for letting him pull me along. Maybe Ray would be home tonight to keep Mama company?

You know he won't be.

I stared at the dripping coffee, and took a deep breath. There was a price for every mending, Gran didn't have to tell me that. I already knew.

I just couldn't figure out if Mr. Vogg was a payment, or if he was something else.

• • •

HOMECOMING

Mama bit her lip, her fingers quick and deft. "These seams are always so… there, I think. How does that feel?"

"Okay." I had to whisper.

Ray, sprawled on the couch with a beer Mama pretended not to notice, snorted. "I never did this shit." He didn't flinch at the swear, and neither did I.

"Well, your sister's a different person than you are." She didn't sound sharp, though, only weary. "Oh, honey." She gave me a once-over, while I tried to figure out what to do with my hands since the wrist corsage was already on. I finally just let them fall, running my fingertips nervously down the seam on my hip. Dove-gray watered silk, blue chiffon and velvet in subtly toning shades, a daggered hem, shoes dyed to match, and spaghetti straps. Marcie had loaned Mama her flat iron, so my hair was full of ringlets, and a tiny rhinestone butterfly perched in the updo.

I felt ridiculous.

The corsage was simple, tiny roses closer to purple than blue with a little bit of greenery and baby's breath. It probably cost more than the fabric for the dress. My calves already ached a bit from the heels, and I was already wishing this was over with.

Mama studied me, a small line between her eyebrows. She looked about as nervous as I felt. "What time is Alex coming?"

"He said five. We're going to dinner."

Ray took another swig. It was a bottle, not a can. "Alone?"

We could afford bottles now, I guess. "With some of his friends." *Other couples.* Including girls with teased-out hair and those shiny smiles, real Populars. It was a little surprising, the way none of them mocked me openly. Instead, Alex's personal planet seemed to cover me as well, and even Tawny McDonnell, the biggest snob in school, talked to me during lunch. Or rather, talked *at* me. I just found myself listening to the same subjects recycled over and over again, wishing I could get Alex alone and talk about real things. "Melody and Marsellus, I bet, and Bruce and Anabella. Maybe some others."

"Where's he taking you?" Ray stretched his legs out.

I glanced at Mama, whose lips had thinned. "Hathaway's."

"Fancy." Ray snorted, and took yet another gulp. He'd come home with a case of Pabst and a six-pack of the more expensive bottles, and Mama hadn't said anything.

I wondered about that. And I kept thinking about him telling Alex that Daddy was some sort of saint. Did he not remember? Was I crazy because *I* did? Or when someone died, did everything just get erased? I wanted to ask Mama, but...

Yeah. That wouldn't go over well. Besides, she was busy. Mr. Vogg kept her late, and sometimes she brought papers home to study, distracted and muttering legal terms to herself. She was getting a crash course in all sorts of stuff, she said, it was good experience.

I'd peeked at her pay stub while she was in the shower this morning. It made me feel sort of weird—hot and cold at the same time. It was good money, but something about it didn't seem quite, well, *right*. Of course, it kept us fed, right? And Mama had said that maybe next time she'd buy me a dress instead of making one.

If there was a next time. And Mama was already mentioning maybe looking for an apartment in a better part of town.

Ray might have been about to say something else, but he didn't get the chance. Light, distinctive raps on the front door made everything inside me go fluttery.

Mama's grin was a sight to behold. "He's early. Stay here, Dez."

I don't think I can walk. So I just nodded, and hoped I didn't look ridiculous. There was a full-length mirror in Mama's room, but that seemed a little too far away at the moment. I heard the door open and murmurs in the kitchen, and I looked steadily at Ray. "How is it?"

He still wore that faint, nasty smile. "You look like a high school dance."

It was the sort of thing Daddy might have said when he wasn't angry but he wasn't happy with you, either. "If you can't say something nice, Ray-Ray, shut up." I restrained the urge to pinch the bridge of my nose the way Mama sometimes did when he got this way. "You're mean, and you shouldn't be drinking all that."

"Can't tattle on me, Mama's already seen." But a hint of shame crossed his expression now, and if I hadn't been so nervous I might have been able to figure out what was bothering him. Just this morning Mama had been sharp with him over ten dollars for gas. *You have your own job, Raymond. Really, you're irresponsible.*

"Dez?"

I turned.

A dark suit, an indigo tie his mother probably tied for him, and his boutonniere matched my corsage. Black spit-shine wingtips, and his hair tamed and darkened with what looked like gel. He must have shaved, because he was all red—but no, that was a blush, one echoed in my own furious-hot cheeks. We regarded each other for about thirty of the longest seconds of my life.

"Wow," he finally breathed. "You look amazing."

Relief, hot as Granny's stove, lit behind my breastbone. "So do you. You, um, you have the tickets?"

He reached up, tapped at the left side of his chest. "Right in my pocket." His hand stayed there for a few seconds though, like he was feeling some sort of pain. Second thoughts, maybe?

I found out I didn't want to know. "Good. I, um… just let me get my purse and we can go."

"Do you have a coat?"

"Yeah." It was Mama's vintage fur wrap, and now I wondered if it would look silly. I couldn't wear a hoodie, or my parka, for God's sake. Were they going to laugh at me?

Well, so what if they do? After all, none of them were Granny Iyaga's students. They didn't know about the secret things under the skin of the world, and they couldn't watch a lightning storm on the horizon and predict the strikes, *feeling* where the next one would flicker.

There were times thinking like that helped. This wasn't one of them.

My bedroom was painted soft yellow now, the walls full of sunlight all day. I scooped up the wrap—Mama had taken it to the dry-cleaners special—and the tiny, beaded purse just big enough for lip gloss, ID, and a twenty-dollar bill Mama had tucked in there. *This is your ride-home money, just in case. You don't ever have to do something to pay a date back for a ride home. If I don't come get you, this will at least get a cab to bring you partway. You mind me now, Desiree.*

I did. And the flashes inside my head, sneaking through the knot's tight anxiety, when she told me that were enough to make me wonder why she was so excited for me, but I had to go. I figured it would keep for later.

Coming back down the hall, my head full of humming expectancy, I almost stumbled, righted myself on the heels, and stepped out into the living room. "Mama, I..." The words died on my lips.

Ray's face was set and sullen. He sat bolt-upright on the couch. Alex, standing near the half-wall to the kitchen, was blushing even harder, and he looked just about as uncomfortable as it was possible to. Mama's cheeks were flour-pale, except for two spots of high color. Her eyes glowed dangerously, a fierce blue I could only remember seeing once or twice in my entire life.

"Mama?" Two breathless syllables. "What's wrong?"

She shook her head. "Nothing, sweetheart. You go on with Alex now. Raymond and I will be having a talk." A small, set grimace that was supposed to be a smile, and the knot in my head turned slippery. I couldn't tell what they were feeling when my own insides were all in a riot.

"Mama—"

"Let's go, Dez." Alex stepped forward, and just like a gentleman, he held the wrap for me. "This is beautiful. You look really... you look beautiful."

It was nice to hear it, but his tension stole into me, grabbing my back and calves and throat.

"Curfew is 2 a.m.," Mama said, steadily. "Not a second afterward, Mr. Carr, or I'll come looking for you."

"Yes ma'am." A nervous laugh, and Ray just watched this. Thunder was gathering around him, the same black bleakness I knew from *before*. I should have said something, but Alex had my arm, and he pulled me out into a late afternoon with the sun hanging bloody on the Rockies, and it wasn't until we were about ten miles down the road I finally got out of him what had happened.

He'd asked how Ray's new job was going. Mama, momentarily confused, asked *wasn't he working for your daddy?*

That's how it came out that Ray was fired from Carr's weeks ago, and he hadn't told Mama.

The whole rest of that night is a blur. I don't remember a single thing, even dancing with Alex under spangled tinfoil stars in the gym, and him kissing me while slow sweet music played. That was the night I became a Popular, but everything in me was just noise and splinters.

PART THREE: WINTER

CHAPTER SEVENTEEN

Freeze Long Enough

SNOW CAME EARLY, and everyone at school reasserted their place in the pecking order with parkas and boots. Alex put chains in the truck, and it was a good thing I always scooted over to sit next to him. The floor on the passenger side was taken up with the metal box for the chains, a folding shovel in case he needed to dig us out, and a plastic box I wondered about, stealing suspicious little glances at it until he laughed. *Mom packs emergency boxes. Snacks, toilet paper, candles, and space blankets. She worries.*

Mothers worried. It was what they did. I understood that much, at least.

Mornings were best. Mama would be up, dressed for the day, but she didn't talk much before her morning coffee. She wasn't smoking anymore, and the tests had come back from the doctor—the envelope, secretive and prim, sat in her pile of bills and watched us all for a week or so before I came home one knife-cold afternoon and found her sitting at the table with it, tear-tracks on her cheeks and her relief filling the whole house with a different kind of warmth.

It didn't last, though. There were other things to worry Mama now.

Where are you working, Raymond Sarpe? Who are these friends of yours? Where are you going?

And Ray's grunts in return, or—worse—the explosions, terrifying while I locked myself in my bedroom and listened to them yell at each other.

Leave me alone! I fucking hate you!

Don't you talk to your mama like that!

Fuck off! Bitch!

Raymond Jonathan, I should tan your hide—

Now I know why Dad couldn't stand you!

And the unsteady silence, until the door would slam and an engine would gun. I didn't know where he was getting the gas money; he wasn't working, we knew that much. Somehow he always had enough to fill the Camaro's tank.

And enough for the whiskey bottles that showed up empty in the garbage, the sight of them sending an unsteady feeling through my knees.

Jim Beam. Daddy's brand. Ray wasn't even turning them back in for a deposit, either.

The mending wouldn't come. I tried, rocking back and forth on my bed—Mama had helped me pick out a frame with high iron curlicues, and glowed as she bought it cash, no credit—and tried to find the edges of the bad feeling, tried to find the way through it. There was a secret seed of harmony in everything, you just had to find it, Gran said.

But I couldn't.

The worst was suspecting that *this* was somehow the price for Mama's mending, the knotted root I didn't remember digging up from Gran's garden wrapped with red ribbon and slipped under my mother's bed on a fullmoon night, with a roaring passing through me and her steady sleeping breathing above not missing a single beat.

I tried mending when they weren't fighting, too, but the knot in my head just turned slippery and splintery, trying to contain something huge. It didn't make any *sense*. It was like they were still angry even while they were sleeping, still glaring at each other through closed doors and eyelids.

It was enough to make me wish I could go to Alex's house all the time and let the warm blanket of someone else's life fold around me. How awful was it to wish for safety like that, to wish to leave behind Mama's worry and Ray's sullen rage?

I trudged down the gully's slippery side in my new snowboots, my parka hood pulled up and flakes catching in the fake fur edging. Alex had just dropped me off, and I'd watched him drive carefully away under a sky like beaten, infinite iron, chains biting already packed ice-slush. The weather report said more snow, a lot of it, and the plows were already out on the highway. *Whiteout conditions, folks, so get your supplies now!*

I didn't have to look for the path. I could *feel* it now, unreeling under my bootsoles. It was weird, how it had seemed to jump around before.

Maybe I just hadn't been in the habit of seeing.

Which brought up an interesting question—who else might be in the habit as well? What you could see you could take a stab at mending, but Gran said most people didn't want to mend.

Easier just to twist, or to outright break. *They take a pleasure in it,* Gran said, her face darkening a little, and I hadn't dared to ask more. It made sense, though. I knew what it was like to be around someone who liked to break and twist and hurt. I knew the joy someone like that got from it.

I'd seen it up close.

The creek was still a trickle, not a sheet of ice yet. Moving water didn't freeze as fast. If Ray slowed down a little, would he freeze long enough to listen to someone? Not Mama, maybe—though how he couldn't listen to her was beyond me—but maybe me? Or Alex? Or someone, *anyone*, who could get him to stop pulling Daddy's black cloud over himself like a sheet?

Not a sheet. A coat. One that looked like it fit him pretty well, actually. Or at least, he looked comfortable in it.

Too comfortable.

If that was the price for Mama's mending...

It's not. He was doing this before you went to Gran.

But what if the price was making it worse? Thinking about it that way made a hot, unsteady feeling bloom inside me.

Gran's garden, cut back for the winter under three and a half inches of snow, closed silently around me. I tapped at her door, felt the welcoming shift in the air, and twisted the knob. "Hello?

"Come in." Softly. "But quiet as mouse, Dasya."

I edged into warm dimness and closed the door softly, the good scent of seasoned wood from the potbelly stove and strong-spiced tea from the samovar closing around me. A tug on the knot in my head, and melted snow sloughed itself from my boots, evaporating in little steam-curls.

It was so easy and satisfying to do, but you had to be careful. People didn't like the unusual. Most of them just plain don't want to see it, but if you made them see, they got... afraid.

And angry.

When I straightened, there was a thump, and a rattling buzz. Gran, a gray shawl pulled close around her thinning shoulders, stood in front of the butcher-block table, her back to me. She was losing some of her summer weight, less of a round old lady now and more an angular picture of one. Her hair was almost completely black. Behind her, I could just see the edges of an antique glass aquarium, iron scrollwork holding panes turning milky at the corners, like cataracts. The buzz made me shiver, and when I approached, quiet and careful, I could see why.

Alex was right.

Inside the aquarium, coiled into a tight spiral, a rattlesnake lifted its wedge of a head. The buzzing was its tail, blur-vibrating, and the thump was it darting forward, banging on the glass. The aquarium was huge, but I didn't wonder how she'd managed to lift it onto the table, or how she'd gotten the sere, dried grass matted inside. It radiated the sleepy baking heat of a summer day, a large oblong dish of water on one side and a rock carved to look like a cave on the other.

"This fellow should be sleeping." Gran cocked her head, her black hair glossy and thickening each day. "Granny chose a fine strong one, and brought him in last night. Dasya should say hello, hmmm?"

"I've heard them." I matched her quiet tone. "In the field behind the house, all the time."

"Yes." Gran shifted her weight from foot to foot, like a mother with a sleepy baby. The rattler followed her movement, its rattles blurring-quick. There was nothing human in its flat unblinking gaze, its supple curves beautiful even if the skin all over me roughened instinctively. Each scale was perfect, even the dulled ones, and when it struck at the glass again I saw the fangs distending.

I realized I was shifting just like Gran, side to side.

"Good, Dasya," she whispered. "Eyes. Always the eyes."

The pupils were slots, and behind them was an alien.

Buzzblur fear, instinct moving, quickstrike. Body long and flexible, each small scale harsh fluid music. Sleeping to dream in the cold, waking to bask in the sun, sliding through grass to hunt. Small things quivering, sensing the drydust rasp over rocks, the strike a flash of lightning, the consummation of folding around a warm lump of frantic, venom-frozen hotmeat. Rumbles in the earth, every inch alive, a long jointed wave...

I surfaced slowly, weaving bonelessly on my useless booted feet. My eyelids fluttered, shutterclicks of motion as I saw my hand stroking along the glass. The rattler followed, a long sinuous curve, sliding into the cave-rock and curling up. Deathly silent, I *felt* its relief at a place to hide, and a warm lump of food in its gut.

Gran fed it. My throat was dry, but I kept stroking the glass until nictating membranes flickered and I felt the alien thing relax fully.

Funny, it wasn't so different than anything else. It just wanted food, shelter, sleep. If only people were so simple. Were they? Or did they want more, and was it that wanting that made them hurt each other?

I exhaled, hissing, and for a moment wasn't sure how to walk. Gran caught my arm, strong ancient fingers gentle, and I found myself in a human body again. "Very good, Dasya." She nodded. "Come, tea. Then you go home. It will snow deep tonight."

I blinked, found words again. "Wow. Are you... do you have enough food, Gran?"

Her teeth showed, a wide white grin. "Tonight I have snake. Makes me strong. The rattles are for my Dasya, a pretty bracelet when she is old enough."

Oh, man. Are you really going to eat it? I knew better than to ask. I followed her meekly to her tiny round kitchen table, settled on my familiar stool, and she made her hot, strong, sweetspice tea. We drank in silence, and before I left, I dared to put my arms around her and hug. Gently, as if she was fragile, feeling angles and corners that weren't there before.

She hugged me back, and I didn't have to ask anything.

I knew she was leaving soon.

• • •

CAN'T STAY HERE

I woke up the day afterward with a scratchy throat and a stuffed-up nose, shivering under my blankets. Mama, late for work because of the snow, took one look at me and told me to go back to bed. I guess Alex stopped by to pick me up for school and shoveled her car out, fussing at her about the chains on the Ford's tires until she gave him a mug of coffee and a *Young man, you go along to school, I know what I'm doing.* I didn't hear any of it, because I fell back asleep and dreamed of soft thumps against thick cataract-clouded glass, a buzzing hiss, and summer sun baking outside cool, dark holes.

Slam. Footsteps. I jolted into shivering wakefulness, but then I realized what I was hearing. A familiar tread, he used to be so light on his feet. Now he clumped in big heavy boots, jabbing the heels down like Daddy used to.

I rolled out of bed, taking the sunset-colored comforter with me. Wrapped it around my shoulders and trudged softly down the hall. His door was open and I caught sight of his messy bed, the curtains pulled just enough to let a thin crack of bluish snowlight in, and Ray sitting on the edge with his head in his hands.

He didn't move when I knocked. My head was too stuffed up to use the knot and figure out what he was feeling, but I pushed the door open a little more with my sock foot and edged in, wrapping the comforter even more securely. He still didn't move, even when I settled next to him. I sniffed a couple times, wiped under my nose with the back of my hand.

"Sick?" He sounded like the old Raymond, mostly.

"Yeah." I leaned my shoulder against his. He'd taken down the rock posters. It was pretty bare in here without them. We hadn't had a chance to paint his room, not wanting to open the door while he was gone. His closet was half-open, but I just saw empty hangers. The teak dresser—antique, refinished, bought for a song at a garage sale, one of Mama's particular projects to turn into an heirloom—had a couple of its drawers lolling open as well, and they were bare enough I could see the striped contact paper in the bottom. All those clothes weren't in his hamper either, and his stack of Chilton's manuals and magazines wasn't in its expected corner.

It didn't take a genius to figure out he'd carried everything out, little by little. Daddy's glass ashtray stood on the windowsill, exhaling a breath of rotten Camel smoke from a forest of short, stubbed-hard filters. Ray's beanbag was gone, too.

There didn't seem to be anything to say that wouldn't make him furious, so I just sat there.

"I'm sorry." Finally, two short sharp little words, with an angry punch to them. They fell onto the sad orange shag carpeting—Mama didn't go in here with the vacuum because his door was always closed, and he'd taken this room partly because of the carpet. *Look at that,* he'd said. *It's amazing!*

Or did Mama sometimes come in, and stand in the middle of the room, and wonder at the diminishing volume of his stuff?

I wiped at my nose again. There was a jar of spice-tea in my bedroom, with Gran's spidery handwriting on its yellowing paper label. It could have said "poison" for all I could read, in Cyrillic for that language she spoke when she didn't want to talk American. I knew how much boiled water to add, and I suspected it would fix me right up, if I could just get up the energy to make some. I even knew what to get to make my own, but that thought made me so tired I sagged a little.

Maybe he thought I was expecting him to say something else, so he did. "It's gonna be okay." Muffled, into his hands.

Even though I couldn't know for sure, I guessed he was probably talking about losing the job at the garage. It was cold in here, so I pulled the comforter closer. Little curls of sweat-soaked hair stuck to my forehead, just like Mama's. "Alex didn't mean to tell."

"I knew she'd find out anyway." He sighed and straightened, the mattress creaking. His big panther blanket, ultra-king-sized plush we got for thirty bucks in singles and quarters at a roadside stand one dusty summer afternoon in Missouri, was still here. Was he keeping that for last? "Dez…"

I waited. The rock wasn't in my throat, but it might as well have been. "Don't go," I said, finally, curling my toes inside my socks. "Please."

The wind mouthed the edges of the mobile. His room was in the back corner—bigger than mine, but that meant he heard that soft low moaning all the time. What was it like to sleep through it?

Not like he slept here much. Or did he rest during the day? In a cave-hole, while the world went on outside?

Where did he *go*?

"Can't stay here." Short and sharp, but not mean. Just like he was telling a customer *I can't fix that, we need a whole new part.*

"Why not?"

That got me a sigh and a patented Raymond eyeroll. Bloodshot eyes, his nose red and chapped. His hands had engine grease on them, so he was working *somewhere.* Why didn't he tell Mama? Or me?

"I just can't. Be better without me, anyway." An absent-minded kneading, cracking his left-hand knuckles, his right. "Quieter."

Maybe it would be quieter, but the thought of a hole in the house where he used to be wasn't *better.* "Don't go."

"I *have* to, Dez."

"But *why*?" If I could just hear the reason I'd know what to say to sort it out. Or so I hoped.

"For God's sake." A helpless shrug, his muscle-wiry shoulder bumping mine. I swayed. "I just got to."

"Mama will cry."

"Mama's always crying."

Not a lot, not anymore. "I'll cry."

He winced. "Don't."

But I will. Mama won't see it. "Ray—"

"Do you miss him?" He paused, his hands knotting together, staring at the teak dresser. "Daddy, I mean."

I know who you mean. What could I say? Another time you can't tell the truth and you don't want to lie, but this time I thought of Gran and my mouth fell open.

"No," I whispered. I looked at the dresser too, its bulk wavering and blurring as I blinked and a hot drop of salt water slid down my flushed face.

"Me either." Ray's arm slid over my shoulders and squeezed. But gently. "You stay in school, okay? You're smart."

Why did you tell Alex Daddy was such a saint, if you don't miss him either? "You can visit." I swallowed hard. "Please? You can come back. Anytime. Mama will—"

"Maybe." He let go, rocking up to his feet. Behind the door was Daddy's old duffel, stained and worn but tough as iron, and full to bursting. "You just stay in school, Dez. Someone has to get out of this."

"Out of what?"

"The entire shithole." He shook his head, dots of melted snow in his black hair glistening. The wind keened, taking on a fresh urgency. "I gotta go, I'm late."

For what? I didn't say it, though. I watched him heft the duffel and tap a Camel up out of a battered pack from his jacket pocket, and he lit it like he'd been smoking all his life instead of just a few months. The rock was back, filling up my throat, and I could see trembling streaks of the black thundercloud trying to paint the air around him. My head ached, a sharp edge folded into my brain, and I listened to his boots clump through the house. He didn't slam the front door, just closed it gently, and the little click of his key in the lock echoed all the way down through me.

With my eyes closed I could hear the Camaro rouse itself, and the slipperiness of the ice. He had chains too, though, and they bit, throwing up chunks of frozen gravel from the driveway before he made it out onto the indifferent paving. I listened as long as I could, seeing the car inside my head, Ray's hands clutched on the wheel shaking a little, and that black thundercloud filling the interior when I tried to catch a glimpse of his face.

When I went back to bed I dragged the panther blanket too, and curled into the tightest ball I could make. I cried until my hands were full of snot and I had to scramble out of bed, stumbling through the cold house for the bathroom, where I threw up nothing but bile over and over again while I sobbed.

CHAPTER EIGHTEEN

Puzzle Pieces

MAMA CAME HOME AS EARLY DUSK TURNED THE WORLD OUTSIDE to a resonating cave of flying ice. The Ford's engine noise swallowed under the wind's keening, the slam of the car door and a few minutes while she got the engine block heater situated, the stamping when she finally got inside and got snow off her boots. Crackle of plastic as she hung the suit she'd worn at work—too thin to wear on the drive home even with the heater blasting—on the hook behind the door so she could struggle out of her coat, her sigh as she saw the frozen chunk of beef stew I'd put over low on the stove so she could have something warm. Her footsteps, light but slow, as she headed for her room to change...

...and the way she halted, probably seeing Ray's door open. She walked down the hall.

Two mugs of Gran's spice tea, and I was feeling a *lot* better. But so, so tired. And cold. I curled into the panther blanket, the knot in my head just a miserable swelling, one of those zits that sits way under the skin and won't pop. Just swells and hurts even when you don't touch it, until you want to scratch yourself bloody just to get it *out*.

She stood there for a long time. I squeezed my eyes shut.

Finally, she turned away. A soft but urgent tapping on my door. "Desiree?"

It was my turn to pretend to be half-asleep. "Mama?"

Her relief was a sharp wine-red flood, filling up the darkness of my room. I'd shut my curtains tight, trying to keep the killing cold out. Now I was the one in a cave, curled up and waiting.

So gentle and hopeful, her wistful words. "Did you see Ray, honey?"

I stirred a little. "I was sleeping." It wasn't quite a lie. It still stung me a little, but what else could I say?

Nothing, that's what. Nothing at all. Even if I wanted to.

"How are you feeling?"

"Tired." *And cold*. And like I was a box of puzzle pieces knocked off a kitchen table, scattered everywhere. You couldn't ever be sure you'd picked them all up, not even with Daddy standing over you and glowering because you'd made a mess. *Every single one, girl. Or I'm gonna tan your hide.*

Mama stepped delicately through the door, in her sock feet. She smelled of snow and a car heater, of the fancy new perfume Mr. Vogg had said she should try, of the soft purple grape-scent of heartbreak with a bright orange edge of guilt. It was amazing I could smell through the dried snot rimming my nostrils.

The back of her hand against my forehead, cold and wonderful. "Still a bit of a fever." She smoothed the panther blanket, and maybe she noticed it. Maybe she didn't. "Dez, honey..."

Silence. The snot in my nose could be from sickness, not crying. The burning in my eyes could be the same. The wind's song teased through the quiet, adding a silver stitchery. Was the whistling man out there, dancing on iced-over telephone lines, peering into empty car windows, tiptoeing across snowdrifts? The sudden certainty was unwelcome. I didn't want to see what he was doing right now.

I finally moved again a little, watching her through my eyelashes. "Huh?"

"Nothing." She smoothed my hair, the quietest, kindest touch in the world. It could make everything right when I was younger, why not now? "I'll bring you some soup and crackers. I stopped for NyQuil on the way home."

"Thanks." I tried to smile. It felt fake on my flushed, messy mask of a face.

I didn't even try to get up for dinner. She ate alone, and when she brought me a tray later I pretended to be asleep. She left my door a little open, and I heard her speaking softly on the phone, the broken hitching of her breath as she cried. The wind howled, and before I fell asleep I heard the front door open again, and padding male footsteps.

It wasn't Ray.

I lay in the dark, stiff and sick, while I heard an oily voice whisper to Mama. I heard her soft breathless sobs, and the relief in her as he soothed. *There, there, let it out. It will all be all right.* That faint ghost of an accent in his words, and his greedy weasel-musk attention tiptoeing through the mobile home as it rocked and shuddered. It lingered in Ray's room, but it couldn't get into mine. Each time it tried, the knot in my head would twitch and I would think of Gran's eyes turning fathomless black from lid to lid, fans of wrinkles at the corners.

Get out, I thought. *Get out.*

It stopped trying to tiptoe in. Mr. Vogg came through ice and snow and dark when Mama called him, and maybe that was okay. Maybe she needed that.

But I didn't like it.

• • •

MAN LIKE ME

The storm was bad, but it was already losing its sharp keening edge by the next morning. Mama called Alex to tell him not to pick me up, and let me sleep in. She would have been gone to work by the time I got up, but her boss's boss was at our house anyway.

That was how Mr. Vogg knew there was a position open, I guess.

I put on two pairs of socks before I padded out into the kitchen, as quietly as I could. It was no use, he stood in front of the coffeemaker, smiling his bright-white smile. The badger-tufts in his hair were also smiling, and even though his silken button-down shirt and gray wool suit pants were a little crumpled, he still looked... plastic. Shrink-wrapped and burnished, soaked in oil.

Slick as gooseshit, Daddy would have said. Was I wishing he was here? We wouldn't be in this mobile if Daddy was still alive. I wouldn't ever have met Granny.

I couldn't tell if things would be better or worse if Daddy hadn't been blown to pieces. My mouth went dry, my head stuffed full of cotton. I needed more of Gran's tea, and I was hungry. But I just stood there, looking at his back, and something occurred to me.

There was mending, and there was also... the other. Things Gran said people came to her more often for. *Bad* things. Breaking, twisting, hurting.

"I know what you're thinking," Mr. Vogg said, quietly, with no trace of an accent. A pleasant, light baritone, as American as apple pie. Did the accent only come out when he talked to Mama late at night?

I grabbed at the wall, fetching up against it with a bump. I wished I'd brought the comforter out to wrap around myself, too.

He kept staring at the coffeemaker. "You're thinking that it's awful strange for a man like me to do so much for your mama."

That's not what I'm thinking. I leaned against the wall, shakes beginning in my legs as if I was way sicker than I knew I was. Thermal bottoms, a pair of thrift store boxers, a tank top and two sweaters, and it wasn't enough even with the heaters on. It didn't even make much of a difference; the cold was inside as well as out. All the precious heat in the house was just egg white around a yolk of ice inside me.

"Your mama's special, Desiree." He said my name like it was candy, a piece he'd already licked poison all over before offering to a starving child. "I know you know how special she is."

The sickness turned specific, settled in the pit of my stomach. It threatened to crawl up into my throat and sit there just like the dry rock that wouldn't let anything past. My eyelids fell halfway, and I peered at him, trying not to look at the surface.

Trying to look *underneath*.

He turned, noiseless and with a weird rippling movement all over his plastic, perfect exterior. Even in winter he had a tan, but it wasn't the weathered good look of someone who's been under the sun a lot, or the orange of the popular girls. Instead, it was a perfect even tone, burnished and expensively false.

Where had he slept? On the couch?

In Mama's bed?

I didn't want to think about it. The knot in my head tightened, and... a *ripple* passed through him, like the stagnant part of the creek in high summer, choked with weeds and crawling with mosquitoes and no-see-ums and other biting, flying insect bits. Even those chomping little bloodsuckers had their place, hovering above the water so the birds could dart through and scoop them up, but still, I didn't like them.

A white gleam was his teeth, nice and sharp. His eyes were dark coals, and I spilled against the wall again, my breath coming high and hard and fast. The ripple went away, a swift snarl crossing his mask and disappearing underneath.

He doesn't like being looked at, I realized, and the cold all through me twitched a little.

"*Very* special," he said, softly. "I think we can agree on that, can't we?"

I nodded. No reason not to. Fear-sweat collected at the hollow of my back, under my arms, under my jaw. How can you sweat while you shiver?

"And special things need protecting, don't they?" That white, white smile widened, those teeth sharp enough to cut metal. Like bones of some metallic creature, wrenched free of the carcass and ground to pearly edges. A perfect smile, one you wouldn't see the tarpit behind until it was too late and you were already sinking past your nose.

I stared at him. My eyes burned, but I didn't blink. He took one step towards me.

"Very careful nurturing." He nodded slightly. "Sometimes even saving from themselves."

I couldn't breathe. The rock was in my throat, but it wasn't the dam catching all words behind it. It was a dry stone, shoved past the back of the tongue and pressed in while a man smiled a wide white greasy smile.

"And discipline," he continued. "Like your brother. So sad, to break a mother's heart."

I swallowed, twice, my throat clicking. The rock shifted slightly, and before I ran out of oxygen I saw how to shift it. Just a little.

Enough for a small hiss to escape.

That stopped him. The coffeemaker gurgled, and my hands turned into fists. My hair crawled, each separate one trying to stand straight up. My head filled with soft *thump, thumps*. Blunt snouts hitting glass, striking again and again.

It shoved him back, only a step or two. His side hit the kitchen counter, and I realized how short he was. Just a few inches taller than me. Alex would tower over him.

Gran was about his size, but she would probably cut him down with a single glance. Or hiss at him, her hand flashing out and jabbing, two forked fingers and—

"Is that coffee?" Mama said, from the hallway, a sweet lilt to the words. "Everyone's already up."

The ripple vanished, and his oily, oozing smile came back. He grinned as Mama touched my forehead and told me I should be back in bed. I shook my head and said I felt better; I hugged myself while Mama fussed him into a chair, then set about making breakfast. She got out the bacon we'd been saving for Sunday, too.

Soft cloudy snowlight came in through the kitchen window, bathing him and turning Mama's face into a tired angel's. She poured his coffee, added sugar and milk, apologized because it probably wasn't what he was used to, and started the bacon.

She fluttered around nervously, as if it was Daddy at the table in one of his rare good moods, with his hands curled loosely and that black thunder just threatening, not filling the room. Mr. Vogg complimented her eggs and bacon like it was pure gold, winked at her when she poured him another cup of coffee, and grinned his shark smile at me when Mama scolded me for not sitting down and sent me back to my room and said she would bring me breakfast in bed.

I went. What else could I do?

CHAPTER NINETEEN

What He Was Selling

"**Y**OU DON'T LIKE HIM.**" In her recliner, her feet up, Mama still looked like a queen, with a blue and white crocheted afghan from the Salvation Army tucked all around her and dark shadows under her blue, blue eyes. "Is that it?"

Mama had spent the whole day in the kitchen after Mr. Vogg left, except for when the snowlight started to fail and she stepped outside onto the porch, bundled up and standing in the wind, a cigarette clutched in her gloved hand. The slamming of the screen door afterward was just like Ray leaving, so much that I got up and came out wrapped in a blanket to find her at the sink, staring out the kitchen window, her cheeks red from the wind and the ghost of cigarette smoke turning her gray around the edges. Dinner was reheated beef stew, again. No fancy garlic bread, and Ray's empty chair at the table glaring at both of us.

And now, the first thing she asked about was *him*.

The loveseat smelled like summerbaked air with a ghost of long-ago cigarette smoke and spilled beer. I curled up on my side, my head pillowed on my arm. My sunlight-colored comforter, full of fabric softener and a hint of fresh paint from my room, wasn't enough to keep me from shivering occasionally. At least the water heater was working again, which meant no frozen showers. "I dunno," I mumbled. I didn't want to talk about Mr. Vogg, but it was better than the questions about Ray.

"And you have no idea where Ray went?"

"No, Mama." *If I did, I'd tell you, probably the first three times you asked, or the next six.* Would it make it better if I did, though? Or worse? I just kept wondering about things like that, trying to decide.

School was back on tomorrow. I'd made up my mind to go, but I called Alex and told him I'd ride the bus. Well, actually, I just left a message with his little brother, because I didn't want him to talk me into letting him come out and pick me up again. Too much ice on the road.

Even if Mr. Vogg had somehow gotten his sleek black car out of the driveway. Mama didn't notice there was no snow on the hood, that the car was as sealed and pristine as a wrapper on a shelf in a grocery store, all arranged to show the best side. Every inch of it whispering *buy me, buy me*.

It was enough to make you wonder what he was selling. And why she didn't notice. Was it really that hard to see what stuck out like big sore thumbs?

"He was just gone?" There it was again, the *I-don't-believe-it* tone. She suspected me of knowing. Maybe if Ray had taken off a year ago, I would have. I used to know everything about him, right?

He'd left a long time ago, just not physically. The worst thing was I hadn't even noticed.

I struggled with myself, and lost. "I heard him. He left his panther blanket." I almost said *remember when we bought that?*

"What did he say?" Mama stared at the dark-screened TV. Its ancient wood-paneled bulk crouched near the cable outlet, and Mama had mentioned maybe getting someone out here to hook it up. When she wasn't thinking about a better mobile. Or even an apartment, a nice one. With parking.

"Not much." *Just that he was leaving.* "I don't know where he went, Mama. Honest."

She shifted a little, sighed. "He didn't leave a phone number? Anything?"

"No." My throat ached, so did the rest of me. "He's working, though."

"Where?"

"I dunno. But he had car-grease on his hands."

"Well, at least that." The line between her eyebrows deepened as she stared at the television's blank eye. The wind had fallen off, and with it, the cold threatening to creep into every corner. The heaters were beginning to make some headway. "He's eighteen. I can't keep him here."

She kept saying that. Was she trying to convince me? "I know."

"Oh, honey." Now she wasn't looking at the TV. Instead, she turned her head a little, and her worried blue gaze rested fully on me for the first time that day.

I was visible again. I pulled my knees up, tried to look sleepy and warm so she wouldn't worry.

"You're a good girl, Dez." Now she just sounded sad. "If Ray calls, you can tell him this is his home. He can always come back."

"I will." *I don't think he will, though. Do you?* I couldn't say that to her. It sounded mean even inside my head.

"You're not going anywhere, are you?"

"Mama!" I sounded shocked even to myself. "Where would I go?"

"I don't know, honey." Still studying me. "I just... he's always been... I don't know. Sensitive. Maybe I should have... God."

"It's not you." Why did I feel like I was lying? Of course, there was only one thing I could say after that. *It wasn't you. It was Daddy. Grief or relief, Mama? Which one are you feeling, and why do you let Mr. Vogg in the house?*

That sad smile of hers said she didn't believe it, and maybe it was the wrong thing to say. Because she stretched and got up, slowly, folding up the afghan with her quick, capable hands. "Go brush your teeth. I'll get you some NyQuil. Sure you don't want to stay home tomorrow?"

I never thought I'd ever hear Mama ask me that. "I gotta go. I don't want to get behind." My hair was stiff with sweat and sleep, I sat up and ran my fingers through it, wincing at the tangles. Maybe I could be warm in the shower tomorrow morning; even tepid was better than the ice outside. "Mama?"

"Hm?" She looked back over her shoulder, framed by the golden light in the hall.

"I love you." I got it out without the rock swelling in my throat. I wanted to say it, sure, but I wanted to say so many other things. *Are you happy Ray's gone? Are you happy Daddy's gone? What is that man selling you, what do you think you're buying? What are we going to do?*

Will you be happy if I go, too?

"I love you too, baby." She came back, and when she hugged me, it was her perfume and softness, salt and an edge of fried food that never left her even though she wasn't working at the diner now. I buried my face in her shoulder and tried not to cry, because she trembled worse than I did.

It was the first time I felt alone with Mama hugging me.

And all over her was a steam-scrim of Mr. Vogg's cologne.

• • •

FAULT

I tried to be cheerful, I really did. But in the middle of lunch, while Kara Muldowney was in the middle of talking about how she hated her mother because the bitch wouldn't move her curfew out past 1 a.m. on school nights, I just couldn't. I just got up, my chair scraping on the caf floor like bad brake shoes, and ditched my uneaten lunch in the overflowing garbage near where I used to sit. Wasting food was bad, but I couldn't help myself.

I kept going, head down and my steps quicker and quicker, until I found myself in the big gym. The floor had been freshly sealed before school started, and even after all the scuffing and skipping, it still glowed with a lovely mellow wooden shine. The bleachers were all folded back, but you could tuck yourself almost-behind them, near the doors to the soccer field. Which was now just a white wasteland, the baseball field in the distance with its chain-link batting cage and foul walls its own Siberian sculpture.

I slid down to sitting, against the wall, hidden from view. Or maybe I wasn't hidden as well as I thought, because of course he'd followed me.

I found myself wishing he hadn't. The dim lighting in here, because the big gym wasn't used after fourth period this semester, highlighted the gold in his hair. He had the same loping stride every other guy in jeans had out here, an almost-bowlegged cowboy strut. He'd changed the shitkickers for expensive hiking boots, like all the Populars. And like me, too, except mine weren't expensive. They were quality, though. Just good enough.

Ray had worn hiking boots while it was still summer.

Alex saw me, hesitated for just a second. I hugged my legs, put my forehead down on my knees. Closing my eyes didn't shut the world out anymore. It just showed me everything underneath, everything I didn't want to see. Like cruelty, and indifference, and the twisting, shifting pain too big to mend. Like the worry following Alex around, a cloud of silent static just like Mama's.

He settled down next to me, that worry filling me up to the brim, chasing out my own damn feelings and leaving me at the mercy of his.

"What happened?" So softly, as if I was sick. Or going to break.

Or as if he thought I might yell at him.

I had to lift my head a little bit, open my eyes so I could stare at the lines on the floor. "Ray."

"What'd he do now?"

What do you mean, now? I took a deep breath. Why was I so *irritated* at him? "He left."

"Left?"

"For good. Moved out. Took all his stuff."

"Oh." Alex mulled this over. "I thought he already had, I thought he was living on Hawkins with that…" The words trailed off. "I'm sorry, Dez."

You didn't do anything. But he had. If he hadn't told Mama, would they have started fighting so much? "It isn't your fault."

"He didn't tell you? I thought he would have, you know. He's your brother."

"Do your brothers know everything?"

He acknowledged it with a shrug. "I wouldn't go without telling them, though. They need me. And you're Ray's baby sister. The one he's proud of."

"He doesn't have another one." I rested my chin on my knees. Breathed in, breathed out. Gran said if you could breathe through a problem, a solution more often than not showed up. "Alex?"

"Huh?"

"Does he talk to you?"

"He used to. Not now, though. And, you know, I hear things."

"How?"

"From the guys at the shop. Ray's a good kid, you know? Magic with an engine. Dad was sad we had to let him go."

"Why did they?"

He shifted a little. Looked away.

I get it. "Is it a secret?"

"Not really. Just… he's real friendly with Stark, that's all."

"Who's Stark?"

"Another mechanic." He looked pretty miserable, as if giving me even that much was somehow against the rules. His eyes had darkened, and it hit me all at once that he could throw me off his personal planet at any time, and then where would I be? Not back where I started, that was for sure.

But still... each mending had a price. If I could mend Mama and Ray, would losing Alex be enough to pay?

Maybe, maybe not. There were different things, darker things, that could be done. Gran said that if you couldn't harm, you couldn't mend. The answer might not be in mending at all. That seemed like an option where Mr. Vogg was concerned, but still... was it something I wanted to do? Would Granny be proud of that? Or would she look at me that way again, grimacing with narrow eyes, dangerous sparks dancing in her pupils?

"So? Alex, *please*." My eyes were full again. "Where on Hawkins?" *I could find a map. I could go out there, talk to Ray. Find out more.* "You could... I mean, maybe you could drive me there, right?"

"Dez..." An unhappy blue cloud, something secret locked up in his head. "It's almost time for class. I'll walk you."

I couldn't help myself. I glanced at the wire-caged clock near the scoreboard. Ten minutes of lunch left. "You go ahead."

"Dez—"

"Just go. Get to class. Better hurry." I didn't mean it to sound so snide, but it was like Ray's voice in my mouth, each word with a sharp edge.

"I just think it's better if I don't, you know. It's just better, Dez." Was it *shame* he was feeling?

Since when do you get to decide? "Okay." I put my head down on my knees again. "Fine." Maybe I was okay to be friends with, but Ray wasn't. I'd been assuming Ray had been the one to cut things off with Alex, but what if he hadn't?

"Come on, Dez. Let's go back to the caf. Or we could skip and go to the Tasty Freez." Offering me a treat now. Like I was one of his dogs.

I don't want to. "That's okay. You go ahead."

"They have the best chili dogs around."

That was probably when I decided what I was going to do. I took a deep breath, my jaw clenching like Mama's when she had to take us in for shots. Something had to be done, and it wasn't pleasant, but sometimes you just grit your teeth and walk right on through.

Ray could hide things, and so could Mama. Why couldn't I? Of course, I'd already hidden so much. Like Gran, and the mending. And the ribbon-wrapped root under Mama's bed—if I took it out and threw it in the creek, or burned it while untangling the knot in my head, would Ray come back, along with the... the cancer?

So I pushed the weight in my throat away, tightened the knot inside my head. It made my eyes dry up, which was good, because my nose was full of that hot runny saline you get when you can't afford to cry. I sniffled it, not caring if it sounded unladylike, and when I uncurled myself, pushing myself up the wall even though Alex wanted to lend a hand, I had the mask back on. "Sorry." It sounded unnaturally loud in the gym's dark hush, with the wind scraping at the walls outside. "I'll walk *you* to class this time."

"You're the lady, though." Was it uneasiness, shading over his now-handsome face? He'd changed from a kid near my age to something else, a little more self-assured, a little more filled-out. "Look, Dez… I'm sorry. It's just not a good idea for me to say anything."

I shrugged. *It's only my brother, dammit.* But no shadow of that escaped my expression. "It's fine. Come on." I grabbed for his hand and set off across the gym. He let me tow him, and when I got him to the door of his Integrated Math classroom I even kissed him, proud of the way I could disconnect, my mouth and tongue doing what was necessary while the rest of me watched. We had a few minutes before tall thin disapproving Mr. Browning or any of the hall monitors showed up, and we used them. By the time I let go of him, he was smiling, and I walked away through the crowd with my head down.

Then, for the first time in my life, I skipped school.

CHAPTER TWENTY

Get In

THE SKY, a milk-blue lens this morning, was now a sheet of iron-gray; the wind had picked up even more and was scrubbing tiny pellets off the tops of drifts, a sandblast scourge. They hadn't given any weather warnings, but I thought one would probably start to blatt from the radios soon. It was beyond me how people actually *lived* out here year-round instead of hibernating all winter or fleeing south.

Of course, it cost money to leave. Less money to stay, maybe. They burrowed in wherever they could find a crevice and curled tightly around themselves, conserving any heat they could steal or breathe, in one way or another.

County transit had a stop across the street and two blocks down from John Wayne High. The houses here clustered the school, with wide sidewalks and fenced yards, just like chicks around a hen. It was no use; the wind roaring across the plains drifted snow against them anyway, and there wasn't a whole lot of warmth to be found even when they grouped up. I always wondered what it would be like to live in one of those houses, all new and shiny like Alex's, a place for everything and no sagging floors or holes in the drywall, broken doors, ovens that needed their doors propped closed with a yardstick. Kids who didn't play barefoot in the dirt road, parents who didn't yell *get your ass home or so help me I will beat you within an inch*, no sirens or flashing lights on paydays or fifth of the month when the rent was due, or when the Social Security checks came.

Base housing was sort of in-between, no holes and the appliances were usually okay, but there was always the suffocating static hiding in all the corners, even while Daddy was gone. Always the breathlessness, and Mama's worry everywhere, a sticky suffocating blanket.

I stood without stamping or fidgeting, waiting for the bus. Out of the wind it wasn't so bad, even if little tiny snow-pellets, whipped up from the ground, stung the sides of the shelter with small whispering *pockpock* sounds.

Besides, the cold inside me, all the way through, was worse.

I studied the timetable, squinting through the sheet of clouded plastic and ice it lurked under. It was only about ten more minutes waiting for the 370 bus, and I was beginning to wonder what I would do if the bus was late, or had broken down, or if it broke down on the highway, or something else. Go back to school? Walk home?

I don't care.

Out in the wind you could probably freeze to death, just like in Arctic stories. I was already shivering so hard my jaw felt like it had been wired shut to keep teeth from breaking against each other. Under the susurration against the shelter's walls, a different noise began fitfully, a thin silver string. My head jerked up; my breath turned into a cloud whisked away once it left the shelter. I wiped at my nose, stuffed my hand quickly back in my pocket. My thick green knitted mittens were at home, sitting on top of the low blue dresser I'd sponge-painted clouds on. I'd looked right at them this morning, too, and thought *I should take those.* Somehow I'd gone out the door without them.

The sound became a ribbon, weaving through stinging snow-pellets. I squinted, peering down the road. Ice and snow scraped high on the sides, stick-markers piercing the crust with reflectors on their top so the plows didn't go over into someone's yard. Sand and salt striped the piles in geologic lines, and the paving was even clean in places, scoured to gray leprosy patches.

The ribbon-whistle became a clanking and the rough cough-splutter of an engine Ray would wince to hear. The truck wheezed, melding out of gray stormlight and flying grit. One headlight busted, its ice-blue coat scabbed with primer gray just like the road and its tires jangling with rusting chains, it limped along with condensation-clouded windows. It jalopy-rolled to a stop right in front of the bus stop, and I heard the *chuk* of a lock popping up.

The whistling threaded through the sound of the engine, intensifying as I listened. I took a step towards it.

Don't do this, common sense whispered inside my head. *You don't know what's in there. It could be anyone.*

I could just open the door and look, though. Couldn't I?

Are you sure you want to see?

I could wait until the bus came, right? Once I did, there was no reason to do anything but go home, make my apologies to Alex when he showed up, keep eating at myself about Ray until there was nothing left or someone decided to throw me another bone to worry at. Wait for Alex to decide one of the Popular girls without a shameful secret of a brother was less trouble.

I stepped forward, out into the full stinging force of the wind again. Groped for the door handle with my jacket sleeve folded over my fingers so they didn't stick to cold metal, found it, pulled up. The hinges were rusted; they squealed.

The cab was a dark cave. I blinked several times, tears stinging my cheeks along with the flying ice, and saw a familiar lean shape, almost vibrating in place. Thin, bony, corpse-white hands clutched the ancient steering wheel, and his battered cowboy hat pulled itself down low, low over his face. The shade from the brim, and his lank, stringy, dishwater hair, hid his features, except for the tip of a long nose and a flash of white teeth.

Very sharp white teeth, square like a horse's.

"Hi," I whispered.

The whistling man didn't answer. The glow of his teeth vanished, and his lips pursed. He began to whistle again, a high drilling note.

In other words, *get in and shut the damn door.*

I would have hesitated, but there, on the seat next to him, were my mittens. They were dry, and I scrambled into the truck with a faint breathless *thank you.* The door slammed, the entire truck lurched, and we skidded off, the wind's sharp moan vanishing.

The windows were all fogged. There was no way to tell where we were going, or even if the Whistling Man could see to steer. I yanked my mittens on, biting back ridiculous questions. *Can you see? I didn't know you could drive.*

And, stupidest of all, *Are you real?*

Gran would have proud of me, maybe, for not filling up the air with useless words. Right now it was time to *do.* Which meant just sitting there, peering at the window, and feeling each shudder in the truck's hitching as if the gears were attached to my stomach.

My breath made a cloud, but without the wind it actually wasn't that bad. My mittens helped, and I just stared at the fogged-over windshield, watching billows of condensation shift across the glass.

• • •

ONLY MYSELF TO BLAME

Time passes weird inside a cloudy truck cab. However-longer later, the glass began to clear in streaks. We slowed, gradually, and the truck hitched sideways as if it had hit a patch of ice. I grabbed for the dash, trying to brace myself, but the movement stopped almost before it began and condensation melted off the windshield in wide angry claw-stripes.

I peered through the glass, blinking rapidly as winterlight rippled outside the truck's frayed, bleached cabin. The seats were sprung and the engine sounded like a sleeping asthmatic now, heavy wheezing and soft coughs. The whistling man tapped his flour-white fingers on the bent steering wheel, as if he was playing a keyboard as well as the air in his mouth. There were no keys in the ignition, and the gearshift looked like a stick taped to a broken-off chrome handle. Little nubbins of green leaf on the stick quivered, way out of season.

It wasn't important. Through the clearing glass, I could see a ramshackle apartment building—*Harrison Arms*. Three stories, peeling brown paint frosted with icicles and snow-spackle, the covered parking listing to one side and Ray's prized Camaro in one of the slots. It had wide, shiny-new tires now, and I wondered if he put chains on every morning. The parking spot had a faded, painted 2B on the crosspiece over it, but that didn't have to be his—

I reached for the door handle. The man beside me let out a slow, low sound—not quite a whistle, but not quite a hiss either.

I didn't have to use the knot in my head to know it meant *if you get out, I'm not parking and waiting for you.*

It must have been Hawkins Avenue, but no slice of it I'd ever seen before. Of course, there was nothing on Hawkins but rundown apartments and pawnshops, a liquor store or two, a grocery outlet store we might be driven to shop in every once in a while because you could find good stuff among the spoiling produce if you didn't mind digging.

Like dumpster diving. We never had to do that, but sometimes Daddy talked about it. *When I was your age,* he would say, as if such a thing was ever possible. I couldn't imagine Daddy as a kid. *My daddy beat me every day, whether I needed it or not.*

I couldn't imagine *that,* either. If it was true, why would Daddy spread the pain around? Or maybe it was true, and it still hurt him, the way everything was still hurting Ray, or Mama?

"Ray's here." My voice sounded thin and tinny, wavering. Little icy clouds accompanied the words.

The man nodded. Pointed one long, thin finger. I decided I didn't want to look at the fact that he didn't have fingernails, just a smooth seamless glove of... was it skin?

Don't ask if you don't want to know. I leaned forward, studying the address number, craned my neck to look for landmarks so I could find this place again. Between this and what Alex had let slip, I could get a bus out here. Talk to Ray, maybe... or even just...

The knot in my head twitched. A door opened, a long slot of golden light piercing the unnatural gloom under the beaten-iron sky. Second floor, apartment B.

Ray appeared. I'd know that battered parka of his anywhere, and he wore Daddy's Army scarf, faded green looped a couple times times, his jeans stuffed into the new hiking boots. Right after him, closing the door and locking it, came a stocky older man, hatless in spite of the cold, with thinning dark hair. The glass rippled again, and I could see every line on his face. He looked, in fact, a little like Daddy, from the dark eyes to the cruel downward twist of thin lips at rest, the wide shoulders and his way of walking, jabbing his heels down like the ground personally offended him.

My breath came short, whistling past my teeth as if I was running. The knot quivered inside my head, its strands shifting into a different pattern, and all of a sudden I understood, even before the man caught up with Ray, slung an arm around his shoulders, and nuzzled at my brother's neck. Just like Alex sometimes nuzzled at mine, or Daddy had at Mama's, or Mr. Vogg...

Everything inside me went turned to loose mud and steam. A dry rock jammed itself far back into my throat, the memory of ancient black thunderclouds and Daddy's yelling. *You little faggot! Gonna whip you into a man if I gotta!*

And later, the stealthy footsteps, and Ray's soft sobs. I hadn't precisely *known* before, had I? It was just there, like the anxious static or the shape inside my teeth when I ran my tongue along them, or the burn-shiny scar on Mama's arm.

You knew. The accusing certainty, even if I didn't know then I knew *now*, and why hadn't I done something? Daddy had stood over my bed in the darkness, but he'd never done more than watch as I pretended to be asleep, my heart in my throat turned to that rock over and over again, just like Gran could turn a clump of mud into dry sand with a single look.

This was why Alex thought it was better I didn't know. Because even if people around here didn't precisely know, they would *suspect*, and once they suspected something like that about you, well.

Vomit, hot and acid, crawled up my throat, met the rock, fought with it. My stomach cramped, even the back of my nose burning from bile and the peanut-butter toast I'd eaten this morning making an unwelcome reappearance. My wrists ached, and the whistling man grabbed the stick shift again. The truck groaned and creaked, but Ray didn't seem to notice. I saw the older, shorter man push him playfully, that cruel down-curve lengthening his lips, and I shut my eyes.

Don't ask if you don't want to know, Dez.

I had only myself to blame.

CHAPTER TWENTY-ONE

On My Own

ANOTHER STRANGE, shuddering silence lasted for a little while before the truck juddered to another stop, not gradual like before but a sudden stomach-loosening jolt. I scrabbled for the handle, not caring if the whistling man left me on the highway or God knows where, I had to get out of there. The ancient metal door didn't want to give, but I shoved and there was a creaking *snap*, the cold hit all along my body like a collection of hammers, and I heaved my guts out next to the wreck of a pickup truck sitting alone and majestic in an empty field the wind screamed over again and again about a mile from our trailer. I'd seen the busted-down vehicle standing out there in the middle of summer, baking in the heat, and now I stumbled away from it and a steaming pool of already freezing puke. I made it through the snow, following the compass inside my head, until a fencepost loomed up in front of me and I found myself staring at our own back yard.

The sky was still that ugly gray, but I made it home before the wind dropped off and the snow began to fall in thick, heavy curtains. Oddly, it warmed up a little before the sky started trying to blot us out.

I didn't care. My fingers, numb inside the mittens, were blocks of ice. I had to stab the key at the lock a few times before it went in, then clumsily twist it. The door was almost frozen shut; I yanked on it, and it finally shivered free of the frame. I had to knock broken ice off the bottom half before it would close again.

Inside, the trailer was a cold, dank cave. The clock on the stove said 4 p.m. sharp; Mama wasn't due back until 6. I moved mechanically, as if I'd just gotten home from school, sliding my snow-crusted backpack off my shoulders—had I been wearing it the entire time? I hadn't even noticed in the swaying, dark, frosted-over cavern of the truck.

The unreality of it walloped my legs right out from under me, and I folded down in the middle of the dark kitchen, curled into a tiny ball while snow melted off me in trickles. Maybe I was hoping Mama would come home and find me. Maybe I was hoping anyone would.

Nobody came. I was on my own. So after a while I hauled myself up, wiped the snot from under my nose and the hot salt tears from my chapped, windburned cheeks, and got to work.

. . .

INSIDE YOUR OWN BONES

I couldn't warm up, even with three sweaters on and Gran's spice tea stewed in the biggest mug we had, squeezing the last drops of flavor out of the bark, twigs, and floating leaves again and again. The cinnamon stick I stirred it with was noodle-soft at the end, and I nibbled little bits to calm my stomach. I cleaned the kitchen, did my homework, set my empty backpack near the oven to dry off. I even folded all the laundry and considered mopping the floor until I thought of stepping outside to toss the leftover water. At least the shivers only came in waves, their peaks getting further and further apart.

The wind picked up after a couple hours. It was a dilly of a whiteout, the radio said, and cautioned people to stay off the roads. I turned the oven on, hoping we wouldn't lose power, and stuck a frozen lasagna in after it had wheezed up to 350. As soon as I propped the oven door carefully shut again, the phone rang, and I was halfway there to answer when I knew it wasn't Mama at all, but Alex.

That brought me up short. What could I say to him?

Did he know particulars, or just rumor? *That Stark fellow... it's just not a good idea.*

How was I supposed to go to school now? Did he tell all his Popular friends? *Guess what? Her brother's with that Stark fellow, and her mama...*

I let out a sobbing breath, lost under the sound of the wind. Alex wasn't like that. I *knew* he wasn't like that.

But I knew other things too, didn't I? You can't ever be sure when someone will turn, like an apple that's crisp one day and mealy the next. Like a Daddy who can lift you up in his arms and kiss you with a *there's my little girl, my little angel* and who can also hold an arm against blue flame while someone screamed in agony. Who could settle you on his lap and tell you stories about cowboys, but also stand over your bed in the middle of the night breathing like a broken, impatient toy.

The phone rang for a long time, especially while I refilled my backpack for school. He kept calling back. I kept standing there, listening to the wind moan and hiss like it knew something. If I filled my head with the wind, I wouldn't think about a hot mouth on Ray's neck, the man Stark's nasty little smile, Alex telling his friends about Ray, or the fact that Mama was late. So late.

Of course, there was the weather. Maybe she was on the road, struggling home, the Ford wallowing back and forth in drifts, finding her way with luck and what she called moxie—

The phone rang again, and this time it sent a thrill right through me. I ran the last few steps toward it, scooped up the handset. "Mama?" High and breathy, like I was a little girl again, instead of sixteen and practically grown-up.

"Desiree? Oh, thank God. Listen, honey, the storm's real bad, they've closed the highway a few miles from the park. I'm staying in a hotel near the office tonight." The line crackled, stretching her voice out into a tinny ghost of itself. "You still have power?"

"I got dinner in the oven, Mama." *Please come home.* The words trembled on my lips. But she couldn't, now could she?

Someone said something behind her. Or maybe it was the wires crossed, a man's voice, low and rough. But Mama continued, as if she was alone in a room with just the phone. "You eat dinner and close up the house, honey. Leave the heat on all night, the last thing we need is for pipes to freeze. I'll call tomorrow morning, okay?"

"Okay." *No. It's not okay. Where are you really, Mama? Come back. I need you.* But that was selfish, wasn't it?

"I'm so sorry, honey. I shouldn't have gone in today."

"We all gotta work, Mama. It's okay." Who was the brittle stranger using my voice? She sounded just like normal.

If not for the throb-whispering in my head, I would have believed Mama was in an anonymous hotel room we couldn't afford—except with her new job, maybe we could. I would have believed she'd do anything to get home, and gone to bed feeling a little weirded out but still largely okay. I wouldn't freeze to death even if the power went out.

But what do you do when the cold is coming from inside your own bones? And when the whispers inside your head tells you more than you want to hear, scraping softly and subtle inside your skull, showing you all sorts of things you knew better than to disbelieve?

Her voice crackled out of the phone. "I'll be home tomorrow, sweetheart."

"Okay. I love you, Mama." The words squeezed past the rock in my throat, dripped out one by one.

"I love you too, Dez-baby. You keep the heat on, and get the blankets from my bed, you hear?"

"I hear you, Mama." *I hear everything.*

"Good. Don't worry, honey. I'll see you tomorrow." Maybe she even believed it herself.

I made my voice work, loud and clear. One tiny word, two syllables. "Okay."

After she hung up, I listened to the emptiness of the dial tone for a long time. My fingers cramped around the handle, and the timer dinged for the lasagna in the oven. When I finally forced myself to put the phone down, I knew even before it touched the cradle that I wouldn't see Mama the same way ever again.

I knew where she was, and it wasn't a hotel. It was a place full of a creeping, expensive cologne and a man's low, imperious voice. It was a house, and behind her as she talked on a sleek phone was a dark oily head with two badger-streaks at the temples, and a satisfied, self-congratulatory grin.

CHAPTER TWENTY-TWO

No Rhyming Song

THE STORM LASTED ALL NIGHT AND HALF THE DAY.
That happens a lot around that part of the country, I found out.
Pale blue snowlight filtered in past the cracks left in drapes and
blankets—got to close up all the holes, glass just becomes something
you lose heat out of. Make yourself a dark cave and coil up inside it.
Conserve the body heat, don't think about the icicles dripping down the
side of your trailer. Just listen to the wind. Hear it scrape past the walls,
a fur-scaled creature with its own chill breath, rubbing and rubbing.
Even the wind wants a pet now and again, a caress across the ears, a
who's a good boy to make it purr.

The phone rang off and on. Once I thought it might be Mama. The
sensation was faint and faraway, the ice like thick glass making everything
blurry. Another time I knew it was Alex. But mostly I just curled up tight,
knees and elbows, and let it ring.

I knew Ray wouldn't be calling.

I only got up to pee, and there was a bit of ice in the toilet bowl. I had
the cabinet doors propped open a little so the heat would keep the pipes
from freezing solid, and the kitchen faucet made a steady drip-drip-drip to
keep everything moving.

Back in bed. No spice tea, no food, nothing, and when the thundering
knocks on the door came, shaking the whole trailer, it jolted me out of a
thin, unsteady doze. I couldn't even tell who it was, and the idea that
maybe the door was iced shut and Mama needed help opening it, or Ray
had come back, got me out of bed and all the way through the mobile,
running in a dreamlike slow-motion.

The door was half-frozen, but it didn't matter, because when I
unlocked it, it burst free and a large shape barged past me on a wall of
frigid air. I gasped, he slammed the door, and Alex stamped on the mat
just inside, his boots shedding water and crusted ice. "Jesus," he said.
"Thank God. It's nasty out there."

I stood in the middle of the kitchen, my hair a wild mess and my
mouth full of sleep-taste, clutching Mama's blue comforter around my
shoulders, staring at him. His jacket fit him perfectly, a new parka with a
furry hood and buckles instead of buttons, the kind the Populars were all
wearing now.

Like mine, even. Mama had asked me what the other kids were wearing, and brought one home. I tried to tell her it was too expensive, but she'd just laughed. The new job paid her enough she could do things like that.

I didn't want to think about what Mr. Vogg might be thinking he was buying when he mentioned—oh, very subtly, of course—that the law office was hiring.

Alex's breath was a white cloud, even in the kitchen. Had the heat failed, or was it just that cold? He finished stamping, and I wondered blankly how I was going to clean up the mess on the floor. The thought of mopping just made me want to curl up right there and go back to sleep.

"Dez?" Kindly, his blue eyes all lit up. His face was a familiar stranger's, here in this dim dankness. It was a shock to hear someone else's voice in the empty mobile, instead of the wind's throatless hum and the cottonwool rasping inside my head. "You look sick."

I swayed. I couldn't decide what I was feeling. Relief? Anger? Both? There was no rhyming song I could make out of the tangle. My cheeks burned, but the rest of me was a faraway mess of ice-threads. As if wet hair had frozen all over me, and the strands were the only thing keeping me together. Little glassy filaments, and if I moved the wrong way they'd shatter.

"Where's your mom?" He stepped forward again while I stared at him, trying to find the words. My head felt too big on the inside, stuffed with empty space like a closed restaurant, all the chairs up on the tables and everything echoing. "Are you... Is your mom here?"

"She's in town," I managed, a colorless whisper. "The storm."

He nodded. "Okay. Look, you can't stay here alone. There's another front moving in."

I don't have anywhere to go. Except down into the gully, but the thought just tired me out, and Gran didn't have any place for me to sleep. Her bed was huge, but I got the idea she needed all that space. "I'm okay. I can just stay in bed."

He peered at me again, closely, and a decision crossed his face. He'd been filling out pretty steadily since the summer, and now he was just... big. Growing up all at once, the way boys sometimes do. "Can I use your phone?"

Is that what you drove all the way out here for? "Go ahead. It may not work."

"I've been calling."

I figured it was safest not to say anything. Sweat prickled all over me. Now I was too hot, instead of frozen. I turned around and padded back down the hall, shuffled into my room, and fell onto the bed again, burrowing under Ray's panther blanket and my own comforter, and Mama's too. His voice on the phone was a distant murmur, his personal planet pulling away from my solar system. He could do whatever he wanted, as long as he left me alone.

But he didn't. After a while I heard footsteps, and I shut my eyes.

"Dez?" He was in the door. "Desiree?"

Go away. I have to think.

What was there to think about, though? Just things I didn't want to—Ray and the man, Ray and Daddy, Mama and her scarred arm, Mama with Mr. Vogg.

He started moving around my room. My eyes flew open. "What are you doing?"

"You can't stay here alone. I called my mom. You're coming with me."

What? I couldn't leave, I had things to do here. Responsibilities. "You can't—"

"There's another front moving in. This place is already freezing. You can call your mom from my house so she doesn't worry. We've got the guest bedrooms downstairs, Mom's getting one ready for you. She's all excited. Someone else to cook for." He was in my *closet*, for God's sake. "You got a suitcase?"

"Alex. No. I'm not leaving." I tried to burrow even deeper into my nest, but getting up had robbed me of the small bit of feverish heat I'd been able to hoard. My tongue felt too thick for my mouth.

He wasn't listening, still in my closet, grabbing things. "Mom'll drive out here if you don't want me to take you. You shouldn't be alone."

"I'm not—" But I was, wasn't I? He couldn't know just how alone I really was.

He wasn't listening, anyway. "Safer for *your* mom in town, safer for you at our place. Come on. You got a suitcase?"

Alex was touching my clothes, and I should have been angry about it. I felt only a weary irritation. "Mama won't—"

"She will. Come on, Dez. If you don't I'm gonna have to stay with you, or my mom will. Your choice."

He *couldn't* stay here. That was just too much. Mama would give me that disappointed look when she came back.

If she came back. "I don't have anything for you to—"

"So that's decided. Where's your suitcase?"

I should've fought harder, I guess, but I was too tired. Maybe if I gave him my suitcase he'd go away. "Look up. It's orange."

He craned his neck, peering at the shelf above the hanger rod. "Good God, is it ever. Okay. Come on, get dressed, and pack. I wanna get home before it gets any worse."

I gave up. I was moving through a thick, slowing-down sludge, even mentally, and I threw what I could into the battered, bright orange nylon ripstop we'd found at the thrift store. Almost a whole set, and nice and cheap. I also stuffed my library books in there, but I forgot to go down the hall and get my shampoo or toothbrush. It didn't matter, I was dizzy, sweating and shivering by turns. The cold had come back with a vengeance. I managed to get into a pair of jeans and a sweater, my still-damp jacket, and my mittens.

Alex took the suitcase from me as soon as I got outside my bedroom door. "Okay, so now we—Dez? You okay?"

No. I haven't been okay for a while now. I struggled between saying a polite yes and a truthful no. "I don't know." My teeth chattered through it, and something in his face changed.

"Here." He grabbed the new, blue, thick-knitted stocking cap off his head and smoothed it down over my messy hair. It was still warm, and smelled like him. For some reason that made my eyes well up. The shivering wouldn't stop, and now that I was upright I could barely breathe.

"My backpack." *Have to go to school.* Why I was so concerned about that, I'll never know. I didn't even remember what homework I might have had, or if I'd done it. All that mattered was that I had to go, and the backpack had to be stuffed full of its usual cargo, I couldn't forget that.

"Yeah, I put it by the door. Let's go."

I was stupid. I left the heat on.

It was my fault.

. . .

FIX IT

It wasn't a cold, it was a bad case of influenza. Their house was so *quiet*, the wind closed outside its weatherproof walls, stilettos of blue snowy light robbed of any chill coming through the thick curtains. Mrs. Carr brought me chicken soup that wasn't from a can, and fresh towels, shampoo and toothpaste, and crackers for the soup. DayQuil and TheraFlu and fancy bottled water I felt bad for drinking, but I was so thirsty. So I kept saying *thank you* and *I'm fine* and *no, please, I don't want to be any trouble.*

"I talked to your mama," Mrs. Carr told me that first, weird, fever-dark afternoon. "She's so polite, I can tell where you get it from."

"Is she all right?" I sounded drunk, all slurred. I'd given Alex the office number for the big shiny building downtown, the one I only knew about because Mama described it to me. She hadn't ever let me come to work with me.

Not there.

Mrs. Carr's hand was cool against my flushed forehead. "Of course. Jim Vogg got hotel rooms for his staff in-town, since the roads are so bad." Her forehead creased a little, but I couldn't tell what she thought of the badger-man. "Don't you worry, honey. The adults can handle this, you don't have to. You're such a good girl."

You don't know. But I accepted it, and closed my eyes, and she left.

The room was so pretty. Soft blue carpet, a pillowy, royal bed with a canopy, a dresser with pumpkin spice sachets, a closet full of padded hangers. Sometimes I thought about how easy it would be to stay there, in a dreamy sort of way, pretending I belonged, hearing them move through the house around me. What would I be if I'd been born here? One of the fashion-skinny Popular girls, with their cheerleader skirts and their expensive coats and their teased hair? Maybe one of the brainy Populars, with their trips for science clubs and their glowing scholarship prospects?

Later, as afternoon wended towards evening, I woke from restless tossing to a familiar thread of perfume, and an even more familiar half-cough, a recovering smoker's unconscious clearing of a rough throat. My eyes flew open. "Mama?"

She stood in the door, her head cocked and her hair spilling to one side, and for a moment she was a stranger. I blinked, hazily, thinking the fever had done something funny to my brain. She was so... thin. Not her body, but thin like a tissue, like a piece of paper. Her hair was different, somehow. Oh, it was brushing her shoulders still, thick and black as ever, but it was... like when a television screen is just a few degrees of color *off*. You can't really see it, but you know it's wrong. Something deeper than your eyesight keeps trying to inform your brain, but the brain won't listen.

Brains are stupid like that.

"Oh, honey," she said. "Thank God." Her voice, but... I don't know. Just off by those few shades. Not softer or louder, but less rich, maybe? Less weight to it.

"Mama?" I sat up, held out my arms. "*Mama*."

She glided into the room, painfully out of place. Her knee-length red work skirt, a pair of black L'eggs, the ancient boots held together with duct tape because Ray and I always got new shoes first, her fresh red nail polish, the silk shell we'd found at the Salvation Army store and marveled over its construction and quality... she *looked* all right, I guess. My head, stuffed full of snot and aching, throbbed painfully.

Mama sank down to sit on the bed, touched my forehead, hugged me so hard the breath whooshed out of me. "Oh, baby. I shouldn't have let you go to school."

"I wanted to go," I said into her shoulder. It was probably walking home from the brokedown truck that made me sick, but I couldn't tell her that.

So many secrets. *I saw Ray, Mama. I know why he doesn't want to come home.* Everything inside me shook and blurred. If I told her, would I have to tell her about Daddy's wandering in the middle of the night, too? The sounds, the soft snuffling sobs when it was over and the black cloud vanished, how I knew Ray would never talk about it in that same way I knew gravity was down and water was wet.

Did she know about Daddy? She couldn't have. If she knew, she would have stopped him. Done something.

Right?

"I should have come home." She shook her head, biting her lip, cuddling me close.

Her feeling-bad crashed into me. Poor Mama. I couldn't tell her *anything*. She would break, and then where would I be? I was too tired and too sick to hold this all up on my own, even though it was my job. Who else could she depend on?

But I was so *tired*. "It was okay. I had blankets and food and everything. Alex made me come here."

"It's a good thing he did," she said, a little sharply.

"I got to get dressed." I sounded nervous and fretful even to myself. "I want to go home. Can we go home?"

"Oh, honey..." She hugged me even tighter, and I couldn't tell if the sick feeling was the influenza or my other way of knowing, trying to warn me.

In the end it didn't matter, because she told me, in soft halting words. Something in the electrical wires. Something in the mobile, something falling apart or heating up and by the time anyone noticed, the whole place was burning. A torch in the middle of all that ice. I listened to her say it, haltingly, how everything had... burned. How the whole mobile had been involved, and we couldn't get out there for a while to find out what was still left. Some of the snow helped damp the flames, and the firefighters eventually got there and put it out, but that just meant there was water damage too.

When it finally got through to me, my chest began to ache as well as my head. *Oh, God.* "I left the heat on," I whispered. "I'm sorry, Mama."

She stroked my hair. Just a touch too lightly. Like her hand wasn't as heavy as it used to be. "Oh, honey. If you hadn't, the pipes would have frozen and the whole place would be flooded when the thaw hit. Something always happens in weather like this, it's not *your* fault. It'll be all right."

No, it won't. "Where are we gonna live? How are we going to—"

"You don't worry about that, Desiree." A flash of her old self, anemic winter sun breaking through heavy cloud; it almost tipped me into tears again. Something was *wrong*, even more than I knew, and I couldn't figure out what. "You're going to stay here a few days, Mrs. Carr says you're most welcome, and then... don't you worry. *Don't* worry, honey. Mama's going to fix it."

How? I didn't ask. Maybe I should have.

"You're staying here, while I make arrangements. You're too sick for a hotel." Mama stayed for another half-hour before she had to chance the road back into town, petting my hair and singing to me in that soft voice she used when we were sick, chiding me softly when I kept asking her to take me with her. "A hotel's no place for you right now, honey."

My head was so full of bad noise I could almost pretend she was just the same, that it was bad but Mama could fix everything. I maybe even believed some of it.

What else did I have to cling to?

CHAPTER TWENTY-THREE

Shining Path

IT FROZE HARD THAT NIGHT, the sky warming even though a layer of cold stayed near the ground. Freezing rain laid a half-inch of glass over everything, and when morning dawned it was gold refracted through crystal. I know because I woke up during that dawn, that liquid metal light spearing through the curtain-crack and warming the center of my forehead. A sunlight-finger, slipping between curtains and stroking just above and between my eyebrows, warmth spreading from its impersonal touch.

I lay there, the knowing inside my head masked by snot, and listened. Not a sound, everyone in this strange pretty house sleeping. Ice-filtered sunshine faded, it clouded over, and the hazy idea that it was going to snow again occurred right before I dove back into blackness, surfacing later when there was a knock at my door and Alex crept in, his arms full of a bulk that turned out to be a blank screen and dangling electrical wires. I struggled out of the bed and retreated to the bathroom in the hall—unused, pristine, the toilet bowl so white I felt guilty for peeing in it—and found out that someone had washed my clothes, even though they were perfectly clean. They were stacked in neat piles, folded by unfamiliar hands and smelling of expensive fabric softener.

Sweat-sticky hair clung to my forehead, the back of my neck, turning stiff down near the ends. My nose and lips and cheeks were chapped flaming red. I couldn't stop coughing, and my entire skull sloshed with mucus. I was hoping Alex would be gone by the time I trudged back out, down the hall that seemed funhouse-wrong, all its angles off by a few degrees.

"I can read to you." Alex perched on the chair next to the bed. There was a stack of three Kleenex boxes on the nightstand—the good ones, with lotion. "I carried the TV down, too. There's movies."

"Okay. Thanks." My throat was dry and slick at the same time. "I'm fine." I made it to the bed, pulled my feeling-unfamiliar legs up, hugged my knees. My tank top and boxers, freshly washed and coated with rich-girl smells, were soft little traitors next to my skin. I didn't need an extra sweater, their house had good heating. Frostflowers on the window—you could leave the drapes open and not freeze to death, looking out on the white wasteland. It was another kind of secret power, and one I didn't understand. "It's so quiet here."

"This is quiet?" He made a face, and I was surprised into laughing, cupping my hand over my mouth to trap the inevitable, chest-thumping cough it caused. Somewhere in the house, Jesse the basset hound was baying, and I could hear Charlie yelling excitedly and galumphing on the stairs.

When I could talk again, every word had to be forced out through sandpaper. "It's nice. Peaceful, even when it's noisy. You know?"

"I dunno." He scratched at his hairline. With his hair all messy from sleep and his sloppy Broncos sweatshirt, he looked a lot less Popular and a lot more like just-Alex, someone familiar. "Every time Charlie and Jess get going, it's like World War Three. When Sol lived here, she used to call it the 'morning scramble.' Better than an alarm clock."

"Soul?" I rubbed at the crusties in my eyes. Why was he even looking at me? It wasn't pretty, and even if I could get all the guck off, my eyes would still feel grainy and weird.

For a second he looked like Jesse the beagle, hopeful and eager to please, to fetch something, *anything*. "Solange. Kev's girlfriend. She had some home stuff, lived here for a while. Now she lives with her grandma, but she comes back a lot. You want some coffee? More water?"

So they took in other girls, too. Maybe it was just what people like this did. "I'm okay."

"Wanna come upstairs for breakfast? Mom's doing gingerbread Dutch babies."

"Dutch babies?" The sudden gruesome image of babies shoveled into a hot oven was right out of a fairytale book, one with really lurid illustrations. Mama never got me those, she got me stuff like Little Golden Books. *Fairy tales aren't good for kids,* she'd said once, darkly. *Prince Charming always turns out to be a real hardcase.*

"Like pancakes, only better. She's all excited, she likes cooking for new people."

I slid my legs off the bed again. It had been a little while since I slept in boxers. There were Ray's old blue plaid pair, and the thought filled my chest with an unsteady, colorless feeling, different than the congestion. Everything seemed underwater. "I don't want to be any trouble." I had to weigh doing what he wanted and being nice versus not being a bother, and over it all was the fact that I had to get well and go back to Mama.

Something was wrong, I just couldn't think of what.

"You're not trouble. She really likes you. If we break up she'll probably keep you instead of me." His grin was so wide and easy, blue eyes sparkling. "You want a robe or something? Some socks? Your feet can get cold. I speak from experience."

"I'm fine." I felt greasy, though. The hardwood felt nice and cool under my feet, and I worried about leaving oily streaks on it. Or on the painted walls. The idea of going up stairs, of holding myself carefully so I didn't break or mar any of their fresh new things, exhausted me all at once, and I sat on the edge of the bed, my head dipping forward and my hair turned into fat dark snakes over my shoulders, hissing and writhing to protect my expression. *Just go away. I didn't ask for this.*

"You keep saying that." His head tilted just a little, a handsome stranger's face now. Growing into those cheekbones, and without that beaten-up hat he looked even more like a Popular boy. They all have that same *finished* look, no matter where you go to school. Like they were ironed before being put away, and bought a fresh set of looks each year so they didn't get worn out.

Was this what it was like to not have a secret knot in your head? How did anyone know what anyone else was feeling? Or what to do?

You didn't have it before Gran, you know. You figured out what people wanted then, didn't you?

You get used to a crutch so easily. But still, in a foggy sort of way, I'd sensed things under the surface all my life. Gran made them clearer, more vivid, and I'd gotten lazy when it got easy.

"Sorry." There seemed nothing else to say.

He leaned over, and his hand was ice-cold, pressed under my hair against my sweating forehead. "Jesus. You're burning up. I'm getting Mom."

Oh, God. "No—"

But he was already up and out of the chair. I shook my head, wished I hadn't because it made the whole room spin, and there was a... a *skip*, a sort of absent moment full of movement I wasn't in charge of.

I was tugging at the locked window when Mrs. Carr appeared. I guess I thought I should let some cool air in, because all of a sudden I was burning up. Alex was sent running to the phone with a crisp sentence, and she got me into bed again using that strange tone Mama sometimes had—firm, and no-nonsense, kind but inescapable. It was a relief to hear a mother's voice again, and I collapsed on the bed, watching the ceiling spin for a while as Mrs. Carr told me I wasn't supposed to get up and they'd bring me breakfast. It made me think that she was Mama somehow, and that I belonged here in this pretty, marvelous bedroom in this shining house surrounded by owned property, nothing rented, nothing broken, nothing patched-up. Flavored ice pops, acetaminophen, honey lemon tea, a humidifier—they had so much *stuff* just packed away in those color-coded Rubbermaids, waiting to be dragged out for any emergency.

Sleeping again, while the fever spiked, and all that night I tossed and turned, dreaming. Fuzzily aware that someone was breathing in the same room—sometimes Mama, sometimes Gran, sometimes the badger man with his white, strong teeth. Glowing eyes, dark branches overhead as I ran down the gully's slippery, melting sides, rocks shifting underfoot and the path doing its best to throw me off, curving and hunching. A soft low whistling, the wind trying to get in, to show me something, but I was locked up tight inside a castle, thick stone walls protecting me.

• • •

NIGHT FOR WANDERING

My eyes opened, slowly. The breathing was a round momlady with dark hair pulled back, slumped in the chair next to the bed. A dim glow around her, as if she was some sort of low-level angel, or just giving off the charge all living things carry, even the cold-blooded ones.

That's Libba. *I found her name, and just thinking it made her stir slightly, the glow intensifying a little.*

Everything seemed very clear, but very faraway. I could see how, with just a little push, I could stay here. The castle would fold around me, its walls becoming mine, and in a little while it would seem natural. I could finish school here, I could go to college because that's what you did when you were like the Carrs, and I could know, the entire time, that when I finished there would be a ring waiting, a blond man with laughing blue eyes on one knee. That life was nice and straight and easy, and I could even mend things while I was on it.

Wait. Where's Mama?

My body fell away underneath me. The protective castle tried to snap shut like a Venus flytrap, but I was already gone. I flew, through whirls and buffets of snow, marveling at each big, fluffy, completely unique flake. It wasn't cold or warm, just weightless and full of the dull grayness snow is at night when there's no sun or moon to make it sparkle. Dirty electric light, slush frozen into asphalt-striped mountains, strata of melt and freeze. I coasted, here and there, searching, but all I saw were empty streets. Nothing to hold onto. No place to go.

Slowing down. Straining against heavy air, the snow turned treacherous, massing in front of me. Shapes I vaguely recognized, whisked away by the silent wind, and I realized I couldn't even hear the whistling man, though I knew he was somewhere in the dark, maybe looking for me.

Maybe not. I couldn't be the only one he danced past, could I? Gran knew him—

As if the thought summoned her, I heard a scratchy, deep old voice. **"Get back in."** *The crinkles at the corners of Gran's eyes, fans built from laughing and other things, and thudding pops as blunt triangular heads hit glass aquarium walls.* **"Now you get back in, Dasya. This is not a night for wandering."**

A streetlamp fizzing overhead. Glass edges rising, a shape I thought was a huge aquarium until I realized it was a house, all modern and sharp-edged, its wide windows black as tar. It crouched, and I didn't feel the night's cold, but everything inside me shriveled and every winter-naked tree clustered around that cubist fantasy of a house was dead. Even if they leafed out in summer, they were still dead, clockwork approximations of living things, blasted by a hatred so fiery-frozen all weather was just a teardrop on its hateful, shaven cheek.

A snap, Granny Iyaga's capable, knotted hands breaking the seal on a jar of preserves. A spoon dipping in, and her crooning. The bedroom window was open, a snowdrift sparkle-pouring through as moonlight danced on its surface. Granny hunched over me, her yellowed teeth strong and her breath foul-vital, her hair skeins of black just like mine now, with only token streaks of gray. "**Here, child. Listen to old Granny.**"

I didn't want to, but the spoon made of horn was in my mouth, and its cargo was so cloying-sweet I gagged before it liquified, pouring down my throat. I retched, Libba Carr twitching restlessly, but she slept on and Granny Iyaga cackled soundlessly. She wore her familiar red shawl knotted around shoulders slimmer, firmer, and more muscular than they had been before. The window's vomited snowdrift began to reverse itself, pouring up and out the window like a pressure washer was pushing it away.

Granny Iyaga, the green sparks in her pupils swelling hungrily, glided across the hardwood. The pointy toes of her ancient boots dug pale furrows in polished tree-hearts as she floated to the window. Ice shivered into spikes, spearing the drifts below with jagged toothshapes, and the window's slam was the door to her round little trailer kicked closed.

The cough-retching went on and on, I curled on my side and hacked until my mouth was full of something that wasn't the preserves. It was a solid clot, and I spat it into a handful of tissues, sagging back on the pillows while Mrs. Carr murmured in her sleep. I closed my fist around the slippery, hot nugget of illness, squeezing as hard as I could.

When I woke up in the morning the fever was gone. The only thing remaining was a smooth white stone, clutched in my aching fist. I looked at it for a long while, until Libba Carr woke up and felt at my salt-sticky forehead and said the worst was past.

I didn't bother to ask for who.

CHAPTER TWENTY-FOUR

Home Truth

"**N**OW YOU STOP THAT." Libba—she flat-out *made* me call her that—took Charlie's plate firmly out of my hands. "Sit down and finish your dinner."

"It's no use, Mom." Alex grinned as he swung by, a stack of bowls cradled in his capable grasp. Jazz played softly, and the bright icy glow falling through the skylights turned the entire kitchen into a stage set. "She keeps cleaning things."

"I'm done, ma'am. I like to help," I said. "You did the same thing at our house, Alex." *Before it burned down.*

There wasn't even an awkward silence after that. Or at least, if there was, it was covered up by Mr. Carr bringing the pan with the remains of the roast from the table. "Libba, damn, you outdid yourself. That was some mighty fine cow."

Libba pushed a few strands of graying hair back and looked pleased, even when he nuzzled at her neck. They were always at each other, it was kind of weird to see. They'd met in high school and been in love ever since. It was amazing, like they had found some secret key and just couldn't share it with the rest of us even if they wanted to.

Libba didn't ever seem frightened, or more than mildly irritated. I kept watching, but they were just what they looked like. Mr. Carr was big and loud but not mean, and she was small and round and quick and he clearly thought she hung the moon. There was no static filling the corners, worried *or* angry, and even when Charlie stamped mud and snow-water in from the fields outside there wasn't a big fuss made. He groaned and rolled his eyes when told to get the mop and the vacuum, and that was all. The worst thing Charlie could envision was being grounded, which meant no video games played on the bigscreen TV in his daddy's den.

Jess snuffled at my ankles, her big brown eyes hopeful as she gazed up adoringly. With her big floppy ears and her little croons, she begged all day long for food. I'd never seen a dog so determined to get a mouthful of anything that might possibly have any caloric value, no matter how slight. Daisy, the elderly German shepherd, waited by her bowl when food-time was nigh, but Jess was always at ankle or appearing when anyone headed kitchen-ward. Butch, of course, just wanted to be where someone would pet him. *We had to give him a fierce name,* Libba remarked. *Otherwise the other two would just walk right over him.*

"Mom?" Kevin shouldered past his father. "Can I go see Sol?"

"Kev, it's still icy. You can call her after you finish your chores."

"I *did* finish my chores."

"Then go call her to see if she's at home." Libba rolled her eyes, scraping the plate into the covered garbage bin with efficient swipes. "Alex, will you and Dez go see what's in the freezer for dessert? No, Charlie, you may *not* go along, leave them alone!"

Charlie, mischief all over his broad blond face, contented himself with making wet kissy-noises at us as Alex led me away from the kitchen. Butch trooped after us, his nails clicking on mellow-shining wood. Through the big bright dining room, where Libba would change the tablecloth on the big maple table every two or three days. The two matching sideboards crouched, full of china and linens, waxed once every few months, the art-deco chandelier was dusted too. Libba just seemed to naturally keep things clean; she even ironed her lace doilies. *Got to keep them crisp. Like apples.*

What would it be like, to have a mama that could do that? A mama who had *time* for all that? It was enough to make anyone wonder. The boys had chores, and even Mr. Carr had things to clean. Everything got ticked off the list Libba had on a hanging chalkboard in the kitchen. I kept glancing at the list to see what I could do, since they were feeding me.

"You okay?" Alex held the door open for me, and the entire world slipped back into its rightful proportions.

How did he *do* that?

"Yeah. I guess. I'm just a little..." I shivered, even though I had socks on. The utility room wasn't cold, but the change between wood and linoleum made it *feel* colder. "I dunno."

That was maybe the wrong thing to say, because it made him stop and look at me, *really* look at me. It was sunny yellow and smelled of fabric softener in here, the same scent that clung to me now. "You're not used to people giving a damn, are you."

Well, don't put any sugar on that home truth, boy. It was something Daddy might have said, if he was in a good mood. "My brother left and my house burned down and my mama's dating her boss's boss. It's like a country song, only worse." I didn't mean it to come out so sharp, but he didn't even wince.

"*There* you are." He swung the door closed, first making sure Butch was well clear, since the dog had a habit of standing in doorways. You could bang him right in the middle if you weren't careful. "Hi, Dez. Been a while since you piped up."

Oh, dammit. "I didn't mean to say that."

"I wish you did. I like it when I get to hear what you really think. I was wondering when you'd cotton on that Vogg's after your mama." He slipped past me for the garage door, glancing back over his shoulder before he stepped down onto frigid concrete.

In the garage, you could hear the wind. I stood on the step, shivering, my arms wrapped around me. Did Alex think I was an idiot? He'd been there and seen Vogg and my mama in our trailer. "I don't like him." There. It was out, it was said.

"Yeah, well... you're not the only one. Dad calls him an oily SOB." He popped open the chest freezer. "You like cheesecake?"

Like Sara Lee? With frozen cherries on top. Except theirs is probably expensive. "It's okay." I bit at my lower lip. The sweater was Alex's, heavy blue wool and silk, and it smelled like him. *You get cold,* he said. *Here.* And he just handed it over. Maybe like the letterman jackets Mama told me about. Class rings and doo-wop, be my steady yes please. Like that show Daddy would watch and heave with laughter during—what was it? *Happy Days.* "I'm worried. About..." Was I just going to stand here in his garage and say it out loud? Say something, anything, except once I began describing a single worry, the others would probably pour out of me too.

"Well, he's never been sweet on anyone before. Didn't stop some from trying. Mom used to call him the Widow Flytrap."

It sounded like something Libba would say, fearless and adult. My guilty little laugh puffed out on a frigid cloud. "He came out to our house. The night... when Ray left."

He found something he liked in the freezer, let it slam shut in that weird way chest freezers have, a cushion of air making the sound flat, a padded chop. Butch nosed at the back of my knees, lipping the flannel pajama bottoms. Alex's gaze met mine. To my right, their shiny automobiles crouched, safe from the weather outside. Even Alex's truck had been pulled into shelter. Each one had its engine block warmer plugged in, the extension cords all neatly labeled.

"Your mom might get an apartment in town." He said it gently, like it didn't matter. "Hopefully you won't switch schools, but if you do I'll come visit."

How long would you do that? And now he'd seen me all chapped and gross from being sick. "You're planning everything out."

"Can't help it. I'm a natural planner."

"Me too." Except I didn't have a damn idea of what to do next. Every time I thought I was safe for a little while, another rope snapped and the tide kept dragging me out toward the sea.

"You could stay here. We've got the room."

Guests are like fish. You don't keep them around forever. "I don't want to be a bother." *I don't want charity, either.* Or did I? It would be so nice to stay here, to pretend I wasn't...

Well, what was the alternative? Would Mama get an apartment? Could we afford it? And without Ray, we didn't need a three-bedroom, right?

Alarmed at the mental direction I was heading, I backed up, almost tripping back into the utility room.

"You're not a bother. You talk books with Mom, she loves that. Dad doesn't read, and the rest of us, well."

Boys. "I'm only sixteen, Mama won't let me stay here forever." *Even if I might want to.* Did I?

"I dunno. She might want to keep you in our school."

Not when we've been moving around all my life. That's what military means. I decided we'd better get the cheesecake, or whatever it was, back into the kitchen before Libba thought we were making out in here or something. Of course, she kept giving us things to do together, like she *wanted* us to make out. I tried not to, in case I was contagious. And also...

...Well, something had *changed*. Maybe it was just because I got the idea I was just a piece to slide into his perfect life, checking a box. Why he hadn't chosen one of the Populars was beyond me, but maybe he was just stubborn. Or maybe he liked that I came from the trailer parks, because I was so goddamn *grateful*.

That thought made a spiky, uncomfortable irritation well up inside me, one I did my best to keep throttled all the way back. So I gave the little whistle they used to move Butch along, and coaxed the prancing dog back through the utility room. I even bent down when we got to the dining room, scratching behind his ears until he flopped over, all four legs in the air, and begged for bellyrubs. I leaned against the larger sideboard, not looking at Alex as he trooped past. He went around barefoot, like he didn't feel the cold.

Maybe he didn't. Maybe it was just me.

The phone rang just as I got Butch drooling, his eyes rolled back in his head and his doggy smile big enough to park a semi in. I actually laughed, everything in the world bright and happy in that one moment, the knot inside my head loosening to take in his joy.

"Dez? Honey, it's your mama." Libba's voice, cheerful enough, but there was that undertone.

As if she didn't like Mama. Or as if she saw something I didn't. Maybe she had a secret way of knowing things, too.

I scrambled to my feet and ran, Butch scrabbling to get his legs underneath him so he could follow, and Libba handed me the phone, her face set in that bright, pretty smile. Was I the only one who would see the unease under it? "Mama?" Breathless, my entire chest filling up with happy. "Mama, are you okay?"

Alex gave the box he'd pulled from the freezer to his mother, and they both retreated to the other side of the kitchen to give me some privacy. I carried the cordless towards the French door to the deck, Butch at my ankles. His hot tongue lapped, begging for more attention, each lick a little wet star of joy as it cooled.

"Hi, honey." Blurred and faraway, like she was under clear, heavy water, neither hot nor cold, just skin-warm. "I'll be out to get you as soon as I can."

"You sound tired." I stared out at the white waste, the fancy grill and the covered patio furniture just suggestions under a thick white blanket. "I'm okay here, really I am."

"I know, honey. Libba and Fred are good people." A long pause. Slow and sleepy. "Are you feeling better? You sound better."

"I am, Mama. I could come out to you now, except the buses aren't running. Are you eating? You sound awful tired. Are you okay?" *Talk to me.*

"Honey, don't you worry about me. I'm... fine. Just fine." Of course it was her voice, just a little tinny from the wires. Just exhausted, as if she'd been up worrying and chainsmoking again, those lines around her mouth as she looked at the bills, or as if Daddy had been drinking again, or had taken all the money from the account and done something. Again.

I knew every shade and tone of my Mama's voice. Why did I feel like I was talking to a stranger?

"Mama..." What was I going to ask?

"I'll be out to get you as soon as I can," she repeated. "I've found us a nice place. You'll like it. Windows all over, and it's warm."

That could be here. "Okay." My fingers were cold. So were my toes. Butch pressed against my calves, like he could tell. "I love you, Mama."

"I lo—" The connection fuzzed out for a moment, and when it came back, the voice was different.

"Little Miss Sarpe." It was the badger-man's voice. "I look forward to seeing you soon."

Cold all over, I glanced at the kitchen—Libba looking at the boxed cheesecake, her forehead furrowed a little, Alex saying something to her. She swatted at him, but gently, and her smile was a sunrise forgiving him even as she half-growled. He mock-cowered, but that just made the cold worse. It was like looking in a magic mirror, where things were better than they could be out in the real world.

I swallowed, hard. "You've done something," I whispered, to Mr. Vogg, the Widow Flytrap.

"I do a lot of things." An oily chuckle. "Be a good girl now, *Desiree.*"

And for a moment it wasn't Mr. Vogg, it was *Daddy* hissing through the phone, and I swayed. There was a low thrumming sound, and I found myself clutching a cordless handset that had gone dead, and Butch the cocker spaniel, who didn't have a mean bone in his body, was staring up from my ankles, the fur all over him standing up. It would have been funny if his eyes hadn't been wild and white-ringed, and if he hadn't been growling. It was a deep *I mean business* sound, and it almost rattled the glass out of the French doors.

Nobody heard it but me, though. Butch shook himself, gave me an apologetic look, and wobbled off for the kitchen and his water bowl. He drank a lot, noisily, and I walked, slow and wooden, to the breakfast bar. I set the handset back in its cradle, and stared at it until Libba asked me what was wrong, and I had to think of something polite to say.

That was how I found out Mama was living with Mr. Vogg, and that she wanted *me* there, too.

Or he did. Which ended up as the same thing.

• • •

HOUSE ON THE HILL

The yellow SUV—during the winter out here, their taxis were bigger, just like everything else—banked like a plane. Its tires crunched on wet rock salt, grinding on sand. A scrap of paper with an already-familiar phone number clutched in my sweating fist, and Libba's words still ringing in my ears—*you call us, anytime, sweetheart, and someone will come pick you up. I promise.* Along with a meaningful look, brushing a strand of graying hair out of her face, her eyes just like Alex's, kind and worried. *Also, call us when you get there, so we know you're safe.*

It was the same thing Mama might say to one of my friends, if I ever could have had them overnight. When Daddy was home, I always had the fuzzy idea that it wasn't good to ask, and even when he wasn't it just didn't ever seem reasonable. Girls were supposed to stay home where they belonged, unless they were *that kind of girl.*

Boys were different. Ray could have friends over, if he didn't mind Daddy humiliating him sometimes in front of them, but never to spend the night. I used to hear other girls planning slumber parties and sleepovers in middle school, and wonder what their daddies thought about it. That was the first time I realized things in other people's houses might be different than ours.

I peered out the window, marking the turns and noticing street names. We'd gone all the way through downtown and swung south a bit. The skyscrapers loomed behind us, a silent headache of steel and glass. A funky, antique residential section came next, with small yards and older houses, obviously expensive but kind, too. Then the houses began getting bigger and more expensive according to some weird mathematical law. There's always people who like being close to the big towers, and are willing to pay for the privilege if only to show that they can. Mama sometimes talked about living in New York, the throb and pulse of the city, and Daddy sometimes called her *city girl*, as if that was an insult.

The way he said it, it was, I guess. She didn't talk that often about where she came from, and Granny Avi only left her comfortable Manhattan apartment to visit us twice that I knew of. Both times Daddy stayed silent, almost anxious, but after she left the last time, well, that was the summer of Ray's broken arm. I ended up being sorry she'd ever come at all, even if she sent marvelous Christmas presents and Mama was brighter and happier whenever Granny Avi called.

Girls need their mamas, she would say, hugging me extra tight.

The driver, a stained red baseball cap firmly clapped on his balding head and a divot on his left third finger where his wedding ring should be, hummed along with Christian rock on the staticky radio, occasionally mumbling a *Praise be!* Mr. Carr had slipped him a folded bill with a meaningful look, while he took the man aside and Alex put my suitcase in the trunk. My backpack sat on my lap, and I caught myself hugging it each time I thought about where we were going.

Another turn through a gate made of high iron spikes, and a slight rise. The driveway was sealed black and glossy as the Carr's place, under a thin hazard-layer of ice and slush. I craned my neck, and there it was. Glass cubes stacked on top of each other, a chunk of expensive, soulless modern architecture. All lit up like a Christmas tree, and there was no front yard. Just concrete and a fountain, frozen into a cascade of icy spikes.

My throat went dry. I swallowed, hard, and wished I'd stayed with Libba, even if I was going to see Mama again. It surely wasn't disloyal to like another momlady that much, was it? It was just that I didn't want to see Mr. Vogg.

"Carry your stuff up to the door, Miss," the driver said, and popped the SUV into park. The huge front door was up two wide granite stairs, overhung by the first glass cube, made out of something black and shiny as well. A burst of frigid air broke the car's warm bubble, and I didn't wait for him to open my door.

My boots slipped a little, caught on the grit. I swung the door shut at the same time the driver slammed the trunk, and he clucked his tongue at me, motioning towards the door as if I was a chicken needing herding.

I don't want to go in there.

Too bad. There was nowhere else to go. And Mama—if she was in *there*, she needed me. *We girls have to stick together,* she might say.

"Unless you want me to take you back, Miss," the driver bugled at me, his nose already red from the cold.

I jumped, a little guiltily, but he paid no attention.

"Cos that's what I'm paid for, too, if you wanna go back. Mister was really clear on that."

Which Mister? As far as I knew, Mr. Vogg had called for the cab to pick me up. So I said a quiet, squeaky "Nosirthankyou," pasted on a smile that had to look sickly, and began picking my way towards the door.

It took forever, even though the footing was nice and solid. The sky was a solid iron mass again, but the snow was tapering off. Busy people were back at work now that it had warmed up, or clearing away the mess, bundled up like bears—"warming up" being, well, only a relative term. The green knitted scarf Libba had given me scratched a little, comforting, under my hair. She'd wanted me to take a matching hat, too, but I didn't.

The black door was some kind of wood, but none I'd ever seen before. I looked for the bell, found it, and was halfway to pressing it when there was a *click* and a buzz. The right half swung back, slowly, and warm electric light spilled out.

Mr. Vogg beamed at us both, the white streaks at his temples glowing. Behind him, there was a confused impression of space, light, hard glossy edges. He extended a hand, but I stepped aside, suddenly sure I didn't want him to touch me. He wasn't going for me, though. He took my suitcase, the light picking out every shabby stain and worn spot on the orange nylon, and tipped the driver a ten before stepping back hastily, as if to let me inside. "Safe and sound, thank goodness! Care for a cup of coffee, to warm up?"

"Nosir." The cabbie gave me a worried look, his bushy eyebrows drawing together, but I stepped over the threshold, and that seemed to relieve him of any responsibility. "Thank you, sir. Miss." A tug on the bill of his cap, and he crunched back towards his still-running car. The knot quivered inside me, and I suddenly knew the indentation for his wedding ring was there because his wife was gone home to Jesus and he had a daughter in college even further west, and both things occupied him so much he didn't have time for even vague suspicion at being tipped at both ends of a fare like that.

Mr. Vogg smiled, and smiled, not moving a muscle. The door moved, without his help, almost clipping my backpack. I had to skip forward a little, slipping as my wet soles squeaked on stone tiles. The foyer was all granite and marble, stairs going up on the left and a single table, what Mama would call lyre-shaped, at the end between two doorways, holding a stone vase and a spray of white flowers.

Flowers. In this weather. Even at this distance I could tell they weren't artificial. I could hear their wilting, sad little voices lost in the wide cold spaces.

The door closed, a heavy, final sound, like bowling balls clacking together. Mr. Vogg stood there grinning like a fiend, the very same wide plastic expression. I hitched my backpack higher on my shoulder and waited. Something told me opening my mouth first would be a bad idea.

We stared at each other. His gaze crawled over me, probably noting every rip and stain, even if my clothes were clean and smelled like quality now. There's a way people look at you when they can tell where you're from, if you have to prop your oven door closed with a yardstick or if you've ever sat in the dark because the power company likes to be paid and is deaf to anything but cold hard cash.

"Welcome," he finally said. "Your mother is upstairs."

That was probably the first warning I had that this wasn't just bad luck. A squirrelly trembling began inside my ribs. *I thought she was at work.*

But the boss's boss could excuse her, right?

"Come with me." He turned on his heel, a faint squeaking against the stone, and I was suddenly sure the tiles were paper-thin and when I started moving, they'd tear and I'd fall into a black pit. He set off up the stairs, the back of his gray suit jacket floating above matching pants, his shoes gloss-shiny. His hair didn't move. A ring gleamed on his right hand, pale metal and a small black stone. I caught a small, vivid red spark in those black depths, blinked and lost it. My head was closed up tight, walled off. "How are Frank and his lovely wife?"

I was going to have to talk to him. I took a step, another, cautiously, waiting for the ground to shift, then sped up when it didn't. "They're, ah, good. They send their hellos."

"So polite." A rich, burping chuckle. "I realize this is a bit... sudden. You must be feeling a little adrift."

Is that what you'd call it? "Sir?" Carefully, the same tone I used to use when I wasn't sure what Daddy wanted. Soft and as uninflected as possible, so that he wouldn't think you were "gettin' uppity."

"You'll go to a more... appropriate school when the weather cooperates. Until then, why, you'll have time to spend with your mother. She's anxious to see you. I'll show you your room—this way, my dear—and then you can see her. She's been very anxious about you."

"Sir?" I figured I could make that one word carry a lot of weight. It could be a *yes* or a *no*, or an *I'm not sure*. Or anything else. How was I going to sleep here? Why wasn't Mama the one showing me my room? What the hell was he doing, telling me where I was going to school?

How many rooms did he have for sick secretaries, even if they worked in his office? Or was he really truly sweet on Mama? It should have been good for her—a rich man in love, just like the romances with their pink and purple covers. Mama was beautiful and kind and sweet, and if anyone deserved a rich husband it was her, wasn't it? If this was a romance she'd already be happily settled.

Nobody in the romances lived in broken-down trailers or ate from cans, though.

"Here it is," he said, sweeping open a door made of dark, heavily carved wood. I caught a glimpse—a tree, it looked like, and it sent a shiver clear through me. Something about it was flat-out wrong, as if the carver had decided to make every dig with his chisel just a slight bit *off*. Not only that, but trees shouldn't...

Well, they shouldn't *leer* at you.

I shouldn't be here. A sweating, dozy certainty, as if I was sick again. I coughed, a little—the deep racking almost-retches had gone away, but my throat was still scratchy.

The carpet was cream-colored, and thick enough to lose small change in. The bed was a white-painted four-poster swathed in pink and more white, a striped comforter like a candycane and the gauzy curtains blushing. A whole bank of windows with a long, wide seat built in front of them looked out on the glassed-in pool below, a blue jewel under its clear protective shell, the rest of the yard around it smothered under white. There was a rolltop desk of pale wood with a green-shaded, antique lamp on it, a dresser of that same wood, two empty, matching bookshelves, and a mirrored closet big enough to park Alex's truck in. The bedside table was black wood—I was irrationally certain it was real for-true ebony—and held a stained-glass lamp Mr. Vogg remarked was a genuine Tiffany, whatever that meant. The closet was slightly open, and I saw hangers full of different, muted colors, enough to confuse me as Mr. Vogg put the suitcases down at the end of the bed.

"Your mother and I ordered clothes for you, since... the fire." Did he have to sound so cheerful, like he was rolling every word inside his oily mouth? Savoring each syllable of someone else's broken life. "She seemed quite happy. We're discussing colleges for you, too. We want to make sure you have *every* advantage. A young lady as smart as you are." He turned, slowly, those badger-streaks glowing. "No doubt you have questions."

The rock threatened to fill my throat up again. His paralyzing glare, as if I swallowed against the taste of dirt and stone, willing it to go away, and stared at him. He finished turning, those dark eyes aimed right at me, two gun-holes.

Shoot 'em up, Dez!

"Do they know what you really are?" My voice took me by surprise. I didn't even sound like myself. It was Mama's bright, cold *you're a stranger and going to stay that way* tone, the one she used on traveling salesman and debt collectors.

Was that a flicker of anger, crossing his wide, happy face? It vanished, and the smile was just the same. "I'm just a businessman in love, little Desiree." Lingering over my name, those lips touching every consonant and vowel, and that made me want a hot shower to wipe off the skin-crawling taking over every inch of me. "Your Mama is so very, very special. Would you like to see her now?"

That was the exact moment I realized just how trapped I was. So I looked down at my boots—even though they were new they looked shabby on the carpet; I was suddenly sure I was tracking mud and snowmelt everywhere, just like Charlie.

Except the punishment here was likely to be worse than anything Charlie Carr ever got. I could *feel* it.

You couldn't live with Daddy for as long as we had without knowing when you'd come across another man who would make you pay for smudges or breaks or just-plain-breathing. It didn't even take a special sensing, or anything Granny had taught me.

"Yes, sir," I mumbled, exactly as if he was Daddy, and I stood stock-still to let him walk heavily past me. He lingered just a little too long, right inside my personal space, then glided out into the hall.

CHAPTER TWENTY-FIVE

Warm Wax

M AMA'S ROOM WAS JUST AS SPACIOUS, but it was blue. The carpet was indigo, the waterbed covered in robin's-egg velvet, and I couldn't see what her windows looked out on because the cerulean drapes were pulled. I almost ran across the carpet and stopped dead at the side of the bed, staring down.

Mama lay on her back, which was the first wrong thing. She said it hurt too much after a long day's work, and always slept on her side. When I was a little girl I would curl up on the inside—*the little peanut inside the shell*, she'd say, and nuzzle my black hair, so much like hers. Her eyes were closed and her breathing came in long, deep swells. She was sleeping, maybe? There were roses in her cheeks, her black hair lying lustrous over the cobalt pillows, and right there on the azure-varnished nightstand was a glass cup of water and her wristwatch, dainty gold with the engraving from her grandmother, Granny Avi's mother, on the back, its ticking suddenly loud.

Daddy had never managed to break it, though he'd probably wanted to.

"Wake up, my dear," Mr. Vogg said, very quietly.

Mama's eyes opened sleepily, sightlessly. She sighed, staring at the ceiling. The rock lodged itself in my throat, dry and heavy, my breath whistling around it.

She just... she just *laid* there.

"Your daughter is here, Edie."

Her lips moved a little. That was all.

"Say hello."

"Hello." A reedy cricket-whisper from a doll's mouth. She stared at the ceiling, her gaze floaty, her blue eyes swimming a little. Refusing to focus on anything.

"Good, good. You can rest now." Mr. Vogg clasped his hands in front of him. "Desiree and I will get along so very well, don't you worry. I've already shown her the room."

What have you done to her? The words died behind the stone in my throat. Like the white egg-shaped one tucked in my backpack, the one I'd woken up clutching after dreaming of Granny Iyaga. Except that hadn't been a dream, not really.

Neither was this. I stared at Mama's face, willing her to blink, to look at me, to *recognize* me.

Nothing happened. I reached down, touched the back of Mama's hand against the velvet coverlet.

It was familiar and warm. Warm clay. The knot in my head didn't throb with the sense of... personality, maybe? Or life? Something was *gone*, and every sense in me, regular or special, knew it.

My stomach turned over, hard. Bile filled my throat; the rock right behind my voicebox was a plug holding it back. I swallowed again and again, trying to dislodge it, trying to push my stomach down.

"You'll be very happy with me here, Desiree." Lingering over my name again. "Edie and I have agreed. You'll go to school, and you will stay away from strangers and... undesirables. I have no objection to you remaining under my roof for a while. At least until we've agreed on a college for you. Education is important for a young lady."

I stared at Mama's face. No, not her face. This was a woman who looked like her, but was empty as a washed-out glass. "This isn't her." I could barely get the words out past the obstruction in my throat. At least the hot stomach-juice had retreated. "This isn't my Mama. Where is she?"

Mr. Vogg gave his hearty, well-bred chuckle, sticking his thumbs in his belt. Standing there, solid as a brick wall—or a window a butterfly would break itself against, its wings freezing as it beat ineffectually at an invisible barrier keeping it from nectar-laden flowers. "Now, now, you'll hurt her feelings! This is Edie Sarpe, your very own mother, my dear. She's simply... tired. Resting."

"What did you do to her?" The rock kept swelling, I could *taste* it, earth and minerals pressing at the back of my tongue. It made me think of the stripes in the gully wall and digging in Gran's garden in the cool of the morning. Then it soured, a damp rank smell, and I knew what I was tasting.

Deep down, we all know what grave-dirt smells like.

"Now, now, little girl." He stepped back, turned on one heel as if on parade, and clicked his heels together once. "There are things that don't concern you, and our relationship is one of them. Now, if you ladies will excuse me. I have so much to do! This weather, you know. Dinner is at six, Desiree, and I expect to see you at the table on time." He minced out, and I heard heavy footsteps in the hall before all of a sudden they cut off. The silence was a big, roaring beast, filling my head, and it occurred to me that he'd done that on purpose, so I knew he could move quietly.

When he wanted to.

My knees hit the floor next to the bed. I grabbed Mama's warm waxen hand in both of mine, put my forehead down, and tried loosening the knot inside me.

Nothing. It was like yelling down a well. Except in a well, there's an echo.

He'd had days and days of her here to do... whatever it was. How could you do this, scrape a person clean dry, hollow them out? What did you do with what you scraped out of them? Did you keep it, or did you... did you *eat* it?

Had he eaten my mama? Of just some parts of her, the parts that made her special like everyone was special? The parts that made her my *Mama*, with her way of shaking greens and stirring ravioli without breaking and her soft perfume and her cool hands that could fix any hurt and her beautiful, beautiful voice?

I sank my teeth into my lower lip, the pain a bright little star not as nice as Butch's licking but giving me something to focus on. There was Mending. I'd have to be careful. Very careful. And protect myself. I couldn't count on any help—could Gran get into this place of sharp corners and hard edges? She'd probably already helped me as much as she could, somehow breaking my fever. And the smooth white stone, would that help?

Oh Mama, I wanted to whisper. *Mama, I'm sorry. I should have made you come home.*

I should have started the Mending then. But I couldn't when I was all full of whirling and sick-scared trembling. I knelt there, next to the bed, and sobbed as quietly as I could.

• • •

WOMAN'S HERB

My head was full of cotton wool, my eyes red-rimmed, and my cheeks raw-chapped. I stared at the square black plate—even his *plates* looked expensive.

Mr. Vogg wielded a serrated knife with gusto, carving himself a bite of pink-in-the-middle steak. "Medium rare is the only way to eat, don't you agree?" He didn't wait for any answer I would have made. "Now, don't think you're in any... danger, little Desiree." A faint frown, as if his dinner wasn't all he expected. "You are... how shall I put it? Not to my tastes."

You only eat mothers? I stared at the rosemary potatoes, the strips of steak, the handful of something I only knew was arugula because Libba had put it in a salad yesterday, and Charlie had groaned like he'd found a wriggling bug on his plate. There was a dollop of dressing situated right next to it, vile yellow like a clot of infected snot.

He took a small sip from his water-glass. "Besides, you've already had some training, haven't you? You are remarkably difficult to influence."

Because of Gran, I bet. What I wouldn't give for some of her spice tea right now. She'd fix this right up, wouldn't she. An image of the snowed-in gully, the space where her trailer stood just holding a trailer-sized divot and the remains of her blanketed garden, wouldn't go away. Had she known? Did it matter? I'd known she was going to go elsewhere, probably for good. She'd finished what she set out to do, I guess.

Or she just went south for the winter, like birds were supposed to. Except all I could think was that she had gone to another place as cold as this, her trailer suddenly looking different but holding the samovar and her big bedstead and her funny handpump over the sink. I could almost see the trailer perched in a clearing near trees as big around as it was, and bigger. The signposts in that place, if there were any, would all be in that funny lettering on her favorite tea mug.

Cyrillic.

"Desiree." Mr. Vogg laid his fork and knife down, crosswise, on his plate. "Come, now. I am not a monster."

You sure do look like one from here. I shifted my gaze to the glass of milk, slightly bluish because it was skim. Had he cooked this? He didn't seem the cooking type. Who cleaned this place? Was that going to be my job?

"In fact, I think you might be quite useful. I'll bet you were only taught the, let's say, less *practical* aspects of exercising power. Am I right?"

I don't know. I shifted to staring at his plate. Imagined the steak knife rising, jetting forward, burying itself in his meaty neck. That wasn't Mending. Probably wasn't even possible. Maybe I could try?

His rich, fruity chuckle. "You'd like that, wouldn't you." A wide white grin, just caught at the top of my peripheral vision. "Imagine the blood."

A shudder went through me. The potatoes were still hot, steam lifting from their thin jackets.

He kept going, softly, inexorably. "Ah, young girls are so transparent, and so troublesome. You'll find I can be kind enough, if you don't cross me. Children need discipline, don't you agree? It's good for them. So. You will go to school. You will work diligently. You will visit your mother daily. In return, I will feed you, and shelter you, and continue to make your mother comfortable."

"Comfortable?" I couldn't help myself. *You call that comfortable?*

"She's safe, and warm. Come now, how long did you think she was going to live anyway? She was very ill."

I Mended her. I stared at him. The world had tilted sideways, and I was sliding off the surface. Ray leaving had pulled the plug out, and now I was adrift on the swirl going down a big black hole. *She was fine. I made her fine.*

"Such a pity. Very special, your mother. A bright soul, like a burning coal in the stomach. She gave birth to such wonderful children. Tell me, how is Raymond?"

I don't know. And even if I did I wouldn't tell you. I shifted back to staring at the plate in front of me. My stomach ached with hunger, and the potatoes smelled good. I wished I could drink some of the milk, at least. "He's gone."

A brief silence. I *felt* something change, like a weather front moving through. It chilled me all over. If my hair hadn't been pulled back in what Daddy always called a horsetail, it might have tried to stand up all over my head. Just like a dandelion puff.

Mr. Vogg picked up his fork and knife again. He sawed at his steak. "How troubling. Surely you have some idea where he went?"

I shook my head. The man nuzzling Ray's neck, the cataract-clouded windshield, the cold all through me—that belonged on another planet. Ray probably didn't even know the mobile had burned down. Would Alex tell him, if they ever saw each other again?

Alex. I hadn't called. Were the Carrs worrying about me? Or glad to have their house back without a guest stuck in its craw? Was the rock in my throat just a guest, instead of a permanent feature?

If I ever got rid of that rock for good, what would it feel like?

"Well." Mr. Vogg kept sawing at the steak, lifting mannerly bites of it, and chewing them with great relish. "Of course, if he wishes to visit, he's more than welcome."

I wondered what Ray would make of Mama lying there, breathing and staring, blinking slowly, then sinking back down into whatever was left of the body's processes when the person who inhabited it was... gone.

She's not gone. I can bring her back. But I've got to think. It would be easier if Mr. Vogg would just shut *up*. Every time he talked the shakes went through me.

"Or do you think your brother won't care to come? He hurt your mother very badly. No wonder she wanted... rest." Very soft and reasonable. If it wasn't for him chewing up his meat so happily, you'd think he was sad, or something. "Now you, my dear... all you want is to help your mother. Correct?"

That I could answer. So I let myself look at his face, and at his dark, dark eyes. Slightly bloodshot, fringed with black lashes, and cradled with fanlike wrinkles that looked planned, crinkles in cellophane. Didn't anyone notice how, well, *plastic* he looked? Or did they not care, because the general features were in the right place? Just like the people who can hear a woman crying through thin military housing walls, but don't say a single thing. "Yes."

He lit up, those eyes sparkling. "Then we're agreed!" Another forkful, this time of potatoes. "Do as I say, Desiree, and your mother might... regain some of her health."

A muscle in my cheek twitched. I heard Granny Iyaga, suddenly, clear as a bell, the rasp pronounced as if she'd just finished one of her pipes of sweet, strong tobacco. *Rosemary throws off evil, little Dasya. It's a woman's herb.*

I stared at him while he chewed. His expression changed slightly, and even though I was sitting there wishing something would happen, I wasn't prepared for him to suddenly choke and spit the mouthful back out, reaching for his water glass with a clawed hand. I had that same shifting, melting sensation of seeing *underneath*, the flash of whatever lived under that perfect plastic shield peeking out for a second, and it made my heart go cold and leaden inside my ribs. Time and world both skipped sideways, like I was running down the gully again, and my chair hit the ground as I was on my feet, backing up as he hacked out a few more loud coughs.

Go ahead. Choke on it. My hands were fists, but they felt like something strong and supple-scaled was writhing in them. In my *mental* fists, the ones Granny Iyaga had taught me how to make, how to use, how to *squeeze*.

I stood ten feet from the dining table's high-polished gleam, the square plaques of glass on the chandelier overhead tinkling, and when he started to laugh the sweat on me turned to ice. It was just as cold as the wind, really, but with him around, the temperature drop was all... inside. Inside your own skin.

"It's a pity you weren't born a boy." The mask was back on, and he ran his hands over his lacquer-black hair. Was I imagining it, or were the white streaks bigger now? His suit jacket was creased, too, a long wrinkle down the left side as if he'd crumpled. "You could have been very special to me indeed. As it is, I'll overlook this one incident, since you're no doubt... adjusting. Go to your room, Desiree." He laid his hands on either side of his plate. "School starts again in two days."

There was a lot that could mean, but I didn't wait to find out. I fled, and the echoes of his nasty, jolly laughter chased me all the way upstairs to the white room. The wooden chair at the desk was expensively plain, painted white, and I wedged it under the doorknob before stumbling to the closet and finding the deepest, darkest corner I could, among new clothes that smelled of sizing and yet more different fabric softener.

I cried myself into a fitful, uncomfortable, shuddering sleep.

CHAPTER TWENTY-SIX

Weak to Stand

MORNING CAME UP, bright and sparkling off all the glass and snow, a clawed fist of hunger below my ribs. I emerged from the closet-cave blinking, scrubbing my hands over my salt-slicked face. I made sure the chair was still firmly under the doorknob, even though nobody had touched the tree-carven door, and crept to the window across acres of pale carpeting.

It was just the same as it had been yesterday, except the sky was a pale, endless blue. The sun, a blank white eye, glared over the snowblanket, glittering hard and hurtful off the glass cube below with the swimming pool's blue innocence underneath, like a Lucite paperweight. A jewel within a jewel, but not sitting in some dusty thriftstore window. This was in a high-end shop where the salesladies could smell *poor* on you and followed you around, so you couldn't steal *or* wipe that sticky clear residue of poverty off on their merchandise.

The bathroom was cold and white, too. I washed my face, scrubbed to get the crusted snot from under my nose. *You're not five anymore, Dez. Come on. Tough up.*

"I need a plan," I whispered, chapped lips cracking. It was, as Ray would say, *no shit, Sherlock.*

Ray. He had to be told, and warned not to come anywhere near Mr. Vogg. Maybe he wouldn't be planning on it anyway, but the last thing I needed was him here stomping around. The badger-man would take him apart in way less time than it ever took Daddy to get Ray to cry, even.

Just be quiet. I'll protect you. Ray in the closet, whispering to me. Now it was my turn to protect him and save Mama. But *how*?

What would Granny Iyaga do? Probably just point at Mr. Vogg, sniff, and scare him so bad he'd run away screaming. Did he run, or did he waddle like a badger, too? What was the name for the thing living inside his plastic wrap? Granny would have a name for it. All I could think of was a vampire, but he didn't suck blood.

I husked out a cold laugh, swaying back and forth. My feet ached, I hadn't taken my boots off, even. I tasted blood from my lips, cupped icy, mineral-tasting tapwater in my hand and drank like a dog. Washed my face again, just for the sting of it. Better than coffee to wake you up.

With that done, I peered out into the bedroom again. The knot unloosed a fraction inside me, all through my body instead of just in my head. Bigger and stronger now, the secret knowledge was all through me. When had that happened?

Knock, knock. Anyone home?

My invisible, knowing self tiptoed invisibly through the giant house. The place's sharp edges were dangerous, so I felt around, not moving until I was certain I wouldn't brush against them. There was a warm, breathing stillness just down the hall—Mama in her bed.

Was it really her, though? Or just a doll? I couldn't *sense* her. That body on the bed, was it hers? Or some kind of mannequin, just made to look like her?

I pulled back inside myself, a snail into its safe shell. Stood at the foot of the pristine, cheesecloth-swathed candycane bed in the cold white room. Shaking, sweating like a horse.

Get moving, Dez.

What if I couldn't, though? What if I just stood here until I was too weak to stand, then curled up on the floor? Would he come in to force food down my throat?

No, he'd probably like it if I laid down and died. There wouldn't be anyone stopping him from... what? What did he *want*? He already had Mama on that bed, breathing and just *lying* there, like an empty piñata. If I didn't get out of here, he could do the same thing to me.

Why hadn't he, though?

It's a pity you weren't born a boy. Would Granny have taught a boy?

I swayed a little, hyperventilating, and the lightheadedness threatened to swallow me.

My backpack, lying on top of my battered orange suitcase, looked like a dark mouth when I opened it. I dumped my textbooks on the bed, my notebooks, all the trash that accumulated when you trudged from class to class. Chewed-up pencils and little Ziplocs with the remains of my peanut-butter sandwiches in them, my keyring—I stuffed the key back in, along with my wallet, and began choosing what clothes I could from my orange suitcase.

Everything had burned, and I was going to leave even more behind now. *It can't be helped. Come on. Move.*

I did.

• • •

FAMILY BUSINESS

It had thawed a little, but warming is only relative when you have no place to go and your Mama is just a breathing doll. I made my way through the quiet, empty house, out through the front door—I didn't bother trying to figure how to lock it behind me—and down the long, tar-black driveway. It took me a few minutes of watching the iron gates, my heart racing, before I saw they were just ajar, not closing, no matter how they quivered.

The wind had veered around, and my breath didn't turn into a white cloud. I stood at the very end of the driveway, shivering, my fists knotted tight in my green mittens, and heard a low, persistent drilling whistle. My heart sped up even further, because I knew the mouth that made it, narrow like a single blade of grass, and I knew his pale, narrow hands, their fingers innocent of any ridges or whorls, were clenched too.

He hadn't been able to get close to me all this time, the whistling man, but he was still hanging around. Like a bad habit, or a nightmare biding its time.

I jolted forward, my bootsoles slipping on suddenly-slick sealed concrete, a thin scrim of melt turning it treacherous as a greased mirror. The only thing worse than ice is when it turns sloppy with water over the top; I scrambled like a cartoon rabbit as the gates made a groaning, rusty chuckle, their trembling intensifying. Just like a pair of hands, teasing the little animal trapped between them.

They began to close as I ran, everything slowing to a white nightmare, a harsh cawing sound of effort wringing out of my chest. The whistle peaked, my boots suddenly grabbed, and I shot through, one of the gates kissing my shoulder and almost knocking me off my feet. They clanged shut, a Venus flytrap made of black metal, but I was pelting down the middle of the scraped-clean street, mountains of plowed-aside snow on either side, and I didn't even notice the red Toyota until it locked its brakes and slid, its hind end coming around with slow, majestic inevitability. A woman with perm-frizzed red hair, whiteknuckle grasping the wheel as her mouth lengthened into an *O* of surprise, jammed on the brakes and the slide sped up. I aimed for where the car *was*, fixed my staring gaze, and *ran*. Breath tearing in my throat, the back end of the car missing me by a prayer-breath because it had continued moving, my boots suddenly gripping, a funny floating feeling all through me. I tore down the middle of the street even faster, and it was a pure miracle there weren't any other cars, because luck—or whatever that was—wouldn't have saved me again.

Also because I was screaming, the cry dying as it hit the snow-mountains on either side but bouncing off the scraped, icy pavement. A long trailing yell that only ended when I ran out of air, shot across an intersection at the bottom of the hill, and had to whoop in a knife-cold breath and keep running, keep running, keep running.

• • •

Downtown in a strange icy funhouse, hungry and cold, nowhere to go, nobody to turn to—I wandered for a while, my head down, watching the pavement. Down here the sidewalks were scraped or scattered with rock salt, and the towering buildings sang under the wind. They were teeth so big all sorts of little fish could swim between them, cleaning industriously and eating the waste from a big wallowing city-predator. Thin spots of sunshine managed to slip between glass and iron ribs, shattering on ice. You could almost see the skyscrapers sway, and where the sunlight hit, curls of steam rose.

Finally, it got too cold to just wander, and I began to look around. Even in this weather there were people walking, mostly men. Cars crept on the other side of snowplow mountains, and nobody noticed me. I almost walked right past a bus stop, put on the brakes, and stepped into the Plexiglass almost-cube. The breeze fell off, but I could still hear a tune being whistled, faint and faraway, fading in and out like static on the radio.

It was one of Mama's favorites, about silver threads and golden needles, and how you couldn't buy her love. I was so cold I wasn't even shivering, again, and I stared fixedly at the transit map. The next bus was due in five minutes. If I stayed on it, there was the transit center...and then, maybe I could find a route that would take me... where?

I know where. But how would I *find* it?

The whistling tune faded into a blur. I swayed a little, and when the bus heaved along it was a good thing it was a free ride zone, because my fingers wouldn't work and my backpack felt frozen to my shoulders. It was warm and odorous in the bus; the shaking and jolting bumped everything loose inside me. I kept wiping at my cheeks, even though I wasn't crying—my eyes were dry and hard as the rocks on the banks when the creek turned into a trickle.

It was there, staring at the condensation on the windows, that the rest of the plan came into place. It was so stupid-simple, I wondered why I hadn't thought of it before.

• • •

I dialed carefully, rehearsing what I wanted to say in a whisper. She picked up on the third ring.

"Hi, Mrs. Carr." I couldn't call her *Libba*. Not anymore. "I'm sorry I didn't call."

A splash, and plates rubbing together, as if she was doing the dishes. "Oh, don't worry, honey. Jim called to let us know you got there okay. He says your mother caught that awful flu, how is she?"

He ate her insides. "Still sick." I struggled with the urge to tell her something, anything, but the thought of what Mr. Vogg could do to *her*... no. Just no.

"There's a lot of noise on the line. Are you outside?" Now she sounded curious, and just on the edge of concerned.

Moms have radar. I had to get past her quick, before she cottoned on. "I decided to go for a walk." Lame, but I couldn't think of anything else. "Is Alex there?"

"He sure is. Want to talk to him?"

A burst of relief. I'd fooled her. "Yes, please."

Shuffling, more dishes clinking, Butch's excited yipping, the faint tinny echo of Charlie yodeling as he galumphed through the house. I squeezed my eyes shut.

"Hey, Dez." Warm and comforting. "How are you? Want to hang out?"

I can't. "Maybe tomorrow. I actually... I need a favor, Alex. A big one."

"Sure. Anything." So easily, the two words fell out of his mouth.

"It's about Ray."

A crackling silence. A bus rattled past, I kept my eyes shut.

Finally, he spoke again. "Are you outside?"

"Please, Alex. I need his phone number, or that man Stark's. Mama's sick. Ray needs to know."

"Dez..."

"I know about him and Stark, Alex." *And you probably did too.* "Please. I know you have his number. *Please.*"

Still, he hesitated. "Where are you, Dez? You sound... upset."

"*Please*, Alex."

"Okay. Hang on a second." His familiar footsteps heading away. Charlie was still yelling.

Hurry up. I only have a few more quarters.

It seemed to take forever. But he came back, finally, and picked up the phone. "Okay. I've got it. Look, Dez, where are you? I'll come get you, I'll take you there myself."

Oh, that will go over really well. "It's okay, Alex. It's family business. Stay home." *Where you're safe.* If I showed up with Alex, Ray would just *explode*. God only knew what would happen if Alex stepped into Mr. Vogg's house, too.

"You're practically family now." He said it like it was possible. "Mom's worried."

I winced. "Tell her not to be. I'm okay."

He was unconvinced. "You don't sound okay."

"Sorry. It's just... Mama, you know? Can you give me the number?"

He did. My fingers cramped, the ink in my pen sluggish, but I got it scrawled in my History notebook.

"Stark's a drinker." A world of meaning in those three words. Everything from *that's no place for a girl* to *I want to know what's going on.* "I'll come get you, we can go there together."

"No, Alex." I didn't mean to sound sharp, but maybe I did. I tried to scrape up a gentler tone. "Sorry. I just... I don't think it's a good idea."

Did he flinch, hearing me say it this time?

"You can't do everything by yourself."

Watch me. "I'm sorry." What was I apologizing for? I didn't even know. It was cold, and I was tired. It was already afternoon, and when night came, I didn't want to be outside.

I wanted to be *home*, but I couldn't sleep in a smoking, burnt-out shell, now could I? And Gran was gone. Maybe she'd be back in the spring, maybe not. Either way, I was what Daddy used to call *shit outta luck*, it would be too late to save Mama.

Alex's sigh was a gust of static. "I love you, okay? Let me *help*."

For a second I was sure I hadn't heard him right. Then the warmth began, right in the center of me. It flooded out, and for a few seconds I actually thought of telling him... well, not all, but some of it. He'd come and get me, Libba and his dad would ask questions, and maybe I wouldn't have to live with the badger-man.

But Mama. And Ray.

"If you could help," I said, softly and slowly, "I'd ask. But you can't, Alex. I'm sorry." Then I might have made a mistake. Because I said, "I love you too."

I hung up. Stood there for a few minutes, shaking, the warm gooshy feeling fighting with a wind that had lost a few teeth but still had plenty of bite left.

Then I fed the last of my quarters in, and called Ray.

CHAPTER TWENTY-SEVEN

Smoking Cheap

I DIDN'T MEAN TO START CRYING AGAIN. But as soon as I saw the Camaro, its chains biting melting ice and its windshield a familiar eye, a hitching sob worked its way out. I almost tripped running to get to the passenger side door. He leaned over to unlock it, I dropped into the familiar seat, and the heater was on blast. He didn't have tissues, but there were fast-food napkins in the glove compartment, like usual. I dabbed at my raw face, blew my nose with a honk, and the Camaro's purring heartbeat closed around me, warm and safe.

Ray didn't waste any time. "Why ain't you in school?"

Oh, for God's sake. But he didn't know *anything*, he'd been gone all this time. I tried to figure out where to start, my throat closing around its familiar rock. I honked into another napkin, balled it up in my fist, and began to stammer that the mobile had burned down, Mama was sick, and that man, that man—

"What man?"

"Vogg. The one with the badger stripes in his hair."

"Him?" Ray stared at the road like it personally offended him. "What the hell does he have to do with anything?"

"Mama's living with him." I couldn't tell him the rest.

He wouldn't believe me.

"You said she's sick."

She just lays there. "She can't even get out of bed."

Ray feathered the accelerator. He looked like he knew where we were going. Thank God *someone* did. "Did he..."

I knew what he wanted to ask, and the relief of talking to someone who could *understand*, at least a little, was overwhelming. "I don't know," I whispered. *He did worse than Daddy ever did.*

"And you can't stay there." Flatly, with a heavy sigh. "What about..." Slowing down, the thought trailing off as he negotiated a turn. "Weren't you at Alex's?"

"I can't stay there either. They'll send me to *him*." Why did it feel like he was trying to get rid of me? At least now I'd find out where he was working.

Or so I thought. I blew my nose *again*, wondering if I was going to dissolve in a river of snot.

"I'll talk to them. How long were you waiting there?"

"Aw-w-w-while." Now I was shivering. "Ray—"

"You're lucky I was home." He looked different now. All the softness had left his face; a bluish sheen of five-o-clock shadow on his cheeks.

Just like Daddy's. With his blue eyes narrowed and his mouth pulled tight, you could see it. His cheekbones were Mama's, high-arched, and his lashes were too. But his jawline was heavy, and it seemed like his eyes had drawn a little closer together and lightened past Mama's bright summer-sky blue to a colder shade.

Don't turn into Daddy, Ray. I need you too much. "I m-missed you."

"Missed you too, kid." He fished in his coat pocket, dragged out a cigarette, and popped the lighter in. "You can sleep in my room. Tomorrow we'll figure out what to do."

"Thanks."

"You hungry?"

I realized I hadn't eaten in forever. "A little." It was warm in here, and funny to feel the ground slip away so easily underneath. When you walked all the time, you sort of forgot what a car could do.

"Okay." The lighter leapt out with a click that scared me half to death, and he glanced sideways at me, a considering look. "Jesus. Dez, did he—this Vogg guy—did he... *do* anything to you?"

Black boiling revulsion speared me. "N-no. I p-put a chair in f-front of my door."

"But you think he might, if you stay there?"

Yeah, but not in the way you might think. "I know he will. Ray—"

"Okay." His tone warned me. It was Daddy's *don't you say another word, missy,* but not the mean one. In the breathless, scary way that meant Daddy's ire wasn't going to fix on you, but it could if you made a wrong move. The best thing to do was to freeze and let it pass overhead, like weather.

He lit his American Spirit—at least he wasn't smoking cheap, Mama might be proud if she wouldn't be mad at him smoking at all—and cracked his window. The Camaro wallowed a bit, but the chains held her down.

I was just so relieved to see him I didn't even care that the static was settling over him, that black, black anger. It was familiar, like an old coat, so I welcomed it.

· · ·

STARK

He pulled up in front of a long row of brick townhouses, squeezed together like base housing, and I swallowed a surprised blurt of *this wasn't where you were before.* Reversing into a parking spot like he'd done it a million times, his arm over the back of the seat and his smoke-tarnished breath against my wet hair, I almost tried to believe he was Alex. Or that he was the old Ray-Ray, the sweet brother who had taught me how to build a ship with Legos and held my hand on the first day of kindergarten, while Mama held the other. Sandwiched between them, I'd felt safe.

Now I felt a little safer than I had, and it was such a kneeshaking relief I wasn't sure I could stand up.

"Home sweet home," he muttered, his chin not thrust so far forward now. "Come on in. I've got Ramen."

"It looks nice," I managed, clutching my backpack. Everything I owned in the world, now. I was travelin' light, as Daddy would say.

"Should be, for what I pay." His chin dipped.

"I thought you were living with... someone else."

He glanced at me, reaching for the door lock, and I wished I could swallow the words.

"Who told you that?" Suddenly wary.

Oh, Lord. A whistling man showed me. "Well, the rent here... you must need roommates."

"Yeah, well." The wariness folded away. "I do some work around the place and they give me a break on the rent. Still high, though. All I've got is noodles and milk."

That curdled the hunger claw-kneading the inside of my stomach. I was full of all sorts of things—fear-fumes, rocks, that spiked ball under my ribs. "I'll get a job."

He didn't roll his eyes, just gave me a brief, paralyzing glance. "You're going back to school. Come on."

I don't want to go back to school. But I followed. I was already starting to get the idea that Ray's idea of helping me out wasn't going to be what I wanted.

I couldn't even name what I wanted. What would he believe about Granny Iyaga, about the mending, about the whistling man, about Mr. Vogg? If I took him to the sharp-edged house, would Mama be up and moving around, speaking in that slurred voice? Would Ray even notice anything *wrong*? Would he think she was just drunk, would they have another fight? Could I get her out of that house and then...

Everything dried up inside me. I was about at the end of my rope.

The door at the end, with a chrome 7 hanging on it, dripped, loosening a vertical sheet of ice from the frozen rain congealed on it. "They say it'll warm up. Weather station's going nuts over it. Sudden thaw." He dug in his pocket for keys, and his boots were splattered with oil, no longer new.

"I hope it does."

"Lots of fender benders. Good money to be made." He shoved black hair out of his eyes, a familiar, irritated motion, and I could have cried with relief, because that was the old Ray, the one I knew.

"I guess so." A glass of milk sounded really good right about now.

A car door slammed, and Ray stiffened, whirling. I turned too, my heart suddenly in my throat and my hands turning to fists inside my green mittens.

It wasn't Vogg. It was a bandy-legged man who looked familiar, his cowboy boots scraping on ice as he hurried across the parking lot.

"Shit," Ray muttered. "Go inside, Dez."

"You got a girlfriend now, Ray?" The man's laugh, a nasty deep sound, bounced off the blank row of beige houses and the cracked parking lot. A thin screen of nervous, shivering pines crowded this side of the row, probably as a windscreen. "Look at you. Bet you don't remember your old friends, now do you, boy?"

"Get inside." Ray drew himself up and pushed past me, blue eyes lightening dangerously. He looked even more like Daddy now, and it would have scared me to death if I hadn't already been terrified. "What the hell are you doing here, Stark?"

"Just wanted to come see you. I got a right to come see a little fagboy if I want to, don't I? Who's that? You decided you like girls now?" The man grinned, a hard-lipped, nicotine-stained smile, and I finally placed him again.

I'd watched through the foggy windshield of a truck that shouldn't have been running, while he kissed my brother's neck.

"This is my sister, Stark. Not that it's any of your goddamn business. Go away."

"Well, since I got fired, there ain't no place for me to be. Sister, huh? That what you're telling everyone?" Another harsh laugh. "Bet she don't know what you *really* like."

The images came, crowding one after another, like he *wanted* them to fill up my head, like this bandy-legged man wanted to show me nasty things he'd imagined doing with Ray—or hadn't imagined. They poured into my aching head, and all of a sudden I was *furious*. I had Mr. Vogg to contend with and Mama to save, and this guy just wanted Ray to... what?

"*Stop it!*" It burst out of me, shrill and surprising, the rock in my throat magically sliding aside. The words shimmered, streaking past Ray, and hit the man square in the chest.

He actually staggered, his bootsoles slipping, and meanness I didn't know I had inside me rose up hot and acid.

Sonofabitch! I heard Daddy hiss inside my head, all one word, with the black nasty that meant he wasn't sober enough to be sloppy-kind or drunk enough to dodge. It came out through my mouth too, a sliding baritone scorching my mouth with the taste of Jim Beam and Pall Malls.

Ray said something, the man Stark's mouth contorted, and I trembled on the edge of unleashing that fiery clot of acid.

My Vasyas and my Dasyas, though, they are not so common. Would she be disappointed in me? Like Mama probably was, if she could feel at all?

Ray poked at the man's chest, driving him back another step. The noise got worse and worse. I was cold, and starving, and the black stormcloud wasn't just around my brother. It wrapped around me, too, whispering, fingering at my skin, brushing all over me, scary-delicious.

Look, it said. *Look at this.*

The man's heart was weak. Part of it was a congenital defect, the rest was black spots of disease. I could *see* it, gristle and muscle pumping along, the arteries around it hardening, a map like the city's concrete veins. The knot inside me turned over, flushing black and red. So easy, just to push and watch him turn purple, flop to the ice-packed parking lot floor, thrash like a fish. There were other things I could do, too—weak spots in the blood vessels. I could turn all his liquids loose, and his body would take care of the rest.

And nobody, nobody at all, would suspect a thing.

Thump, thump. Blunt snouts hitting glass. "Get out of here," I snarled, and it was Daddy's voice again, scraping and burning its way loose.

Ray lunged forward, almost slipping; I lunged too and caught him, dragged him back. Stared at Stark, whose pupils had dilated so big his eyes looked black.

Two harsh coughs, smoker's hacks, chuffed out between my lips. It was a good thing I hadn't eaten anything, because bile whipped up, burning the back of my nose. Stark stumbled back, almost fell straight on his ass, and my harsh disdainful laugh cracked all the ice between us, spiderwebs of force running through the scarred, solid water. They curved, just like a knotted, veiny, ancient hand, and clutched at his heels as he ran for his truck.

I closed my eyes, because if I kept looking, I wouldn't just scare the man. A truck door slammed, an engine gunned, and I thought maybe Stark was going to try to run us both over.

Ray, shouting, leaning forward against my grip. *"Yeah, you better go! Get the fuck out of here! Go on! You* better *run!"*

But no. The truck—a battered Chevy purring like a big tiger kitten, because Ray had probably done some work on the engine—fishtailed out of the lot, almost took the stop sign with it, and tore off down the two-lane highway.

Not fast enough, though. He wasn't quite out of sight when I cracked my eyelids open, afraid I was going to fall down and break my own skull like a rotten egg. I caught one last glimpse of the blue paint, the license plate, and a soft, hissing noise echoed in my throat.

The Chevy's back end fishtailed, something dark and crackling holding onto the fender with claw-knotted hands.

Ray thought *he'd* scared the man off, all by his lonesome.

I didn't tell him otherwise. I was too tired.

CHAPTER TWENTY-EIGHT

Broken Places

"**I** GOT A SLEEPING BAG. Let me get it." He hadn't stopped fussing since we got inside.

"It's fine." My stomach, sloshing-full of Ramen and two glasses of milk, was a warm lump inside me. The headache had gone down, and I felt... well, not fine, but okay. Sort of.

Not really. But better. Problems can shrink a bit when you get some food in you, and when you're finally somewhere safe.

Or just safe enough.

"It might get cold." He pulled the blankets up a little more. This was his twin mattress, set in the precise middle of the empty bedroom upstairs, probably so nothing could sneak up on him.

I could relate.

He rattled around in here like a pea in a can, and I could see why they didn't charge him full rent—the place was falling down. The glass door to a sad slice of concrete "backyard" had to be forced shut with a broomstick in the rails, the oven didn't work but the stove could be coaxed, there was no fridge. Just an empty spot where one used to sit, and he hadn't cleaned out the spot yet, so it was a solid mat of fuzzy black with old primary-colored magnet letters you teach little kids to read with poking through, plastic gems caught in sludge. He kept the milk cold by putting it between the inner and outer metal-framed windows.

The bathroom downstairs stayed closed, but the one upstairs was sparkling. I finally had dry clothes on, and my toes were starting to warm up.

"I'm *fine*," I repeated. "I don't want you to freeze. You can have some of the blankets."

"I'm okay." Sitting crosslegged on the greasy nylon carpet, the weak bare bulb overhead glinting on his messy hair, he didn't look quite so grown-up now. Not so much like Daddy. "I guess you want to know about Stark."

No. I don't. "It's okay."

"Dez..." He kept messing with the pink blanket. It smelled a little, and I was suddenly sure he'd been dumpster diving. Why couldn't he have just stayed home? Resentment, bright purple, swelling inside me. It was hard to keep the knot inside me flipped right-side up, its curves soft and helpful instead of... the other.

The worst thing was, it had been so *easy*. Not like mending. No, the bad stuff was like sliding down a melting hillside.

Little drips and drops of water plinked outside. It was still warming up. Maybe it would just get sloppy and freeze again, and we'd have to stay here for another day or two. He couldn't pass me off on anyone if nobody could travel.

The pillow didn't smell familiar. Nothing was familiar, except him. Or maybe just parts of him. I worked one hand out from under the blankets and the mismatched sheets, trying not to think about where he might have gotten the mattress from. My fingers slid through his, and I held his hand. Warm and familiar, again, the fingers I knew almost as well as my own.

It was *inside* where he was different, or maybe I was. We'd grown away from each other. The thought that maybe we *hadn't* been as close as I thought was awful, and quickly shoved away.

Do you ever really know someone? Even if you're related to them? Or married to them?

Raymond's face crumpled briefly, smoothed out. "He threw me out," he said, finally. "When I didn't want to... I just didn't want to do some things, so he threw me out. But I got lucky with this place. I'm never going back."

"Good." Part of me wanted to ask what *things* he was talking about. The rest of me tightened up the knot in my head and was grateful I was too tired to even hear the whistling man. "Maybe we can go get Mama. Bring her here." *All I have to do is figure out how to bring her back.*

I had an idea. The sickstone, hard and white and impenetrable. Like an egg. It hadn't been Granny doing that. In my dozy half-awake way, I'd done something. Maybe what I'd coughed up could help her.

"She'd hate it." Hunching his shoulders. The shearling jacket was new, and it looked warm. "But we could fix things, I guess. We're good at that."

I nodded. My eyelids were made of lead. "We are." Always painting, sanding, jury-rigging, putting things back together. Glueing, patching, mending. When you landed in the broken places, you figured it out.

That was probably why I felt so weird at the Carr house. Everything there worked like it should, or they bought a new one. So easy, just to discard the broken stuff. Nothing stayed long, unless it was the Antiques. *Those* were different, the expensive things that didn't break badly enough to be replaced.

Ray sighed, again. It was a very Mama-ish sigh. "Tomorrow I'll call Alex."

That was the very last thing I wanted. "Don't. Please."

"You could do worse, Dez. They're nice people."

And we're not? "Will you help me go get Mama? Get her away, bring her here?" *Rescue her?*

Ray made a little shaking motion with his head. Not quite a *no*, just a thinking movement. "You think she'd come?"

"She will."

"She never left *him*."

I stared at the blurring ceiling. A damp spot in the corner, come spring it would probably widen by leaps and bounds. "Maybe she wanted to." *She had us, too. How much did we weigh her down?*

Were we the reason she stayed? Or maybe just me, since Ray's older?

I didn't know, and if I kept thinking about it, the knot would probably show me.

"But she didn't *do* it." Ray slid his hand free, almost roughly. "Get some sleep. I'll take you to that Vogg's house if you want, but if Mama won't come I'm not waiting. I'll drive you to Alex's after that and talk to his dad."

Big man now, aren't you. It was a nasty thought, and one I was slightly ashamed of. But it was what I had wanted, right? Someone else to help. Once Ray was there, it would be easier to call Mama back. She had to be inside that warm, pliant, waxen body somewhere. She just *had* to be.

Ray thumped down the stairs, avoiding the loose one with a leap, and my eyes fell all the way closed.

• • •

INTO MY PARLOR

The day the world ended began with a gray, pearly morning, full of slosh and slush. I still had the address, written down for the cabbie in Libba—no, in *Mrs. Carr's* pretty handwriting, her purple ink. It took a while, threading through downtown to get to the edges of the rich section. It looked different from inside the Camaro's safe embrace. Had I just not noticed the sidewalks while running? They were scrape-shoveled and wet-looking today, the snowplow mountains sagging. It wasn't like anyone walked out here, though. You could just tell the rolling pavements were for show, or for strolling in the summer.

Ray's expression went through surprise, incredulity, straight into wariness. "Holy shit. That's it?"

"Yeah." I shivered, stared at the open gate. It wasn't moving this time. Beyond it, the wide expanse of coal-black driveway shimmered. The clouds were breaking up, midmorning sunshine sinking into that glossy black without a murmur. It was just the shade of Mama's hair, but without the blue sheen and the sheer soft life that filled her. Little curls of steam rose from bare patches on roofs, and Ray nosed the Camaro cautiously through the gate. I watched, but the iron bars didn't move even though my shoulder throbbed from their negligent kiss yesterday.

I took a deep breath. "I'll go in and get Mama."

A sideways look, Ray weighing me in a way he never had before. "You have a key?"

"The door's not locked." *And if it is, I'll burn it right out.* The knowledge sat right behind my breastbone, an uncomfortable, red-hot coal.

Like a burning coal, Vogg's voice hissed. What if Mama had the same way of knowing I did, but there hadn't been a Granny to teach her? Maybe that was what Vogg scraped out of her. I could almost imagine him swallowing glowing-red chunks, settling in his iron-kettle stomach. How long would something like that take? How long would it fuel him?

"Wow. He leaves his door unlocked? Someone's gonna rob the place." Was that grudging respect in Ray's voice?

"In this neighborhood?" *And who would ever steal from him?* I shuddered at the thought.

"Does he have a security system?"

Why do you care? "I don't know. I wasn't taking notes."

"I should come in with you." Now Ray was looking starry-eyed. His raw-washed hands, engine grease lingering under his nails, were tight on the wheel.

"What about keeping the car running?" *And I don't want you to see me do anything... weird.*

"You act like we're robbing a bank."

"We kind of are. Only we're taking Mama."

He sighed, set the parking brake, patted his pocket for a cigarette. "Get going, then."

"Okay. Wait for me, okay?"

"I *will*. Jesus."

I unlocked the door. Swallowed hard. "Ray?"

"Huh?" He bent over the steering wheel, craning to see through the top of the windshield, examining the glass cube.

I leaned over, pressed my lips to his shaven cheek. Under the tang of cigarette smoke and mildew, he still smelled like my brother. A little older now, a little more acrid with puberty finished, but still him. It was pretty comforting. "Thanks."

That got me one of his patented eyerolls. "I'm your brother, Dez. Move it, I've gotta work this afternoon."

If I'd have known... but I didn't. I got out of the car, made my shaking legs carry me up those sharp-edged stairs, and edged up to the massive doors.

I was right. They were unlocked.

It was warm inside, but I couldn't stop shivering. The knot unloosed a little bit, taking in the entire edifice. Nothing but emptiness, and expensive and cloying deodorants to cover up any messy trace of life. Even at the Carr's you could smell dog and the funk of young males, it was nothing like this awful... vacancy, I guess, is the word that applies. Like the whole place was just a stage set for some horrible, pretentious play.

I edged up the stairs and down the hall, the shaking getting worse all through me as I passed the door to the white bedroom. The tree on what remained of its surface writhed a little, because the door itself hung on its hinges, quivering a little just like me. It had been shattered, paler wood inside peeking outside the splintered paint, only suggestions of the branches remaining. My heart galloped thinly behind my ribs.

"Mama?" A breathless whisper. Could I hear her? I didn't *feel* anything, even that sense of an echoing, breathing warmth. "Mama, it's me, it's Dez. Mama?" *I've come to rescue you. We'll get out to the car, and then—*

The blue bedroom's door was wide open too, even though it wasn't broken. I stood on the threshold, staring.

Soft, twilit dark, because the heavy drapes were drawn, sealing the huge windows. How could such a big room suddenly feel so choking-small, again? The rock was back in my throat. Impelled, I crossed the carpeting, moving so silently, the emptiness all around me.

No.

My hands on the heavy drapes. Pushing them open and looking down. *Compelled* to look down.

The pool was below, a blue glimmer. I looked, and through the iceflowers dotting the glass roof I could see a dark shape, floating in the jewel-toned water. Long black hair, the sodden cloth of a white dress swaying around the rest of the corpse, making it a mermaid.

Oh God. God, no. "Mama?" A bird's piping murmur.

"She went for a swim," Mr. Vogg said, from the corner. The two white streaks in his hair were there, painted on the air. He just *appeared*, resolving out of nothingness and shadow. "There was nobody here to help her."

Adrenaline jolted through me, and I jumped. I might have screamed, but my throat was a pinhole. My shoulder rammed the window, another bruise to add to my collection, and just then...

A slam, downstairs. "Dez?" Ray's voice, floating up on a draft of warm air. "Come on, get Mama, and let's go."

"Oh, *good*," Mr. Vogg breathed, and he streaked past me, faster than anything human could move. The world turned over, pain blossoming up the side of my head—he'd hit me, just backhanded me as casually as Daddy might have. "Come into my parlor."

The badger-man's laugh receded down the hallway. I fell, curtain material ripping and tangling all around me. My head bounced off the carpeting, and my ears filled up with rushing noise.

From a long way away, Ray started to scream.

CHAPTER TWENTY-NINE

A Hard Fall

THE CURTAINS WERE ALIVE. Slipper-slithery velvet fat and sickeningly flexible, trying to wriggle under me while I thrashed. I tore at them, black flowers blooming across my vision until I remembered I had to *breathe* and smelled the dusty, nasty rasping of something scaled that had crawled into a hole to die. It wasn't the dry, alien scent of a healthy animal; mental images of roiling white maggots and rotting meat filled my head.

Now, Dasya. Scream.

I might not have, but it was Gran's no-nonsense tone, with the edge of *you'd better* underneath it. Funny how I could be afraid of her, and afraid of Daddy, but the two fears weren't at all the same. The curtains hesitated, probably not used to prey that fought back, and it was that hesitation that probably saved me.

I screamed, my throat feeling twice its regular size for once, and what came out was a high-pitched drilling noise. The window flexed, then creaked, and a crack ran up its water-clear center. The curtains tightened, trying to get my arms locked to my sides, I thrashed some more and heard material rip.

CRACK. A terrific noise, shards of glass falling, the curtains yanked out through the hole, catching on jagged edges and shredding. I heard, clear as day, the whistling that meant someone else was hanging around.

He can't come in. Get Raymond. He's in trouble.

It took me two tries to get my legs under me and monkey-scramble for the door. My parka was shredded, carpet and curtain burns on my cheek and hands. I tumbled through the door right before it slammed shut, barking me on the ankle. I cried out, a hoarse little whimper, and Ray's scream ended on a choked gurgle.

No. No no no no no.

"*Come to Daddy,*" the badger-thing crooned. "*Be a good little boy and come to Daddy.*"

"RAY!" I screamed. "*Ray no fight him, you've got to fight him!*"

But oh God, would he know *how*? I hadn't told him anything, even if he wouldn't have listened I should have *tried*, and now it was clear how stupid I'd been.

We weren't his real targets, Mama and me. He'd been after Ray all along, and I was just bait. I'd done exactly what he wanted, and brought my brother here.

Pity you weren't born a boy.

"RAY!" I kept screaming, tumbling down the hall that suddenly stretched and yawed like a funhouse. *She went for a swim.* Had Vogg taken Mama down to the pool, guided her head underwater?

Had she struggled at all?

My fault. The stairs were treacherous, each one slick as glass or turning to soft mush. I hit the banister, bounced back into the wall, tripped, and landed on the marble floor at the bottom with a nasty *crunch* reverberating all through me.

Did I break something? I scrambled up, because now I could see Ray, lying on his stomach, scrabbling to get away from the badger-thing-man crouching over him. Its claws came down, sinking into Ray's back, and my brother screamed again, a rabbit's cry. Wide white-ringed eyes, I don't know if he saw me. I don't know if he knew I was trying to help him.

I hope he did.

"Little lion," the thing whispered, with its taffy-stretching mouth. "Over soon, little lion."

"Get *AWAY* from him!" This time, it wasn't Daddy's voice. It was Mama's, with the snap of command she rarely used. The one time I'd heard her talk like this was when a teacher wanted to put Ray in special ed, and the principal had agreed because he was Acting Up, but Mama wasn't having any of that. Slightly smoke-roughened, Mama's contralto poured out like fierce honey, and for a moment I could even smell her. Salt and Virginia Slims and fried food, like she'd been working at the diner all day, her cool white hands and her pretty, swinging hair, her red sweater and her quick footsteps, her kiss on the forehead when she tucked us in. "*You get away from my boy, you son of a bitch!*"

The thing tumbled away, howling, leaving long black streaks on the marble. The entire place was shaking, the chandelier overhead tinkling an off-key, jangling little sharp-edged song. Slivers and patters of glass spattering from the ceiling, I made it to Ray on my knees, keeping an eye on the badger-cloud as it writhed against the cold stone. "*You stay away from him!*" I barked again.

"Mama?" Ray's voice, high and dazed, wondering. My hands had turned into claws too, Granny Iyaga's capable, age-veined hands. I hauled on his jacket. *Why did you have to come in, stupid? Why did I have to bring you here?*

I dragged him, or tried to. Somehow I got him upright, and we stumbled drunkenly for the door. The house shivered again, all sorts of noise as glass shattered, and I didn't look back.

If I had, I might have been prepared. But we spilled out into milky-weak winter sunshine, Ray yelping as the steps cut at us both. Snot filling my nose, the cold all through me, but I fished in his pocket for the car keys.

Blood trickled from Ray's nose, glass glittered in his hair, and he looked vacant, his jaw working a little as if he thought he was talking. I was figuring he'd be in no shape to drive, but he got up when I pulled at him and we made it to the Camaro.

I slammed the passenger door just as a thick burping chuckle exhaled from the shuddering house. Stillness fell, my breath turning to a cloud as I jogged around the car, the keys jingling in my fist. Ray wasn't going to be happy about me driving the Camaro, but oh well.

Dropping into the driver's seat, jamming the key for the ignition, my breath coming in huge heaving gulps. "OhGod," I whispered, in between each heave. "OhGod, ohGod, oh *God*."

Ray said nothing. He didn't even reach for his seatbelt.

The engine caught, I twisted the wheel, and the gates didn't try to close to keep us in. Had Vogg just wanted me scared before? Scared enough to run for Ray?

Well, I was. I was *plenty* scared. But I was also past fear, in that funny place where nothing matters but getting you and your own out of danger.

Had Mama ever felt like this?

"Oh God," I whispered. "Please don't be gone. Please don't be gone."

There was only one person who could help me now.

• • •

HURT WHEN YOU MUST

By the time I bounced into a familiar turn the Camaro was running on fumes, Ray's eyes had half-closed, and a string of drool slid down from the corner of his mouth. I should have stopped the car and done something, anything, but I was what Mama and Marcie would have called, with an eyeroll and a grin, On A Mission.

Oh but the thought of Mama hurt. The dark blot in the blue jewel of the pool, just... floating, in its cloud of white lace. Had he dressed her in a wedding gown?

That was the last pretty day of my life, Mama had said once, grinding out her cigarette in an ashtray while she talked to Marcie, the night after the military funeral for Daddy. She hadn't known I was awake to hear, and Marcie's reply had floated up the stairs while Ray snored in his bedroom.

Oh, honey, there are other pretty days ahead.

I swiped at my cheeks, but I wasn't crying. I was done cried out. I'd left Mama there, and Vogg had put her in the pool, confident I was bringing him what he really wanted. Maybe he had scraped out the very last of what was left of Mama and threw her out just like rich people did.

Out here the snowplows had done their work haphazardly, but there were ruts leading into the familiar spine-shape of the mobile park. The pond by the manager's mobile was a giant shimmering ice-jewel, a mirage just like everything else. The wind was picking up, and out here away from the skyscrapers you could see the clouds moving across pale blue sky. They were going at a good clip, too, and all along the northern horizon a band of dull dark gray loomed.

Weather coming. That's what they say out on the plains. You don't know if it's bad or good until it gets to you.

Snow drifted over the bones of our old mobile. Icicles festooned the twisted remains of the kitchen wall; I wrapped my hands around the steering wheel, blinked furiously, and the knot inside me tightened painfully.

He came out here that night. I could *see* the black car sliding along, gleaming wetly, no snow daring to touch its sides. My knuckles were white on the steering wheel, and I was hissing through my teeth, a low furious sound. *I was supposed to be in the house. He wanted me out of the way.*

It hit me then, *that* was why he'd kept Mama alive. With me gone, he only had her to draw Ray in. He wanted Ray. Wanted to scrape him out and eat... but why hadn't he done the same to me?

Pity you weren't born a boy.

The only thing out of place in front of the wreckage of our mobile was a familiar blue truck, sitting obediently in the driveway. It had shoved through softening snow, and something moved in the iced-over clutter.

What the... I squinted.

I pulled the Camaro up a bit, so he could get out around me, and cut the engine. Hopefully it had a teacup of gas left, and I could start it again.

He stepped carefully out on the porch, a furry Canadian hat with earflaps he'd gotten for a birthday years ago clapped securely on his head, and grinned, waving. What the hell was he doing *here*, of all places?

Ray's eyes rolled up inside his head. He twitched a little, his hands moving restlessly on his jean-clad knees. From outside, he'd probably look drunk, or sleeping.

Alex picked his way down the stairs—still solid, but icy. He was holding a blue bag of rock salt. Even at this distance, I could see his eyes gleaming, and I unlocked the door. It took me a couple tries to stand up, and once I did I realized the temperature was dropping again. It was going to freeze hard before long.

"Dez?" He sounded so pleased, so *normal*, my eyes filled with hot water just when I thought I had no tears left. "He let you drive, huh? Hey, Ray!" Waving a gloved hand. He was going to fall over if he didn't watch it.

My mouth hung open. I searched for something to say, a plausible lie to tell. I had to get him out of here and take Ray down into the gully. She had to be there. She *had* to.

If she wasn't, I'd stick the smooth white stone from my pocket into his mouth and hope for the best.

Mama. I want my mama. She was floating in a blue jewel now, though. I was on my own.

A creaking groan was the only warning I got. The Camaro rocked, Alex let out a blurt of surprise, and Ray scrambled across the seat to pile out on my side, hitting me squarely and flinging me down into the snow.

"*Little bitch!*" he crowed, and punched me in the face. It wasn't him, though. His eyes were *black*, and Vogg's leering, canines-heavy smile took over my brother's face. "*Should have burned! Now I'll get you! I'll eat... you... up!*" His hands were around my throat, and he squeezed.

"Hey!" Alex, crunching through the snow. "*Hey!*"

Get away, oh God, get away—Snow and ice ground down the back of my coat. Hot breath in my face, my brother's smoke-and-Ramen-and-engine-grease scent mixed with a deeper, wet-fur reek, and a breath of expensive cologne that couldn't cover up the rot under it. There were no lingering voices to save me this time. Little things in my throat creaked, and I whipped my right hand up, the keys a mass of spikes through a wad of snow and no little amount of gravel. Bright red blood burst, and he howled, his voice not Ray's but Vogg's, spewing obscenities I only partly heard because the snow was in my ear, and those black flowers came back all around the edges of my vision.

A thud, and a crunch, and Ray-notRay was torn off me. "—the *fuck* are you doing, man, she's your *sister!*" Alex yelled, and all I could think was *get up, get up, he's going to kill Alex too if you don't do something, come on, what would Gran do?* Finally breathing again, coughing, rolling onto my side and heaving up to my feet.

Alex grabbed my arm, steadying me. "You all right?" He glanced back at Ray, crumpled in the snow, and maybe he could see the black steam looping around my brother's body. Maybe he couldn't. He turned back to me, as if he thought the fight was over. "Jeez, Dez, what's—"

I shoved past him, my feet planted solidly, and threw my hands out. My wrists ached as if Gran's hands had clamped around them again, fire bracelets that poured heat up my arms. "Get *out* of him!" I screamed, and *threw* with all my might.

Ray screamed, miserably, and snow exploded. He surged up, and Alex started forward. Those black eyes fixed on him, and I *felt* the clot of darkness gather itself to strike.

Alex slipped, his boots flying from underneath him, and hit a patch of concrete with another sickening crack to add to the collection I'd heard today. I couldn't tell whether Vogg or I had done it, and there wasn't *time*—my fingers contorted, and I raked empty air in front of me. Another grinding howl, as something invisible slashed across Ray's face.

Oh God oh god don't let me hurt him—

All those times staring into a bowl of water, while Gran's voice mumbled and whispered inside my head, showing me things. *This is how you mend.* A cackling, her bony fingers in my hair while I stared helplessly, unable to look away. *And this, Dasya my love, this is how you* hurt *when you must.* Grafting the knowledge right into me, all her accumulated study and experience, just waiting for me to need it. Filling me up with the secret ways of knowing.

What had Vogg put into Ray?

Oh, just himself. Was it Gran or my own brain figuring it out? He wanted another body, Mr. Vogg, but not just *any* old corpse would do. Something young, something talented, that he could put himself into just like pouring coffee into a cup. Mama had talent—Gran could have taught her. Maybe she would have helped Ray, too, if he'd come politely to her door.

They hadn't. *I* had, and I hadn't showed them.

Why hadn't I?

"*Selfish little bitch,*" Vogg hissed, and I jerked free of the trap just in time, wrenching my head to the side. He'd almost hypnotized me with those black, black eyes so much like Gran's. He scuttled backwards, throwing up even more snow.

Alex groaned. *Shit.*

I skipped to the side, and Vogg halted. He swayed back and forth on Ray's feet, and stared at me. I heard, faint and faraway, a liquid rill of silvery music. Beating time, the rhythm under the notes, were blunt, venomous snouts hitting glass.

You know what to do, Dez. Change the fight. Go where your power rests.

I turned, my boots slipping in the re-freezing slush, every muscle a symphony of pain, and bolted.

CHAPTER THIRTY

All This Madness

THE JUNKPILE WAS STILL THERE. I scrambled for the top of the frozen refrigerator and leapt, heavy clumping footsteps behind me. Tired, and aching, and hungry, and everything inside me raw-screaming, I was still faster. Maybe because Ray had forgotten what it was like to run, maybe because Vogg had, or because Ray's smoking had blunted the edge of youth.

Of course, I was always faster than Ray, once I got big enough to race and not stumble. We'd go for the corner and back, and he'd give me an Indian burn if I won, so I stopped trying. I let him win, all the time, and he crowed over it, never suspecting that I'd just let him have it. Just like Daddy never suspected Mama would have let him have whatever he wanted, if he'd just been able to decide what it was.

He always kept looking for *something*, forgetting what was right under his nose.

But yeah, I was always faster than Ray. I always knew, way down in me where the secret places remained, that I was, even if I didn't care to try.

Could he ever tell? Or was I just as much a mystery to him as he'd turned out to be to me?

No, you knew him. But people change, Dez. It's called growing up.

Wet snow dragged on me, made every step take the effort of five. I still stayed ahead, sometimes only by a few feet. He didn't know every dip and valley like I did. He'd never trudged along the moon-pale path, and his roar of rage when it threw him the first time might have warmed me clear through if I wasn't already sweating. Even under the snow I could sense the ribbon of paleness, worn thread-thin now but still there, still familiar to me as my own thundering pulse.

The gorge stretched its jaws, swallowed me whole. Its sides, stippled with snowteeth, flashed by. Feet drumming on the path's back, a thin fallen aspen I leapt, my heart pounding so hard it threatened to burst, fire in my veins and a nightmare bearing down on me, I ran.

Evening out, the snow not drifting so much because of the leafless trees and the wind's habit of blowing it right over the gully's top. I pounded along the creekside, made the turn, and skidded to a stop.

It was true. There was the gate and the fence, ice standing up sharp on every picket, and the garden behind it was familiar. But where the shining trailer should be was only an empty toothsocket, a depression of scuffed snow with strange marks on either side, as if big three-toed feet had pressed down to lift the bowl of the trailer up.

Doesn't matter, Dasya. Do what you must.

The whistling got nearer, but no matter how fast the whistling man was he wouldn't get here before Vogg, who was blundering along the path, snorting and heaving, cursing sometimes in Ray's voice, sometimes in his own. I fetched up against the fastened gate, deep sobbing cold-burning breaths filling me, and the thought of just sinking down into the snow and letting him do whatever he wanted was pretty appealing.

At least it would make all this madness *stop.*

"*Little bitch,*" Vogg rasped. "*You found yourself a teacher, did you? Thinking she'd save you? Dried up old hag. I can smell the fear on you.*"

I fished in my pocket for the stone. A smooth, white egg, glowing faintly as the light dimmed. The storm was racing to catch us, now. *Thud. Thudthud. Thud.* The rhythm of the snouts against glass sped up, trying to match my frantic heartbeat.

They need it warm, Dasya. Make it warm.

Fever, then. Not in me, but in the gully. Or maybe just the garden. I closed my eyes, muttering like Gran did. He was getting closer, and closer—

And I fell.

• • •

TO BE EARTH

Down, and down, past the dirt and the rocks, each nook and cranny holding sleepy, coiled venom. They felt me pass, a breathing warmth, and sluggish interest stirred.

No. Deeper.

Falling, frantic, he was right behind me. If he came on my empty body now I could probably fall forever, until the dark and the chill and memories scattered me into the forgiving earth, shattered pieces unremembering a former wholeness.

No. Go deeper.

Another heartbeat, and a hiss faint and low, gathering strength. Warmth, suddenly, and I burst through a crust of rock into scalding. The mountains, pleated high and proud, held fire in their roots. Water held under pressure, long veins of it, the glorious heat just aching to be released. Geology spinning inside my head, Gran holding a mouthful of garden dirt to my slack mouth.

Taste it, Dasya. Know what it is, to be earth.

Slow-sleeping, waking every spring, groaning under the furrow and pierced with roots. They walked upon me, my children, their bodies absorbed into my own when their brief flashes were done.

226

Good, good. Now. Up. *Up*, and give bastard what he deserve, eh?

So tired. It was the season to sleep, to shelter the hidden life in my cracks. A small irritant, a grain of sand, working against my immense weight—but it did not have to lift the whole world onto its tiny back. It was only a small speck, and I could afford to let that one grain do as it pleased for a fraction of a moment.

I was earth, I had nothing but time.

Rising now, the steam racing through hairline fissures, hissing, the buzzing blurring noise filling me all through. A tail lashing back and forth, a warning. Coiled to strike.

POW.

CHAPTER THIRTY-ONE

My Mouth or Any Other

A SCORCH-BLAST OF DAYLIGHT. I screamed, or I would have if my teeth hadn't been buried in something soft and warm. I worried, a rat with a bone, and sweat greased me. Sweat? No. Water. Thick cotton-fog, and that buzzing blur all around me.

They came in answer to the whistling man, who skipped among their undulating bodies. Awakened from their winter nap, finding themselves in a balmy pocket of jungle warmth and lured by irresistible instinct, they burst out between the stones. I had a hazy snapshot of an image—Granny Iyaga whispering to them before it grew too cold, telling them to bed down around her trailer, because little Dasya would need them.

My teeth were sunk deep into Ray's bare hand clapped over my lips. His blood filled my mouth, hot and spicy. Thumps and thuddings as the snakes propelled themselves at Vogg in my brother's skin, some of their bites blunted by his parka or his boots. They went right through his jeans, fastened on his other hand, and his familiar face—he was somehow laying right next to me along the stone-and-trash fence, how had that happened? He had probably tried to hit me again, and my body, quick as a snake itself, had... struck.

Just like a rattler.

The world tilted, and I understood. Geyser-warmth from deep below, melting everything, flash-thawing the dirt and turning it to a soupy pillow.

Ray tore his hand away. "*Bitch!*" Vogg howled with his mouth, and the biggest rattler of all—he looked familiar, or maybe everything looked familiar to me in that state—streaked forward, quick as lightning, and bit his tongue.

I was wrong. I did have tears left. I lay there and sobbed while the snakes swarmed the thing in my brother's body. The whistling man danced, somehow avoiding their heaving backs, and when the thing under the snakes stopped moving his song dropped a few octaves and he led them away, to the very edge of the pocket of temporary warmth, to burrow again. Granny might have let him lead them into the storm, delighting in their struggles as they froze, but since I was here he let them slide below the earth's crust again, opening tiny holes, the plain shifting and swallowing its legless children.

I didn't care.

The body beside me twitched. I hitched myself up, painfully, and crawled to his side. "*Ray*," I sobbed. "Ray-Ray, I'm sorry. I'm so sorry. Mama. I'm sorry. I'm sorry, sorry, sorry." Hot blood slicked my chin. The egg-stone ground between my palm and the wet dirt. My mittens were shredded.

There were holes where Ray-Ray's eyes used to be. His tongue... oh, God. His *tongue*. Everything swollen up black, a low hiss of tortured breath as Vogg struggled to make the body mend itself.

But he didn't have a good enough grasp on it yet, I guess. Or maybe it was Ray, left alone, wondering what the hell as the venom ate him up.

I popped the eggstone in the empty, bloody hole that was my brother's mouth and sagged over him, holding it shut, my torn-open mittens and bruised palms smooshing against blood and sweat and swelling tissue. The white stone grew heavy, and as it sank into Ray's skull two long trails of vicious black steam poured from my brother's clogged, broken nose. They shredded, grabbing at the wind and finding no purchase, locked out, shriveling in the cold.

"Ray," I kept whispering, brokenly. "Oh, Ray. I'm so sorry. Mama. I'm sorry. Ray..."

There was no answer.

I would never hear either of them again, from my mouth or any other. When his body lay there, still and rapidly cooling, the whistling man became a wind that tugged at my hair, pulled at my clothes, slapped my cheeks and stinging hands to get me upright and moving. Gluey mud was already freezing with weird crackles, the sky had darkened, and as I began stumbling away from my murdered brother tiny speckles of snow began to fall, each one a weightless kiss.

• • •

HANDS OUT

Someone had called the cops. By the time I stumbled back around the side of the mobile with the foggy idea that I had to find out if Alex was okay, an ambulance had arrived. Rolled in snow, mud, dirt, and all bloody, I staggered toward the bright lights, my hands lifted like in a movie. *Don't shoot.*

Questions, so many questions, and I heard Alex's voice, harshly. *Jim Vogg*, he said, over and over. *He was here. He tried to kill us.*

Still sobbing, I curled into myself. Alex, a goose-egg on his forehead the size of a baby's fist, grabbed me and hugged me. I clung to him, shut my eyes, and let them do whatever they wanted.

After a while, they bundled both of us in the ambulance. I peered out between my lashes, something bothering me, a nagging at the edge of my consciousness. One last thing I had to check before I could let go.

Where I'd parked Ray's Camaro, there was now a shiny black sedan. No particle of snow or mud stuck to it, and that's when I began to scream. There was a needle-sting in my arm, Alex trying to calm me down. They sedated me, and I fell back into darkness gratefully.

Vogg's Body

*I*T WAS VOGG'S BODY THEY FOUND IN THE GULLY, *where he'd slipped and broken his neck. They found Mama in the swimming pool at his house, dressed all in bridal white, her throat livid with strangle-marks. It was a pure miracle, Libba said, how I got away.*

    I didn't reply.

CHAPTER THIRTY-THREE

Sooner or Later

THE HOSPITAL BED WAS FULL OF OTHER PEOPLE'S PAIN AND sickness, and I sank into it. The knot inside me, overstrained, lay limp as a jellyfish. I didn't have the energy to tighten it up. I had enough to do just keeping breathing, even if I didn't want to. My stupid body kept going, blind and deaf to the fact that I didn't want it to.

The plain fact of it was, I just wanted to go to sleep and never wake up again.

"Poor girl." Libba's face swam into view through the chemical haze. Behind her shoulder, Mr. Carr's dark eyes were somber. He carried a huge bouquet of sun-colored flowers, awkwardly, as if it was a baby he didn't know what to do with. "Shh, it's all right."

I was struggling to sit up. "Mama?" I caught myself. "Libba?" I should have called her Mrs. Carr, but... I don't know. I didn't, and I haven't since.

"It's okay, honey. You're all right, you're safe now." She grabbed my hand while Mr. Carr looked uncomfortably around for somewhere to put the flowers. "Everything's being taken care of. You just rest."

"Vogg," I whispered. There were beeps and boops—machines measuring my pulse, my breathing. "He—he—"

"He's dead," Mr. Carr piped up. "That oily sonofabitch."

I cringed a little, and Libba gave him a Mama Look. "Shh. He's gone, honey. Jim Vogg can't hurt anyone else ever again. You were so brave. You fought him off. Thank goodness Alex could get to the neighbors. They called 911. You're safe now. Some hypothermia and the influenza might come back, they want to make sure you don't come down with pneumonia. Oh, Dez." Stroking my hand, the limp discarded animal that it was, like she wanted to bring it back to life. "We *sent* you there. I'll never forgive myself, *never.*"

"Didn't know, Libba. Had everyone fooled." Mr. Carr fiddled with the blinds. The heavy darkness outside told me it was evening, and I couldn't hear the wind. "Chuck—you know, Ruffio's brother? He says the cops traced him to another murder in Chicago. Bastard picked up and came out west after that, they say. Same thing, mother and daughter. Never did find the son."

"Frank." Libba glared at him.

"Language. Yeah. Sorry," he mumbled, settling the flowers on the window-shelf.

"It's okay," I whispered. "I need to know. Is... Is Alex..."

"Oh, sweetheart." Tears welling up in Libba's eyes, now. Big shining ones, and I watched, the warm haze making everything so distant. "He's fine. They're keeping him for observation, he might have a concussion. When I think of what could have... how close it was..."

"Don't." Mr. Carr loomed over her, his broad capable hands cupping her shoulders, and she didn't look frightened at all. It was so strange, seeing a woman who didn't flinch. "It's all right. We're taking care of everything, Miss Desiree. Don't you worry. You won't go to a foster home or anything like that, we're making arrangements."

I don't want... The world slid away, came back with Libba bending over me, a soft kiss on my forehead.

"She's asleep, poor thing. Come on, let's go get some coffee."

I watched them, Libba leaning into his side, making a comforting four-legged shadow in the door. They pulled it almost-shut.

My eyes drifted closed again, and when I opened them the light had changed. White-gold fluorescent glow came in from the hall, and across the room, Libba Carr curled on a pink-cushioned fold-down chair. The hospital blanket turned her into a sleepy child stealing a few winks on the couch, but the worry and laugh lines on her face made her look as old as she was.

A shadow drifted over the window. I blinked. "I know you're there," I husked.

She melded out of the darkness, her black hair only lightly threaded with gray now. Her nose, however, was still as proud and strong as ever, and the shawl was familiar—black silk, with roses, and the fringe that whispered as she moved. I'd hand-washed it myself in her kitchen sink, in her round little home. I'd hung it to dry in the shade of the garden, and folded it with a sachet in her big wardrobe.

She studied me for a long moment, her arms crossed as if she hugged herself, as if *she* felt the cold. "Old Granny went home, and her little Dasya left all alone."

I longed to move, to get up off the bed. To hug her again. "The snakes. You left them."

Granny Iyaga pursed her lips, shook her head. "No, little one. That was not me. *You* called them. Little Dasya has fangs too, you know."

No. If I had any toughness in me, I would have saved Mama. Known better. *Done* better. "But... the whistling man..."

She touched the back of my hand, a warm, forgiving brush of her work-hardened fingers. "He is your spirit now, little girl. Granny can teach you no more."

"Did you—" My arm moved. I grabbed at her hand, surprising both of us. "Did you know?"

She shook her head again, sucked on her teeth briefly. In this light, and with her hair so dark, she looked older, certainly, but not ancient. Fifty tops, and her flesh was the roundness of a woman who's kept herself in shape for a long while.

Winter has her time. I saw that, now.

"Granny doesn't look beyond her garden. Inside the garden, well, Granny is law. Outside... not so much."

"You left me." I couldn't help but sound accusing.

"Oh Dasya," she said. "Everyone leaves, sooner or later." She freed her fingers from mine, gently, but decidedly.

"Don't go," I managed, though cracked lips. "Granny, please. Don't go." *You're all I have left.*

"Psh. I have arranged things for my Dasya. You have a dowry, and that boy is a good one. He will do." She stopped, regarded me. "We will not see each other again, but I came to..."

"To what?" *To just leave me? I want my Mama. I want you to take me away.*

She leaned down, and I froze. She pressed her lips to my forehead, just where Libba had, and warmth slid down my skin. The machines fuzzed briefly, and Libba stirred across the room.

"Is not all bad." Granny Iyaga's teeth, pressing through the softness of her lips. "You are bright star. What you make of what Granny gave you is yours alone. Old woman is proud of her little Dasya. You are brave, and you are strong." She stepped away. Gave me a critical once over, as if I had just finished cleaning something and my work met with her approval. "More, I cannot help you with."

"Please," I whispered. "Don't leave me, Granny."

Did I imagine the glimmer at her eyelashes? Or did she just blink? "Goodbye, Dasya."

Then she was gone, and I lay stiff as a poker, staring at the place where she had been and willing her to come back.

Out in the hall, someone whistled. A snatch of silver song. I shut my eyes, and meant to look for him, but sleep came back and wrung me out.

• • •

WAIT A LONG TIME

Six months later

The wind-roar stopped, a flood of warm summer through the windows slowing to a trickle. Alex pulled the parking brake, golden hairs on the back of his wrist glowing in sunshine. "You sure you want to do this?"

I nodded. My hands twisted together in my lap. Spring on the plains came with torrents and thunderstorms, and we were back to baking under the hot wind again.

He cut the engine. "I'll go with you."

"No, that's okay." The burned wreck of the mobile had been carted away, and a new concrete foundation poured. The fence was still falling apart by increments. Looked like some people had moved out—the Clarremores, who had let Alex in to use their phone in the middle of a storm—were gone or they'd gotten another used Chevy Nova in a different color. "I want to, you know. By myself."

"You sure?"

"Positive." But I reached over, grabbed his hand, and squeezed.

His entire face lit up. Living at his house wasn't as... awkward... as I thought it would be.

Still, nobody knew about the backpack under my bed, everything I'd need if I wanted to leave. Spare clothes, the roll of cash from working at Granny's, added to in dribs and drabs from the allowance Frank insisted on giving me. *Kid needs an allowance,* he'd said, gruffly, waving off my thanks. *Go get into some trouble, huh? Good trouble. Not that other kind. Oh, hell.*

He was pretty funny, actually, Mr. Carr. Kept telling me, *Call me Frank. Or anything else, just not late for dinner.*

The sun was a fierce white eye, the grass whispering to itself, bowing and nodding. I'd purposely waited for a day with very little wind.

You have to wait a long time out on the plains for one of those.

The path wasn't there. Not even a trickle of it. I walked with my head down, and the buzzing started.

Relax, guys. I'm just walking through.

The Carrs also didn't know about me heading out to the rockpiles sometimes when nobody else was home. Listening to that dangerous, blurring buzz while I sat still as a stone myself, a bubble of quiet around me holding scale-dragging whispers as they slid over my knee, or flicked their forked tongues at my bare wrist. They had their own ways, and I was a stranger. Tolerated, but not loved.

Sometimes, it was even enough.

The gullyside was loose, full of scree. I picked my way down carefully, hopped from stone to stone like I used to, and the creek was back to a trickle. It glittered, but not as sharply as it had last summer.

Libba took me to a therapist once a week. Miss Dodge was a nice enough lady, but I couldn't tell her the important things. Still, she had a name for the shakes and shivers that would hit me crossways with no warning. *Post-traumatic stress,* she said. *You were already vulnerable, with your family history. This is normal.*

Yeah. Normal. My laugh echoed, shook the aspens. I came around the bend.

Nothing. Not even the gate or the stone-and-trash fence. Just a hummocky stretch of green with a shallow divot scraped out of it where the trailer used to be, claw-marks on either side. It was shaded in the afternoon, and the ground probably remembered Granny's careful waterings. Or the water I'd brought up was still there, seeping through those hairline cracks.

My throat was dry. I stood for a long time right where the porch used to be, aspen shade fluttering liquid all over me. Tattoos of light and dark, *grief or relief, grief or relief?*

There were hints in books, of course. I'd gone back to the library and began reading every fairy tale I could lay my hands on. All the old stories. You could find a name for what I did, or for who she was. Or what Vogg was. If you looked hard enough; if you knew what you were looking for.

I went back to where the gate would have been. Bent down where Ray…

Nothing there. Just dirt. No flash of white. My hands were fists.

After a little while, I went back to the creek and grubbed around. I didn't know exactly what I was looking for. A glitter, a gleam—and there it was. A round egg, but not pale.

No, it was a polished chunk of obsidian. The creek's trickle poured over it, wearing it down. As I watched, fissures spread along its smooth surface and it crumbled, as if it had just been waiting for me before it could let go completely. Fine black dust steamed up through the water, and I caught a flash of that particular darkening blue of his eyes when he was happy. I smelled engine oil, and felt the half-serious poke he used to give me in the ribs when he didn't quite want to tickle but he *did* want me to pay attention.

The dust scattered, glittering through the aspens. It would sink in, the trees would take it up, absorb it through their trunks and leaves. When they slept during the winter, he'd sleep too, and little by little all the pain would ease away as their roots drank deep and their branches stretched.

We still ain't found your brother. Not even an address, and that fella Stark had a heart attack…

Mending and hurting. Grief or relief? The Carrs had paid for Mama's gravestone. I visited every Sunday. The tears were a relief. At least, when the crying finished I felt like I'd *done* something, even if it was only producing some snot. Marcie was sometimes there, and she would hug me and say *your mama would be so proud.*

The black guilt would bite, then, and I didn't want to see Marcie, but I didn't avoid her, either. There's always a price to pay.

I cupped my hand, drank a little of the crick-trickle. Clear and cold, just like it used to be.

What did you expect, coming out here?

"Ray," I said, quietly. "This is the best I can do. I'm so sorry."

It hurt. I'd told Miss Dodge I thought Ray was dead.

We can't know for sure, she said. *The not-knowing is pretty hard, isn't it.*

Knowing was just as awful. Maybe I'd tell her that next time, if I was still around.

I thought of Alex waiting in the heat for me. I could have just borrowed Libba's car and come out here, but he didn't want me to go alone, and Libba got that funny look on her face when I told her where I was going.

She looked a little like Mama when she did that. Another flash of guilt, this one rose-red and stinging. She wasn't my mama. I took one last long look around. The aspens made a sound like a lighter clicking, and I smelled Ray, and a ghost of Mama's perfume.

It was time, so I trudged back up the gullyside. I didn't look back, even when the wind played with my hair, brushed at my cheek to dry the tears.

It was best to look back only in private. He didn't like it when I cried. Like a child, he'd get anxious, trying to make me happy again. *Ch'rnvog,* Granny had called him, but I just called him the Whistler. The other name for it was *familiar.*

The buzzing all around me fell silent, long sinuous lengths retreating into their dark holes, sensing it was best to hide for a while until the heat began to leach away.

Halfway up the side of the gully, I hopped from one rock to another, and began to whistle. Someone not so far away did, too, and the two steams of melody blurred into one. Rising, dipping, silver thread flashing under the bowl of a bright blue sky.

I was getting pretty good at it.

• • •

So tell me, little one.
Can you see the wind?

finis

LILI SAINTCROW

was born in New Mexico (which probably explains everything, given the nuclear testing) and spent her childhood bouncing around the world as a military brat. She fell in love with writing in second grade and has done it obsessively ever since. She currently resides in the rainy Pacific Northwest with her children, dogs, cat, and assorted other strays, including a metric ton of books holding her house together.